In Good Faith

A Real Estate Diva Mystery

To Mary!
Thank you for your
support! for
Catharine

Catharine Bramkamp

In Good Faith

First edition copyright 2011 Catharine Bramkamp

This is a work of fiction. Names, characters, some locations and incidents are products of the author's fevered imagination or are used fictionally and are not be construed as real. Any resemblances to actual events, local organization or person, living or dead, is entirely coincidental. It's not about you.

August 2011

Cover design by Stacey Meinzen

Other Books by Catharine Bramkamp

Death Revokes the Offer (A Real Estate Diva Mystery)
Time is of the Essence (A Real Estate Diva Mystery)
Woman on the Verge of Wyoming
Being Miss Behaved
Don't Write Like You Talk: A Smart Girl's Guide to
 Practical Writing and Editing.
Ammonia Sunrise (Poetry Collection)
The Cheap Retreat Workbook

Anthologies
Chicken Soup for the Writer's Soul
Chicken Soup for the Woman's Soul
Vintage Voices Anthology 2008
Vintage Voices Anthology 2009
Vintage Voices Anthology 2011
Pen house Ink
California Women Poets

To Andrew

Good Faith - Bona fide; an act is done in good faith if it is in fact done honestly, whether negligently or not.

-   *The language of Real Estate* – John W. Reilly, fifth edition, Dearborn Financial Publishing, Inc. 2000.

Chapter 1

I found another body.

She was murdered.

This was an even less pleasant experience than both times before. The fact that I have found three bodies in the course of my lifetime must be more than a coincidence. But there was no context to make sense of it. I didn't even want meaning at this juncture. What I wanted then and now is quick closure and a nice glass of Shiraz. And tranquilizers.

What did I think when I flung open that bedroom door? Some options were; horror, revulsion, sickness, shock, but no, my first thought was, I do not need this.

My second thought was perhaps I should switch from selling million dollar homes to only selling inexpensive condos. Nothing happens during a condo purchase. First- time home buyers purchase condos. And first-time homebuyers are too busy working to pay their new mortgage to indulge in mayhem and murder.

For instance, the only thing my client, Owen Spenser, a first time homebuyer, inspires is aggravation, but not murder. Although, our last conversation brought me dangerously close to the latter.

After a year of condo scrutiny, Owen announced that the last condo I found for him had cracks in the soil around the foundation.

"Yes," I explained. "There are cracks in the soil, it's adobe, it shows cracks." I've been selling real estate in River's Bend, California, long enough to be an authority on the solid adobe soil that covers most of the south end of town, I spoke the truth.

Mr. Owen Spenser, who has only been dabbling in real estate (as a perpetual first-time homebuyer) for the last seven years, was obsessed with buying the perfect condo for the perfect price - at the very bottom of the market. Yesterday, he was obsessed with cracking adobe soil.

"Yes," I assure him on a weekly basis, "I'm sure it is a good deal. And, no, you won't be certain it's a good deal until after you've missed the opportunity."

I take that back. I'm not that happy with condo buyers either.

And how do I, Allison Little, know I was looking at a murder scene?

Well, I'm no expert, (I am not saying that to be modest, I am really not an expert of any kind, except for real estate – and am constantly faced with situations where I have no experience, but have to act as if I do, and it's damn annoying) but I do know that when a body has been hacked into small pieces, and those pieces are scattered liberally around the master bedroom, the cause of death was not cancer.

Or suicide. We can rule out suicide and cancer.

Dark stains of brown and red covered the white (of course, white) bedroom walls in fat splotches and horrible arches of smears and drips. One gruesome arch reached to the ceiling. I didn't search for the source of all that abundance, I didn't want to.

The woman's head was positioned dead center of the counterpane; the vicious stains had soaked into the white bedspread. I couldn't tell if the blood was dried or, well, damp. Not that I had any interest in approaching for a better look. Even from the doorway, where I stood frozen, I could see that her beautiful face still held an expression of complete surprise.

I gripped the doorframe and stared at the scene for what felt like an hour, enough time for all those trivial thoughts to flash through my addled brain. At least, it felt like an hour. My stomach finally reacted to what my eyes were seeing and began to heave. I had to move.

I uncurled my fingers from the doorframe and jerked back. I slammed the door closed for good measure, as if she was capable of pursuit (I watched a great many inappropriate-for-my-age horror movies, courtesy of my older brothers, it could happen).

I stumbled into the guest bath. The master bath was accessed through the master suite; I did not want to be that close – to anything. The master bath opened directly to the master bedroom, as if the couple living there rose at precisely the same time so the light in the bath wouldn't disturb the other sleeping person. This master bedroom set up was really a suite for the single. Far too many homes up here have this feature. I never point it out when I'm selling property in the Villas.

I think, in my muddled mind, I was afraid of discovering the murder weapon in the Master Bath. The killer could have very well rinsed off his weapon in the jetted tub and left it to dry on the heated towel rack. Why not? It made as much sense as anything else.

I found the guest bath and guest toilet without a moment to spare and threw up the last eight hours of meals starting with the General's Chicken lunch special and ending with the Caramel Macchiato with too much caramel flavor this morning and too much again this afternoon.

It was disgusting. I needed to clean my mouth and find my phone.

The doorbell rang as I was searching under the sink for mouthwash. I rummaged through stacks of toothpaste, toilet paper and tissue boxes and found two, huge warehouse size bottles of green mouthwash shrink-wrapped together. Perfect, no one would notice if I took some. My mouth was a bitter mess. I spit into the sink.

My phone. Where did I leave my phone? There was probably a phone in the bedroom. No, do not go back into the bedroom.

The doorbell rang again followed by a hello. I risked nicking my polish and ripped open the plastic shrink-wrap with my nails and wrenched the huge bottle from the packaging.

"Hello? Anyone home?" A voice called from downstairs.

I untwisted the hand-size top but the bottle slipped out of my hands before I had a chance to use it. The super sized bottle smacked on the floor and doused the bathroom with a fountain of green liquid. Now the bathroom smelled minty fresh.

"Hello?" Called the intruder.

Oh, that's right. I was here in the first place because I was holding an open house. My efficient system, honed over the years, is to stop on my way to the client's house and place the open house signs through out the neighborhood, so the directional arrows lead a buyer right to my listing. I put out my signs before the advertised time of 1:00 PM. It wasn't really the early bird's fault. But I could blame them anyway because they were egregiously early.

"Hello?" A voice called, a little more irritated.

"Come on in," I trilled, stupidly.

I took a quick mouthful, spit into the sink, flushed the toilet, patted the beads of sweat from my forehead, and slammed the guest bath door. I stumbled as quickly downstairs as my high heels would allow. No sense landing in a heap at this person's feet.

I didn't check to see if I had more minty-fresh mouthwash on my skirt. I bared my teeth at the couple politely waiting at the bottom of the stairs.

"Welcome to our open house," I managed to say. Muscle memory can be your friend.

The man and woman were dressed in matching sweatshirts and sweat pants. They both wore the popular, brightly colored gardening clogs: his in red, hers in shocking pink. Footwear that is both practical and ugly as sin. Neighbors.

"This is lovely," chirped the woman, "I love the color of the living room. What do you think, honey?"

The man kicked at the floor. "I think our cherry wood is better, and look at those uneven jousts, someone did some sloppy work here."

I tried to simultaneously smile and not breathe on them. "You must be neighbors." I glanced around, there was my handbag, bright red against the white carpet, near the front door.

Red. I swallowed and tried to keep my smile in place.

"Yeah, we saw the sign and thought we'd check it out," he confirmed.

"Why is she selling?" the wife asked.

It was with great relief that I admitted I did not have that information.

"Do they have the same master bed set up?" the wife said. She turned towards the stairs.

"No," I put out my hand to stop her. "I mean, probably. All these models are the same." My brain was moving as fast as my mouth, which meant things were becoming more normal. Soon my mouth would move ahead of my brain, and all would be well.

"My client is still dressing," I glanced at my expensive watch, and they noticed. Good. "We're not really open for another fifteen minutes. You understand how it is, with the holidays and all."

The woman nodded. The man looked perplexed, as if the term holiday did not mean twice as much work for a third of the fun.

They stood between me, and the front door. I couldn't blurt out, excuse me, I have to call the police now, there's dead body in the master bedroom, so I came up with another tactic.

"Are you thinking of selling your house?" I inquired with as much enthusiasm as I could. I stepped towards the front table that held a dozen of my business cards. I had to hold onto the edge of the table to steady myself, before I turned again with my card in hand.

"Here, take my card, and here is a list of the surrounding homes so you can get an idea of the market."

"Oh," they were startled out of their peering, critical mode and quickly switched into survival mode. "Oh no, we don't think. . . "

"Of course you keep a close eye on the market daily, don't you?" I continued. The husband, with his critical eye, struck me as one of those men who, because he had worked in installation for AT & T for the last thirty years, automatically possesses complete expertise in the real estate market, and construction as well. Joists my ass.

"I would love to meet with you and evaluate your home. It sounds as if you've installed quite a bit of upgrades, yes?" I pressed my card into the wife's limp hand.

"Umm, that's okay," the husband began to back away. "We would never, I mean, no we're fine, we don't need to talk to anyone. We aren't selling."

"Of course, not right away, but keep in touch. Here, take a flyer on this house to give you an idea. You said your floors are in better shape?"

He nodded, now struck dumb by my torrent of helpful suggestions.

"Great!" I beamed at him. "We can discuss that, too." Their newer floors meant nothing when it came to pricing a house, but my goal was to never see them again, not discuss their home. They were still standing between me and my phone.

"Would you be interested in signing the guest book? Can I get your name? I'll email you later with a custom evaluation of your neighborhood and some statistics on the market." I approached him like a stalking tiger and he, in turn, backed away slowly towards the door like a meerkat, or something. (Animal Planet, last Tuesday, the Tragic Life of the Meerkat, I wasn't paying all that much attention to the show, and can't give you more details).

"No, no, we'll be moving along now," he stuttered.

"Oh, come back, we can do a market analysis. Do you have financing for your next house? Where are you planning to move?"

He shot out the door and dragged his wife along with him.

"I love the carpets," she called, as they exited down the driveway.

I grabbed my phone from my bag and quickly scrolled down the contacts for the police.

The police dispatcher was friendlier than the one I called a long time ago (okay, this past summer) to report an unrelated incident that coincidentally involved the murder of another client, and I happened to be the listing agent for the house. And I sold it, thank you. So, obviously, I'm good at the difficult sale.

This dispatcher and I passed through the pleasantries of who I was, who she was, holiday plans, that sort of thing. But as soon as I told her about the condition of the body, she geared into over drive and barked out so many cautions and procedural instructions I thought she was Rosemary, the most successful agent in our New Century office, in the middle of an escrow. Do this, don't do that. Don't touch. Don't leave.

I nodded, even though she couldn't see me agree. My adrenaline dissipated leaving me limp and strangely lethargic.

"Where are you located?" The dispatcher repeated.

"Follow the open house signs," I said, wearily.

Chapter 2

I collapsed onto the bottom stairs. These things are easier to take in cartoon form. Small brutal creatures eviscerate each other to happy nursery music; you're familiar with those kinds of cartoons. Anyway, the seller's bedroom now resembled the aftermath of one of those nasty skits. Not pretty or even satiric. It was no laughing matter.

Damn. I dropped my head into my hands and tried to think. I looked up and realized Beverley (the seller and now, murder victim) had actually painted her living room walls. Instead of the original lavender color, the walls were painted a clean beige, off white, or eggshell depending on which brand of paint a person preferred. The point was, it was no longer purple. Good for her. She must have worked all day Saturday. Not the best way to spend Thanksgiving weekend, but it was money saving; kept her out of the stores. Judging from my visit last Friday, Beverley Weiss was a woman who needed a break from unrelenting consumerism. She had enough stuff, more than enough.

For me, I needed more mouthwash. I needed lunch again. No, no lunch again. I needed to clean this up.

I slowly walked back to the front door and studied it. I know a great deal more about doors than I used to. To my now practiced eye, there was nothing wrong. No forced entry. Friday, I had connected a lock box with a house key on the water hose faucet adjacent to the front stoop – but the front door was open when I came in this morning – I had walked right in. The murderer had not locked the door on the way out.

Was that surprised expression on Beverley's face because it was someone she knew? Or had she been surprised a stranger had a key?

I checked the driveway. No more visitors.

I stared at my phone, calendar (note, schedule nervous breakdown), cool apps, contact list.

I am nothing, if not generous. To share the pain, panic, and hopefully, the police questions, I called up Ben Stone, Rock

Solid Service.

Yes, Ben and I are an item – a couple of sorts. Our relationship is obvious enough that my best friend, Carrie, is convinced that the best way to celebrate my new relationship is to change.

"Have you thought about losing weight?" Carrie broached the subject last week, Tuesday, with the appropriate hesitation. But if your best friend can't ask that question, really, who can?

"I mean," she continued, emboldened by my silence, aided by the fact my mouth was full of bacon, chili cheeseburger, "I mean, this is a great opportunity to do something different, what with your new relationship and all." She lingered on the word relationship.

Carrie, by the way, is one of those natural beauties who weighs in at an estimated minus 15 pounds and wears a size zero. I weighed more than she does at my birth.

I swallowed. "It's not a big enough relationship to merit weight loss. Besides, I'm not ready to give up the favorite men in my life, Ben & Jerry."

Carrie dropped the weight loss plan as quickly as she brought it up. It's a heavy topic with me. All pun intended. And besides, my current "boyfriend" loves me as I am – many points in his favor.

"So, I need to find another cause," Carrie said.

"You're really off the board of Forgotten Felines?" I asked. She told me she was planning to quit choosing her current love – Patrick Sullivan of Cooper Milk, millionaire, philanthropist and damn cute – over her work with lost kittens, but I hadn't heard the end of the story.

Carrie was devoted to the cause of saving lost kittens. That's the kind of girl she was.

"I do enjoy the kittens and the rescuing and stuff," she said slowly, but this group was so disorganized, it took us twenty minutes to agree on the next meeting time, and right before I left the last meeting, because I had to get back to my own job, the board members launched into another debate on what kind of donuts we should serve at the meetings. Some of those volunteers shouldn't be eating any more donuts. And I had work to do, and I didn't appreciate giving up my lunch for something so silly." She took a drink of water.

"Sorry," she finished, "I didn't mean to burden you."

I smiled. I was the burdener in this relationship; she was the burdenee. I think I have taken advantage of this kind, gentle woodland creature about a dozen times since we met. However, her new relationship with Patrick has given her some more nerve and even some attitude, and frankly it was looking good on her. I was impressed.

"I'm impressed."

"You are?" She relaxed, "I thought you'd start in on how I am violating my principles or something."

"No, I think Patrick is a worthwhile trade."

"He suggested I join this board for the Homeless Prevention League. It's more important work, saving people instead of cats. And he promised they are pretty organized. We're going to their annual dinner next week. Patrick is a donor, but he wants to see what I think."

What a luxury, to worry about weight loss and love. I will remember that.

***

I was relieved that Ben answered his phone on the first ring, I hoped it was because he knew it was me, but since I never examined his phone to see if I have my own ring tone, or if my name or picture comes up with little heart icons, those last speculations were only that. Ben isn't really the type to spend hours choosing exactly the right photos to delineate his callers.

I felt pretty confident calling him. Two nights ago, we had taken the relationship to a new level, so I gained at least some parity. Some.

To a Realtor, the house is the window to the soul. Since summer, it's been about my windows and my soul. Ben has pawed through my bookshelves, riffled through my closets, and slept in my house, all the while protecting his space with disturbing efficiency. I didn't even have his address, so I couldn't look up his property and do a drive by, nor could I look up his records and learn what he owed on his mortgage. I was beginning to worry about what he was hiding. His grandmother, for one thing. He lives with his grandmother.

I know, loser. But he didn't have any of the other hallmarks of a loser, so I was completely mystified. I was dying for an opportunity to gaze into Ben's soul, at the very least, his bathroom cabinets.

Ben, or rather his grandmother, lives in Dry Creek, a few miles west of Healdsburg. Even after I discovered his living situation, he still didn't disclose his address. Okay, fine then.

"Grandma bought dinner," he announced. when he picked me up in his truck the day after Thanksgiving.

"Didn't get enough to eat, yesterday?" I tossed my overnight bag – be prepared – into the back of the truck and climbed in.

"We have no left-overs. Thanksgiving was at Mom's. I drove Grandma down to the City, and we sat around the huge antique Queen Anne table in the formal Queen Anne dining room and made polite conversation about the weather. I think my mother may have brought up the Queen herself. What about you?"

"I enjoyed three hours and seventeen minutes with my brothers and their lovely families," I said. "We had dinner at the Club."

"That seems a little," he trailed off.

"Sterile? That's how mom runs the holiday, organized, proper and color coordinated. The one bit of levity we are allowed is three minutes of clowning around right before the family holiday portrait. Three minutes. After that, we shape up, and smile fiercely, as if we mean it. Those who do not smile; do not get dessert, that's another festive tradition."

"Sounds," he couldn't resist and I didn't blame him. "Festive," he finished.

"About as festive as your holiday."

"Hey, we enjoyed a lively conversation about the Queen."

"How is she doing?"

"Daughter-in-law problems."

I nodded. I hadn't met his mother yet. I suspected she was the queen in her own world. I was not looking forward to that encounter, at all.

"You shopped today?" He must have read my expression

and changed the subject.

"No," I suppressed a sigh. I love Black Friday. I love shopping. But business comes first. "I had a client meeting. I'm listing a house in the Villas. Open House on Sunday."

"Wow, that's fast."

I shrugged; I didn't want to talk about my new, pushy client. I wanted to focus on Ben. We exited at the second Healdsburg exit. Ben turned left to Dry Creek and then right.

When Ben admitted he lived with his grandmother, my first thought was, trailer park. Because, to be brutally honest, when a man his age (he's fortyish) announces that he lives with his grandmother, my assumption is that that man is chronically unemployed, and his grandmother needs help using the toilet. I have visions of them living on only her social security, just able to afford a single wide in a trailer park labeled Journey's End, or End of the Rainbow, or something along those lines. Highly depressing.

That was the mood I was in anyway. The onset of the holidays can do that to a girl.

Maybe some new shoes will make me feel better. The stores were still advertising sales.

Ben pulled into a circular drive and parked. I peered out at the façade of a huge two-story building. It looked to be a high end winery, all bottles costing $60.00 and more. Were we stopping at a winery? If so, why hadn't I heard about it? I thought I knew all the wineries in this valley.

A tall, willowy woman the same vintage as my own grandmother, Prue, slowly pushed open huge double stable-like doors and gestured to us to come in.

The woman wore her hair natural white, and swept off her forehead in an expensive flip. She was dressed in the same casual outfit my mother favored; matched cashmere sweater set and pressed slacks, flat shoes decorated with bows hugged her feet.

I blew out a breath at the sight of her. I wish it had been a winery featuring expensive wine. At least there, I wouldn't have to buy. This was all buy-in.

Ben's grandmother was formidable. She knew it. I knew it.

Ben, apparently, was clueless.

"This is my grandmother, Emily." He pulled out my bag from the truck and gestured to his grandmother.

Emily stood in the enormous open doorway and nodded in my direction. God, the overnight bad was glaringly obvious, but it was too late to snatch it back, Ben swung it back and forth as he approached the front door.

"It's a pleasure," Emily said, calmly.

I reached out to take her hand in what turned out to be a firm handshake.

"It's a pleasure to meet you, too," I echoed.

"Come on in," Ben gestured with his head and gently pushed his grandmother to one side. I waited for her to precede me into the courtyard.

I stepped into the courtyard and took a deep breath.

When I'm wrong. I am spectacularly wrong. Colossally wrong. This was not the trailer park image I had been harboring for the last few months.

It is difficult to impress me, okay, almost impossible. See enough homes and the mansions in the Villas start to resemble the trailers in Journey's End. The only difference is the homes in the Villas are bigger than the trailers in Journey's End, but not necessarily more pleasant.

This home was more than a string of big rooms. So you can compare, Emily's home was built on the same pattern as Michel Schlumberger Winery also located in Dry Creek. Visit the winery, tour around, and you'll have an idea of what kind of house the taciturn Mr. Stone lives in.

His grandmother led us through the huge doors and through a breezeway running the perimeter of the house, enclosing it on all four sides.

"So, Allison, you are from around here, correct?" she said. Her voice was well modulated, the product of lessons, fine living, class.

I nodded, mostly because my own voice is not well modulated. It's naturally loud.

A second story with deep porches hovered to my right; to my left the house was a single story.

"Sorry, yes, I live in River's Bend," I tried to keep my voice low, but it spiked in pitch at the word bend, and sounded like a question. I clamped my lips together.

"Lovely town," she said smoothly. Great, she was a practiced socialite as well.

"You were the one who rescued Ben from the fire." She stopped half way across the patio. She was tall, about five foot nine with the same dark blue eyes as Ben. Or rather, he inherited her eyes and height. She had that effortless patrician air my mother works so hard to emulate. Emily carried herself as if she was born to money.

I glanced at the home – even if she was born into money, it appeared she spent it all on this house.

Lights from the breezeway illuminated the patio area, a fountain played in the center of the courtyard casting water shadows on the second floor. It was very Spanish, very California, quite enviable.

Ben almost lost his life in a forest fire because of me, so I didn't really want to dwell on his "rescue." Since we met, he has been put in the path of questionable situations twice, so I wasn't feeling all that great about my influence. Apparently, she didn't feel I had a terribly salubrious effect on her grandson either.

She regarded me. I stopped gazing around like gaping tourist at the Fairmont and paused to took at her.

"Yes," I couched, "in a manner of speaking."

When Ben and I were up in Claim Jump last September, he was not only kidnapped, but was almost burned to death in a forest fire. It does not bear thinking about. I certainly didn't want to discuss it.

She nodded, "I thought we'd eat in the kitchen. Ben told me you don't mind being casual."

"He's right." I followed her under the porch, through open French doors, into an enormous kitchen. The walls and back splash of the work area were covered with brilliant yellow and blue Spanish tiles. The floor was tiled with rose colored, terra cotta squares. A gleaming copper hood brooded over a five burner Wolf Range. I don't use stoves per se, but I'm great at identifying them. I always list name brand appliances on my home sale flyers.

"Here, Ben, you can help." Emily strode to a huge pot on the stove and pulled out corn husk wrapped tamales and piled them onto a platter.

The dinning table was built of wine cask staves. It would dwarf a normal size room but it barely made an impression in this cavernous kitchen.

Ben carried the plate tamales along with a big bowl containing an avocado and pea salad to the table. He retrieved a bottle of wine from the refrigerator (Sub-Zero, did you have to ask?). The bottle was bare except for a white mailing label with *Pinot Gris* scrawled in ball point pen.

"Here, honey." Ben poured the wine into narrow white wine glasses. Huge, fat, burgundy glasses were already placed on the table for the main course.

"Try this. Cassandra is experimenting with whites this year."

Most people are now familiar with Sonoma County wines. You remember California beat out France in 1976 in a blind tasting, you can name the varietals, you understand the difference between red and white. But for those of you who want to move up to the advance class, un-labeled bottles are the next level of prestige. When you pour wine from a slightly dirty bottle marked with nothing more than a strip of duct tape and *Pinot Gris, 2005*, scrawled in permanent marker, you have achieved the inside track. That wine is likely to hail from a famous wine maker's private reserve – a barrel of something he or she conjured up for fun and is only delivering to personal friends. Delicious, but not for sale, the insider's wine country.

"So, I understand you're in real estate." Emily took a small sip of her white and finally took a bite of her salad, signaling that I, too, could start in.

I tried to eat slowly and daintily, but it was difficult. I don't worry about how much I eat in front of Ben, Carrie's admonishments aside. But here, with Ben's grandmother a ringer for my own mother, God help me, all the rules and restrictions of my childhood rose to the surface. I knew I had to slow down, be good, use the right fork, act like a lady. Why did I agree to this dinner?

"Yes, even though it sounds as if I get myself in awkward situations." I thought I'd go for the jugular; why not say it right away? I have put her precious grandchild in risky situations.

"Well, yes," Emily banished her fork in my direction. "But I'm sure finding a dead body can happen to anyone."

"Certainly, happens all the time," I assured her. I sipped my wine. God, it was delicious. Where did this come from again?

"I'm sure that kind of thing is all behind you," Emily said. "You two certainly seem busy. I don't see Ben as often as I want to."

Ben grunted and poured the red wine, a Preston Zin. You can buy Preston; I had a couple bottles in my cellar.

She rested her fork on the edge of her plate and eyed me. "In fact, he hasn't been here much since July."

Ben shifted and rose to serve the tamales. He picked up each one with his fingers and placed them neatly onto our dinner plates.

Emily did not flinch over Ben's methods.

I met Emily's gaze. "No, he hasn't. He's been with me."

She nodded.

"Really?" Ben balanced a plate of food, three tamales on each, and slipped it towards me. One of the tamales was in danger of sliding off the plate. I caught it with my fork.

"Yes, honey." She turned to Ben and toasted him with the red wine. "I always said you should find a nice girl and settle down."

She glanced at me. I kept my expression neutral. This was between Ben and his grandmother. It was as if Ben was eighteen and arguing with a parent who didn't want him to take off and join the Peace Corps, but stay in town and take over Dad's dry goods business.

Ben groaned, "Grandma."

"I'm being realistic. Ben, honey, three is too many; take one back." She deftly removed the still husk-wrapped tamale and tossed it back into the center bowl.

"Don't you love the holiday tradition of serving tamales to guests?" She asked me. "I get these downtown, hand made, of course."

I nodded.

Dinner went well, I think. Once we moved past the conversation about Ben, and his lack of relationships, the flow of talk was easier for me.

To distract his grandmother, Ben talked about the Pinot Gris girl.

"Cassandra flew home from Adelaide a couple of weeks ago. She is starting up her own winery here, in Dry Creek."

"There's room here?" Emily asked.

"She has about ten acres she inherited from her parents, she's building a small winery where that storage barn used to be."

"You're helping her, aren't you?" Emily said it more as fact than a real question. This was interesting.

"Yeah," Ben admitted, immediately. "I'm a partner in the winery."

Emily rolled her eyes and looked at me, then looked at Ben. "You aren't in need of a partner for any new venture are you?" She addressed me.

"Not that I'm aware of," I said piously.

"Self actualized woman?" Emily said.

"Come on," Ben protested. "I've always been there for Cassandra. What else was I supposed to do? We've been friends since the third grade, and when she inherited the vineyards, I suggested Australia for her MS," he explained to me.

"You help a lot," I said.

"Sometimes, it gets him in trouble," Emily sipped her wine.

"Yes, it does." I felt, of course, that there was more to the Cassandra story, but it probably didn't bear discussion over the dinner table in front of his grandmother. I'd find out more, later. This woman mattered. Whether this Cassandra mattered more than me was something I'd have to explore - very carefully.

Was he caring for his grandmother? Probably. I knew people who shared their homes with a parent, and it often worked well. It was not something that would work for me. My sister-in-law, Mary, once commented that my mother was always welcome in their house. I'm taking Mary at her word. I even wrote it down. I'm thinking of asking Mary to sign it. I may even have the papers notarized.

Even through the house was magnificent and the location divine, why was the man living with his grandmother? Come on, in every *Glamour* magazine article you've ever read, the number one don't sign, the worst thing a boy can do, is still live with his parents – eewww – very failure to launch.

So, as we wished Emily good night and crossed the courtyard to Ben's "apartment", I asked the question, why live with Grandma?

"I haven't found a relationship I want to ruin by building a new house," was his answer.

"Dude, you're over forty." I couldn't help it. It popped out.

I have no discretion when it comes to my personal life. I demonstrate great self-control and tact in business, which makes me think that we must only get a certain finite allotment of tact and diplomacy, and I use mine up selling homes.

He gave me an odd look that I couldn't read at all. "That may change."

"Being over forty?"

"No, you smart ass," he said with somewhat more affection. "Living with Grandma."

"Keep in touch on that."

Calling Ben's quarters an apartment was about the same level of misnomer as calling his grandmother's gracious family compound a house.

Ben lived on the first and second floor directly across the courtyard from the kitchen and, he assured me, his grandmother's rooms.

"We live more separately than it looks," he explained.

"I didn't say anything," I said.

We walked through French doors to his living room a huge library with scattered upholstered furniture.

I stood at the shelves and squinted at all the hardback books. The room was filled, floor to ceiling with books, I was in that scene when Belle is given the Beast's library. How marvelous.

"Yes, the pages are all cut," he said.

I glanced over at him, "You are still surprising me."

"I hope to always surprise you."

His bedroom was large enough to easily accommodate a

king size bed topped by a massive mission style headboard that could have been a carriage house door in a previous life. There was room for a stacked Japanese Tansu chest, two easy chairs, and an occasional table. His bathroom was equally muscular with a walk in shower recently updated in glass tiles in clear green and blue. I could pretend I was underwater. I could hardly wait to try it out.

In his bed, the sex was as good, maybe better, than at my house, there was more room in the bed. But I'm not quite ready to concede that point. I'm very happy with my own, cozy, queen size mattress.

***

Thus, based on that rather idyllic fifteen hours, I felt I could call him up on his only day off and ask for help. If he helped people the way his grandmother claimed, I was in good hands.

"Hi, what are you doing?" I think I kept my voice from trembling. I didn't want to spook him right away.

"Relaxing, are you at your open house?"

"Yes, 109 Silverpoint Circle."

He paused. "Really?"

Before we could explore that reaction, I jumped into the fray. "And I found another body."

His pause was very, long, I could hear a sharp intake of breath. "You what?"

"I found another body," I repeated. I realized, as I said it, that I also covered the entire bathroom with green mouthwash, the police may have field day with that.

Reluctantly I stood, kicked off my shoes – didn't want them to get more minty fresh than they already were – and climbed back up the stairs, while Ben, on the other end of the phone, processed my comment about another corpse.

I didn't blame him. It's not often a person picks up the phone at 12:55 on Sunday afternoon and hears the announcement that there is a new, dead body in his life. Ben was probably watching a football game or lounging in that fabulous library.

"I'm sorry, did I interrupt your game or anything?" I opened the bathroom door, the place was covered in green sticky liquid. The sound of sirens started up the hill.

"Whose?" he asked very slowly. By his tone, he knew the answer already, but that didn't make sense, I had recently taken this listing, and I wasn't all that familiar with the client. "Body?" He finished his thought.

I searched under the sink for paper towels, found them in a three pack, and began mopping up the floor. The siren volume increased.

The client, Beverly Weiss, was one of the most terrifying people in town and she had asked for me.

ASKED for ME. I should contribute at least one chapter to *How to Succeed in Real Estate* titled: *Referrals Gone Bad*. Brian Buffini, the premier guru of real estate relationship marketing aside, I may start cultivating strangers for clients, something along the lines of those afore mentioned innocent buyers of small, inexpensive condominiums. Cheap, easy, and except for lawsuits and arcane HOAs, relatively pain free.

My own referrals of late have wound up, well, late.

While Ben breathed over the phone, I hurriedly swiped at every surface in the bathroom with damp paper towels and listened to the police approach at a disconcertedly rapid rate.

"Whose body did you discover?" he finally repeated. I mopped quickly, clutching the phone with one hand (I keep my headset in the car) and taking broad swipes with the other. I tossed sticky handful after sticky handful of paper towels into the chrome garbage can (very nice style) while I listened to Ben.

"Whose house are you at again?" He repeated distractedly.

"Beverley Weiss's house," I answered honestly.

He took in another breath.

"And where is Beverley?" he asked calmly. I interpreted his voice change as moving from bewildered to preternaturally calm. He did not waver, there was no rise in inflection, no indication of future hysteria and melt down. Besides, he was safely on the phone. I was in the same house with another dead body. This time he was going to share the experience.

"Oh," I said purposefully vague. "Lying around."

"Allison," his tone changed from calm to commanding.

"She's the dead body," I admitted quickly.

"Dear, God," he said. "I'm coming down. Don't touch

anything."

    "Trust me."

Chapter 3

The Wednesday before Thanksgiving is the busiest day of the year for airports and grocery stores, but one of the quietest days of the year for our New Century real estate office. Unlike most of the agents in our office, I did not need to shop for dinner or travel to the far reaches of the country to reunite with relatives. All my relatives were local. I was lurking in the office, trying to look busy, for the benefit of our office manager Patricia and the broker on record, Inez. That is why, when Beverley Weiss marched into our office and demanded the best realtor in the company, there were only two people in the front to appreciate her performance.

Barely an hour earlier, the formidable Ms. Weiss could have had her pick of two of our equally formidable Top Producing Realtors, Rosemary and Katherine. They, too, had no need to travel or shop, but they were both in foul moods, a down market will do that to a person. They had taken to competing in events that did not have anything to do with real estate. Each woman was cranky and ready to rumble.

Today's challenge was the Diet, a feminine favorite. But they were not competing against their own personal best, no. They were dieting against each other.

I lurked by the copy machine to ease drop.

"Anyway," Rosemary boomed, "do we have a bet?"

Katherine eyed her professional adversary doubtfully.

It was one thing, I thought, to be in competition professionally, but quite another to make it personal, as in the case of fitness or diet. I believe a girl should choose to be fit or thin, but not both. The lack of nutrition in the typically female "diet plan" would leave me so weak I wouldn't be able to find the strength to leave the house, let alone indulge in something as odious as jogging, running, discus throwing, caber toss. Fortunately, in the name of keeping our neighborhoods beautiful, jogging was not part of the Katherine/Rosemary bet. Both women are substantial. Katherine is larger than me, jogging wouldn't be a good idea at all.

"Yes," Katherine agreed. She clearly had the advantage over Rosemary. Katherine had less weight to lose, and the weight she did bear was the result of temporary overindulgence overseas. Her latest trip to the Dalmatian Coast had left her relaxed and filled with grilled squid and Croatian beer.

On the other hand, Rosemary was the queen of herbal remedies, magnets and magical thinking. She was not above burying a statue of St. Joseph upside down in the back yard of a house that was not selling quickly. Go to any Christian bookstore, there's a whole kit for purchase.

"Do you think Rosemary has something up her sleeve?" I mused as the two women marched out to conquer their own physiques in the absence of house listings and buyers. Real estate can be very slow in November and December. A person may as well find another project, or a new way to compete. I was relieved they didn't ask me to play.

"Not since she gave up wearing Kimonos to work," Patricia, our office manager, pointed out.

Rosemary loved Japan. Her husband had recently finished building a set of Torii gates in their back yard. The fact that her house is Craftsman and Adobe Mission style is immaterial, the gates were painted an authentic, and bright, orange.

I overheard part of their bet, as well as the contest rules that included engaging a personal trainer. They were not hiring the same personal trainer; that would be a conflict of interest. They had their own. And since that was more important than hanging around an empty office, I had to face the infamous Beverley Weiss alone.

I knew Beverley Weiss by reputation. For years, Beverley was Sonoma County's "it" girl for photos and events. Beverley had the knack and the timing to appear at every important event and in every photo of that event. She was always in the paper, from polo matches to wine auctions. That is, until Carrie became the "it" girl of the dairy world and usurped Ms. Weiss from the society pages. (I am not allowed to call Carrie the Dairy Queen; she's surprisingly sensitive about that.) Beverley even received the *Woman of the Year* award from the Girl Scout Council for her work with the homeless and jolly good for her.

Now, I've only read about the fabulous Beverly Weiss, and seen her many photos in our local paper. More important, I've heard stories about Beverley from Carrie. Carrie is not a fan of Ms. Weiss. Remember, Carrie rescues feral cats. So, I knew there was more to Beverley that met the eye. River's Bend Press reporters, Chris Connor among them, may think Beverley walks on water, I doubt very much that's how the woman cleans her pool.

I was not pre-disposed to love Ms. Weiss, if only to be loyal to my best friend.

Beverley was tall and very thin which is not necessarily the best look for a woman staring down fifty. This afternoon, she was dressed in a leopard print dress and matching shoes. She had the whole stalking feline thing going for her, but she was brittle, not sexy. Her collarbone pushed sharply against the thin fabric of her Furstenberg knock off. A man could get a nasty bruise from her bony hip.

Patricia our office manager/receptionist smirked and gestured in my direction. I hesitated. I was not on Floor (meaning that if a potential client walked into the office, the possible client/sale would not "belong" to me, the client would "belong" to the agent who was working floor) someone else could take this, really.

"Hi," I said reluctantly, "I'm Allison Little."

"I've seen your ads. Good. Meet me at my house tomorrow at 10:00, I want to sell it." She flipped back her dark hair to emphasis the finality of her demand.

"That's Thanksgiving morning," Patricia pointed out.

"Oh," Beverley paused for a second or two, as if calculating what Thanksgiving exactly was, then she dismissed the holiday out of hand.

"How about Friday?" I offered. "I'll be in town." I glanced down pointedly at her footwear. "Love the shoes," I said. "Blahnik?"

"Yes," she eyed me with some suspicion.

"I remember them from last years' collection." I was completely pleasant. "So Friday then?"

"Friday then." If anything she bristled more, as well she

should.

She handed me a card, *Consultant Services for a Better World*, with a home address in the Villas. Lovely.

She stalked out of the office.

"Nice hit on the shoes," Patricia said, happily.

"Wait until the Christmas party," I warned. "I picked your name for the gift exchange."

Patricia's face fell. "I'll make it up to you."

"Oh, yes, you will." I retrieved my laptop and prepared a market analysis for the Villas.

We have two neighborhoods in River's Bend that are distinct and known by name alone. Live in either one, and simply hearing your street address will give an acquaintance a rather accurate summary of your income, taste, and aspirations. I do not live in either area. My neighborhood does not infer any residential reputation, good or bad, which is the way I like it.

The first and most expensive neighborhood in River's Bend is the Villas. It was named a long time ago when there were only a dozen or so homes ground into the foothills overlooking the eastern part of the town. The Villas have since been partitioned off and sold into tiny, tiny lots with great big steroid-smacking houses that push painfully into the few trees that survived the building process in the 80s.

The Villas now comprise of multiple rows of expansive streets and deep cul-de-sacs stacked with homes. Despite the prices starting at one million, the houses all look the same. This is actually part of their appeal. Really.

Nothing says success like a home in the Villas. One of my good friends, Joan, a college professor who should know better, used to have a lot to say about the Villas, until she and her new boyfriend, Norton, bought a condo at the foot of the Villas. Their condo has all of the address without the extra cost. They are inordinately pleased with themselves. Although I appreciated the commission, I wasn't all that excited by their choice.

I sighed heavily. I did not want this listing with Beverley Weiss in the Villas. But times were not great, and only an idiot turns down a listing opportunity. I was not an idiot. But working with Beverley Weiss? I didn't know if that would enhance what was left of my reputation or irrevocably trash it.

I arrived at Beverley's on Friday morning (five minutes early). Beverley was snapping with energy. Her footwear was clearly from this fall's collection, a bright cobalt blue spike heeled pump that matched her formal cobalt boiled wool suit. The suit was by Chanel, and it was not a knock off.

I wore something by DKNY. I don't remember what. I usually dress conservatively, so as not to distract or frighten the prospective clients. My news about the list price (much lower than they imagined) of their house is usually shocking enough without overwhelming them by wearing a crimson suit by Versace, at least in this market.

"I must sell this right away," Beverley allowed me to come in and waved to the two-story high living room stuffed with faux antiques and Chinese inspired furniture found at Cost Plus.

The lilac walls clashed with the dark rosewood of the chairs in the dining room as well as the yellow, uncomfortable appearing couch. No less than five small rugs were scattered on the cushioned wall-to-wall carpet. Magazines and papers slipped and sloshed over the crowd of tables. Plates and glasses covered the dining table. I pushed aside three china plates, all in different patterns, to make room for my briefcase (Coach).

"The average time on the market is ninety days," I pointed out, armed with statistics, real time quotes and a market analysis. I opened my laptop and started up the PowerPoint. My elbow hit a cut glass wine goblet; I grabbed it and moved it carefully out of harm's way.

I glanced up from the computer. There was so much stuff. The place was crammed with crap, and I mean that in a descriptive, non-judgmental way. Crap. Yet, her house would do well on the market listed in the 1.5 range.

"I don't have ninety days." She glanced at the computer screen but didn't focus on it for long. She paced, her shoes muffled by the carpet (white).

"On average," I corrected her.

"Can't we sell this tomorrow?" She marched back and forth; her pointed heels dug tiny half circles into her thick rugs.

"We will need to list it lower than everything else in the

neighborhood," I said.

"Do that," she instructed. "Whatever it takes for a quick sale."

I frowned. I had pulled more than the market comps. I pulled her mortgage and tax information as well. "You're highly leveraged, you may not get enough to make any profit."

Beverley had three loans on the property. So far, the equity had risen enough to keep pace with her withdrawals, barely.

"I also noticed on the tax records that your spouse, listed here as *husband* is still on title," I added.

"Oh, that," she waved her hand elegantly, a practiced gesture to ward off peasants, flies and unpleasant facts. Her nails were long and acrylic, polished with the popular French manicure style, a sparkling pink and white not found in nature, but seen in women's gyms across the country. I had the same manicure, but I'm not found in any gym.

"Don't worry. He'll sign. I'll call him this weekend. He'll sign whatever you want. Leave it," she gestured to the file I set next to the computer, "and I'll have his signature for you."

"He doesn't have a problem with you selling the house?" I have to ask these things, really. If I don't, when the argument comes out later, it's always messy, depressing and by then, I'm out hard cash on marketing, advertising. and signs.

"Oh, no, he only wants me to be happy, the dear," she assured me.

I imagined a soft man, who was originally corralled into the relationship because of her charm, personality, or a pregnancy scare. He did have the nerve to divorce her, which shows he had some balls. I was proud of our Mr. Weiss, whoever he was.

"Can you start the ball rolling, while I get the other signature?" She smiled at me, it was meant to influence people and charm donors, but I was immune, probably because I understand the game.

"You are aware, of course, that November isn't the best time to sell? The holidays are not a traditional home selling season."

"Can you sell it anyway?"

"Of course," I said, without thinking. Sorry, spontaneous reaction. I can close escrow on homes with dead people still on the premise. I am that good. Fortunately, I didn't bring up that bragging right.

"Good, when can we have the open house?" Despite her restless movements, she managed to avoid knocking into any of the antique furniture, tripping on the throw rugs, or slipping on an errant magazine.

"You may want to paint first," I pointed out. "I pastel colors can really turn off potential buyers, especially the men."

A slight exaggeration, my former client, Norton, lived in a house painted in wedding favor pastels. That's how he and Joan met. Joan, a good friend of mine, helped me by posing as a feng shui expert to convince him to paint the whole house a sellable beige. Then they fell in love. That one, I did not see coming.

"If I paint the walls, will you sell the house?" Beverley demanded, hands on her slender hips, perfect nails spread, ready for their close up.

"That, and if you move half of this furniture, and all of this, stuff, to the garage," I instructed. "And remove the throw rugs."

She nodded slowly.

"And if you put away anything precious, jewelry, papers, prescription drugs, anything you don't want strangers looking at or taking." I was dubious about the size of the garage; a two-car garage may not be large enough to pack all this stuff away, and I hadn't seen the upstairs bedrooms, yet.

"Okay."

"I can list it now, and we can run an open house on Sunday. But, by the time I'm back for the open house, I need your ex-husband's signature."

"His signature will be on everything you need, I promise," she said gravely. I expected her to promise with Scouts Honor, but she didn't seem the type, despite her Girl Scout accolades.

That was Friday. I did not think there was any possible way she could pull off getting the house ready by Sunday. More than one wall in that two-story living room was painted luscious lilac. No way.

"Sure," I said. I didn't have to paint; she did. "Why not? Paint."

"No problem," her face was grim.

I'll have your listing on the Internet today," I promised her, pulling out my camera. I never post a listing without photos. I took a few photos for the initial posting and planned to take the rest after the rooms were cleared and re-painted.

"Great." She quickly and efficiently ran down the basics of the house (to her knowledge) and signed the agreements I needed signed with no fuss or wrinkling of her botoxed forehead and asking for more explanation about that paragraph or that boilerplate statement.

I was happy to wrap it up myself; I had that big date at Ben's house. An evening with him was my reward for having to spend Thanksgiving with my family.

* * *

The police arrived in all their glory. Three cars pulled up with lights flashing, but thankfully by the time they reached the neighborhood, they had turned off the sirens. Although, the noise and lights could attract potential buyers right to the open house. That's a thought. For a whole minute, I mused on how I could use a siren in my next open house, but I was distracted by the matter at hand and didn't complete my mental plan.

The River's Bend police were gratifyingly business-like and surprisingly concerned that the perpetrator could be still lurking in the house. I never remember to worry about that part.

Ben arrived ten minutes after the police. He slammed the front door and bellowed my name. He was a wild man, his hair stood straight up from his head, as if he had covered his hands with glue then rubbed his fingers vigorously through his hair.

I discovered later that was fairly close to the truth. He was repairing a chair with   Gorilla glue, and after my phone call, he had agitatedly run his fingers through his hair.

"Hi," he looked at me and took a breath, as if seeing me calmed him.

"Hi," I answered back.

He squinted up at the stairs but didn't move towards them. An officer was already stringing yellow caution tape across the upper banister, blocking off the second floor. I was glad the lilac paint was gone. It would have clashed horribly with the yellow tape.

"She is up there?" he asked.

"Yes. Ben," I began.

"Sir," one of the officers interrupted me. "I'm afraid you'll have to leave, only authorized personnel and next of kin are allowed."

He nodded, "It's okay. I'm her ex-husband."

Chapter 4

The two police officers moved aside, for a third, a man not in uniform but dressed casually in tee shirt and jeans, looking as if his Thanksgiving football game had been interrupted, quickly passed us without a word and raced up the stairs taking them two at a time.

"I need to see her," Ben lunged for the stairs, following the man. One of the police officers stepped forward to restrain Ben, but I reached him first.

"No," I put a hand on Ben's arm. "No, you don't."

He pulled against me, but I held on ready to dig in my heels, so to speak, but he didn't resist further. Maybe, he sensed something. He squinted up the stairs. I kept my hand firmly on his arm, just in case.

"Sir, that is a secured area. Come with us." The young officer gestured with his head to the dinning room a few steps away from the "secured area" but still within sight of the stairs.

Ben looked at me; I nodded and tried my best to look reassuring.

"Please." I pushed back the images that were burned into my own retinas. He did not need that kind of image burned into his retina. I was not aware if, during the divorce, he ever considered hacking up his wife. Many people fantasize about the worst thing that could happen to the ex- spouse. I did. Maybe Ben did, but he didn't need his worst fantasies confirmed.

"Come and sit."

I led him over to the dining room table, cleared of at least the dirty dishes, which reminded me of food, which reminded me of something he said a few months ago about a former relationship.

"Ben," I whispered. The same police officer was approaching again, armed not with his gun but with an official notebook.

"Ben, was Beverley the one who sporked you?"

He nodded. He has used that metaphor to describe a messy painful way of getting your heart ripped out of your chest. Not a knife, that was clean and tidy. A spork, the spoon and fork combination that one picks up in a fast food bin, between the napkins and the catsup. In Ben's case, his heart had been mangled by a cheap plastic spork. If he described his past relationship with a spork metaphor, he did not need to see how his ex-wife had been murdered.

She must have hurt him very badly. We hadn't yet reached the point of discussing at length our past relationships. Hell, I had visited his home. I did peek in his medicine cabinet. The contents were unremarkable. He had no moisturizer or exfoliant, or enhancement drugs of any kind. Not a vain man, my Ben.

The officer sat down across from us. Ben eyed him warily, already knowing what the young man would ask.

I talked first, since I was first on the scene. I explained where I had been and when I found the body. I could be pretty precise, but I had no alibi to speak of, since I spent the night alone in my own house Saturday night.

Ben stared at his hands, as I spoke, and absently picked off the last pieces of dried glue.

"And you sir?"

"I was at home alone last night. No witnesses," Ben said carefully.

The officer nodded and made notes on his notebook.

"Don't go anywhere," the officer, his nametag said Robert Yarnell, counseled.

Ben sighed, "Don't worry; it's the holidays. I don't travel during the holidays."

"Do either of you have the names of the next of kin?" Officer Yarnell asked. They are so young, these police officers.

Ben rubbed his face. "They are in Stanislaus."

"Do you have their contact information?" The nice, young man asked.

"Maybe."

The officer regarded Ben, and so did I.

"I don't have much contact with them. Their name is Spader."

"Her name is Weiss."

"She took my name when we married and wanted to keep it.

I took my mother's name, Stone, after the divorce."

"You changed your name?" I shouldn't poke the bear when he was effectively caged; it popped out.

He sighed, the pain, so long ago, still shimmered inches below the surface. He had not been very good at placing the past to rest.

"Beverley wanted to cut a swath through River's Bend society, and I was not interested in bobbing in her wake, so I took Grandma's name, and retreated."

"That doesn't sound typical of you."

"Well, I've matured some since my twenties, and you have to admit, Ben Stone, Rock Solid Service got your attention." He managed a small smile, a faint copy of the real thing, barely legible.

"Are you saying it was worth it?" I asked.

"Yes," he said simply. "But this."

"This," I gestured to the house (and all the stuff) that surrounded us. "Is now yours. Unless you signed something in the last twenty-four hours."

I stopped talking. Beverley assured me that she would have her ex stop by and sign off on the listing agreement. Had he?

"Did you?" I regarded him. His usually brilliant blue eyes were clouded. Lines I had never noticed before were etched in his forehead and on either side of his mouth. He clenched his jaw, and I could see the strain in his neck muscles.

"No, I haven't signed anything. I've been listed on the house so long I don't even think about it. Beverley let me write off some of the repairs and part of the mortgage on my taxes, but that was it."

I regarded the door, the intact door still on hinges. "You didn't stop by."

"And kill her? No." He rubbed his hands over his face again. "No, I have more sense than that. After the divorce, I became much smarter at recognizing cause and effect." He looked upstairs, as if she could hear him.

"High maintenance, you're familiar with the term?"

"I'm familiar, yes," I wasn't sure if I too, was high maintenance, so I didn't say anything more.

"You know she had a second and third on the house." I said.

"Probably," he agreed. "She was a consultant, but I think it was the kind of consulting that involved too many cocktail parties and not enough income producing seminars. She spent a lot of money. She was excellent at that."

"Do you still support her?"

"Alimony," he agreed.

I must have made a face, because he smiled wanly at my expression.

"I take it you don't agree with alimony?"

"Only if the husband dumps his wife for a much cuter secretary after the wife raised the children to be model citizens, attended all the sporting events alone, and put him through medical school by moonlighting as a Chicken McNugget, then yes, I think alimony is fair, as well as child support. But if everyone works . . ." I shrugged, and his smiled widened.

"You are an independent woman aren't you?"

"Well, yes, you already knew that." I gazed up at the ceiling; it was painted white, fresh paint. I finally focused on the living room and dining area. It was still hopelessly messy. When I arrived this afternoon, I had been too determined to pry the homeowner out of the house, to be distracted by the mess.

"You'll get maybe $10,000 when it's all done." I had to point that out right away.

"Less your commission?" He grinned.

I looked up the stairs at the closed doors of the master bedroom. "I already earned my commission and then some."

"Pretty bad?"

"Ben." He'd find out from the police. I glanced around, only the police. No media? I'd at least expect the River's Bend press to monitor police calls. Where were all the amateur photographers, bloggers, people on the spot? No one. But if I didn't tell him, he'd eventually find out on an Internet posting or read about it in the paper.

I wrenched my attention from the lack of interested bystanders and forced myself to look at him. "Someone hacked her up."

"Why?" He barely got the word out. I understood his

revulsion. I was still reeling from my own.

"I didn't know her," I finally said, a lame answer.

"I did." He closed his eyes and sagged into the chair, but he made no move to go upstairs. I was relieved.

The police took care of the – pieces, and I moved Ben from the Eclectic Living Room into the Spacious Gourmet Kitchen with Double Convection Oven and Wolf Gas Range to prevent him from seeing the grisly procession down the stairs and out the front door. There were still no reporters. And no neighbors, maybe using sirens to attract buyers wasn't such a great idea after all.

Did the police load her into one big bag or a collection of small bags? This is why we weren't watching.

When the front door opened, I could hear the conversations from the gathering of now interested neighbors outside. Ah, there they were. Perhaps there was media as well, which was not good. I wasn't going to say anything.

I heard my looky-loos holding court out on the driveway explaining their version of events in loud, and impressively authoritative, tones.

"We were just in there, we walked right in. Didn't look as if anyone broke in. Maybe it was the Real Estate agent. You can't trust them, you know. Six percent, how do they get away with that kind of money?"

"Thanks very much," I said under my breath.

"The carpets are lovely," the wife chimed in.

"Those are the McMurrys." Ben cocked his head and listened to the running patter outside. "He hasn't changed. Thinks he's an expert on everything and loves to regale anyone unfortunate enough to be caught outside, with details of his latest discovery. When we moved in, he came right over, pointing out every flaw in our new house, because he watched it being built."

"Great, I'll have to disclose about the neighbor."

"No, he'll lay pretty low until the house is sold."

"How can you be sure?

"All these homes were sold in the week we moved in, it was during one of the booms."

"You all bought high."

He nodded, "that was eleven years ago. He won't want to spook the market right now. He wants you to get top dollar to keep his own value up. He'll behave."

"Let's hope so," but I wasn't too sure about the McMurrys.

By two thirty we were asked to vacate the premises. I failed to point out the lock box on the faucet bib to the nice policeman, Robert. A small oversight on my part.

It was the shortest Open House I ever held, and the longest. Ben said nothing about the state of the house, that it was still choked with crap. I was sure that the bedroom downstairs and the second bedroom upstairs were packed with even more stuff. This was the sloppiest Open House I ever held. It was embarrassing, but I couldn't go about cleaning right now.

I checked my phone on my way out. I missed my grandmother's call. I always call her at 2:00 on Sunday. It was a great time to chat, either to fill in a long Sunday afternoon or to while away an open house time.

What exactly was I going to tell my grandmother when she asked about my day?

The coverage in Monday's paper was more discrete than I would have given the fourth estate credit for, ever. The reporter had not been allowed in Beverley's house. The neighbors claimed they heard nothing, saw nothing. She was a quiet neighbor. The article devoted most of the column space to what Beverley contributed to the community. The president of the Homeless Prevention League as well as staff members of United Way were quoted. Her terrible accident was only mentioned briefly. In Chris Connor's daily column, Beverley's good works were highlighted in glowing terms. I suppose that was the right approach. I do admire the new trend in reporting, where the media does not give the random terrorist or disturbed gunman too much publicity, as it seems to play directly into the person's reasons for the action in the first place.

The funeral was scheduled for Wednesday, and there were only twenty-one more shopping days left until Christmas.

I scanned the paper again. Sometimes, I read too fast. I'm so accustomed to already knowing most of what I read: standardized forms, the same financial news, the same war reportage, the same disclaimers from politicians, that I skim right over the words and sometimes miss something. Accident?

I did not attend the funeral, figuring the new girlfriend at the ex-wife's funeral would be tacky.

I knew Ben took Emily, and no, I did not get any feedback from him as to his grandmother's reaction or impression of "yours truly". I didn't expect the man to have a heart to heart talk with his grandmother, nor did I expect him to express his feelings. I'm not that naïve. A word, an acknowledgment, a brief "Emily through your shoes were nice and you have nice teeth", would have been helpful. But it was not to be.

The obituary in the paper was effusive and listed all of Beverley's good works with direct quotes about how lovely and giving she was. Some of the quotes were lifted directly from Chris O'Connor's article. The cause of death was not included in the obit.

"It was tragic." Carrie waved her hand in an excellent impersonation of Martha Anderson, one of the big, and by that I mean an even larger circumference than me, philanthropists in River's Bend.

"It was ALLL so Tragic," Carrie drawled. "The whole funeral was all about the," she dropped her voice to a whisper, "tragedy of it all. She was so young."

Carrie was on a roll, and I had to give her credit. She imitated the second most formidable woman in town with a certain panache.

I leaned back and surveyed the restaurant. It was a Thursday afternoon, and not terribly crowded. The windows of the enclosed patio opened to the vineyards, a few tenacious leaves hung to the bare twisted vines. The vines were beautiful in a stark, artistic way, even in the low light of December. That's why guests are so willing to pay the high entree prices at this restaurant; it's beautiful.

"Are you and Patrick taking acting lessons or something? That was really good."

"No," she lowered her voice to her normal tones. "Since we

quit the personal trainer nonsense, we've been looking for something to work on together."

Carrie won Patrick Sullivan in a fair fight; actually there was no fight at all. Once the young Mr. Sullivan, scion of the Cooper Milk fortune, took one look at Carrie Elliot of the less-said-the-better-Eliots, he was a goner. It couldn't have happened to a nicer man.

"What about those lectures?" I asked.

She sighed and picked up her hamburger, allowing me to snag a half dozen fries. "I was getting kind of fond of those JC lectures, but they don't schedule them during the holidays."

"People are busy."

"Well, I guess we're busy. We have a bunch of parties to attend from now until Christmas, I have your sister-in-law's party, should I bring Patrick? How is Richard holding up?"

"Yes you should, he can slum for one evening. Richard is fine, so far. Thanksgiving was pretty calm. Richard won't over indulge at the club, he meets too many old high school friends there."

She nodded, "What do you think will happen at Christmas?"

"I'm not sure," I admitted. "I have no idea why Debbie insists on organizing a home grown family Christmas."

"Maybe she's tired of the country club scene."

I nodded, "I have to admit, the country club is a good way to keep things civil."

"You're lucky to have civil," Carrie said curtly.

I didn't need to answer her. I knew about her family. They are a long back-story. Carrie works hard to leave her past behind, so I help her by not bringing it up. It's part of our friend code, I consider it our Pirate Code.

"You will do fine this holiday, you have Patrick. Why the glum face?"

"I heard rumors about Beverly's Weiss's death. That it wasn't an accident."

"They said it was an accident at the funeral?"

"That was the assumption, yes. According to the papers. Why?" She narrowed her eyes and abruptly stopped another theft of her fries with a stab of her knife.

"Do you know something?" She asked, suspiciously.

"Me?" I tugged gently at the French fry, but she did not release it. The papers, for once, had left my name out of the article on Beverly Weiss's death, because I am a possible suspect. After all, I did find her, and I had no excuses for the night before. I also have no motive since I hadn't meet the woman before Thanksgiving week. On the other hand, I'm dating her ex-husband.

"Patrick and I were at the funeral because Cooper Milk is a major donor to the Homeless Prevention League and well, it looks good to support those things. I noticed that Ben was there, at the funeral."

"Of course."

"Ben?" She shifted her knife slightly, but didn't quite release the fry.

I sighed and gave up. "Ben's her ex-husband. They divorced years ago."

She released the fry. "Ben Stone and Beverley Weiss?"

"The very same." I popped the fry into my mouth before she could change her mind.

Carrie sat back. She had eaten almost all her blue cheese, bacon burger and some of her own fries. She doesn't often eat that much.

"Ben and Beverley Weiss," Carrie repeated. It was not seemingly to smile at the demise of a rival, but here with me, she could do it. I didn't dare tell her I found the body.

"Dessert ladies?" Cooed our waiter.

We both nodded and ordered. Carrie was on a roll, and it was my turn to pay, so she didn't hold back. I have a better job than Carrie. She is the secretary for the local senior center, practically a volunteer job.

"She was a snob, overbearing and not very nice on top of it," Carrie blurted out.

"I didn't think you knew her."

Carrie picked up a piece of bread and began tearing it into tiny bits. "We use to hold these joint fundraisers with the Homeless Prevention League. I worked with Anna, their marketing director, mostly. The Senior Center and the League had overlapping clients, so we tried to maximize what services we had. Sometimes I helped at the events, the wine auction and polo match, larger events. Beverley Weiss would sweep through wearing a spectacular hat or something and look right through you, as if you were nothing, you understand how that is?"

"Oh, I understand," I reassured her. I did not mention that it was Carrie's turn to sweep into a volunteer event, wear the magnificent hat and be as snotty as she wanted. We were discussing Beverley.

"Anyway, I never admired her attitude. Every one is a person and important, don't you think?"

"Did she help out at all?"

"Doing what?"

"Oh, important activities: rounding up cats, pouring wine, feeding the hungry, that kind of thing."

Carrie shook her head.   "She wasn't all that physically involved. The Homeless Prevention League is having a big party in her honor. The Executive Director, although he calls himself the President and CEO, when did all these executive directors decide to elevate themselves to CEO and President? Why can't they be happy as an Executive Director? What is wrong with the title of Executive Director?"

She looked at me.

I looked at her, and took another French fry, as payment for her outburst. She can get quite passionate about the volunteer systems in River's Bend.

"Sorry."

"It's okay."

"The President and CEO, Steven, announced the event date at the funeral. I heard from Anne that Beverley didn't even leave any money to them, not one dime."

"She didn't have much to leave," I said, "unless there is a hedge fund she's hiding somewhere."

"What do you mean?"

"The house was mortgaged up past its value. Ben will be lucky to clear ten grand from the transaction, maybe less. And it appears much of her income went to the Shopping Network."

"You have a lot of inside information."

I took a deep breath, "I listed her house. And I still have the listing."

"Ben still wants to sell?" Carrie made the immediate and logical jump. I do love that about her. She looks cute, adorable, and in the right light, completely innocent, but I have learned not to underestimate her. Ever.

"Yes, he does," I admitted.

Carrie tapped her lips thoughtfully. "Beverley loved to talk about her things. She couldn't get through a conversation without mentioning how much money she had and all the high fashion items she was planning to buy. She and Cynthia, the ED, sorry, President and CEO's secretary at the Homeless Prevention League were always talking about sales at Nordstrom and the newest designs at Tiffany's. Cyndi wasn't at the funeral. I thought those two might have been friends, but then Cyndi was merely a secretary. Beverley was a board member."

"A secretary and board member can't be friends?"

"What? Oh, God no." Carrie said it with great authority, and I believed her. She knew more about the inner structure and social mores of a non-profit than I did.

"A lack of money does not prevent you from buying more stuff," I pointed out. It was necessary to point that out to Carrie. She was naturally frugal, but she did it with style.

"Beverley's credit cards were maxed out," I continued, not that it was really public knowledge, but Carrie was my best friend. "She had no savings, no IRA, nothing." I shook my head, as a single woman, that kind of attitude was financial suicide, what did the woman think was going to happen? That Prince Charming was coming in to sweep her off her feet and take her to live happily ever after in Mexico or Tahiti?

No Prince Charming will save you. Sometimes, what Prince Charming really wants is a loan. Forget the prince; invest in your IRA.

"Patrick is a big donor, so we'll have to be there," Carrie broke into my thoughts, "at the tribute event."

Our waiter, James, brought a crème brûlée for me, and a chocolate volcano for Carrie.

"I'm impressed." I gazed at her chocolate dessert. No matter what I order, the other dessert always looks better.

"I'm celebrating." Carrie poked her spoon into the surface of the dense pudding, and a small eruption of hot chocolate flowed down to the white plate. She toasted me with her chocolate-mounded spoon. "Patrick fired our personal trainer."

Katherine, who was embarking on her diet and exercise competition with Rosemary, should be so lucky.

There is nothing better than a three-hour lunch (with wine) with Carrie to revive my faith in the world. I floated into the office intending to be seen, then I planned to float out just as quickly, pretending I had a series of important appointments to attend. What I was actually planning to do was nap. There is not much else a person can do with the afternoon after consuming half a bottle of Sauvignon Blanc.

My cell rang, and I foolishly answered, breaking up my euphoria and my immediate plans.

"Come with me."

"Excuse me?"

"Don't ask questions, say yes and come with me," he repeated.

"To the Kasbah, to Hawaii, to Tahiti (once I mentioned it, it was on my mind), on a long cruise?"

"No, to the Homeless Prevention League dinner."

"Why is it a League?"

"League sounds more official. They once wanted to call it a fleet, after the number of RVs for the homeless they have, but I suppose that was too pompous."

"Or someone else already secured the URL."

"That too," he agreed. "So come with me."

"When is it?" I fished out my calendar from the matching brief case.

Say what you want about electronics, I still haven't mastered how to stay on the phone and check my calendar – also on the phone – simultaneously.

He had the decency to pause, "uh, tomorrow?"

"You're kidding."

"It's a last minute tribute, they added it to an already

scheduled event. More efficient that way."

"Well I'm all for non-profit efficiency." I pretended to spend time studying my calendar.

"You are in luck," I said. "I happen to be free tomorrow tonight."

"I'm flattered."

"You're impossible."

"To warn you, they are planning to make a long speech about Beverley and bestow me with some God awful plaque or something, as the officially bereaved husband."

"Ex-husband," I helpfully supplied. "No family?"

"Her parents came to the funeral, but they won't attend an event that's so formal. They don't drive at night."

"They could stay over."

"They don't drive at night," he repeated sternly. I wondered how long he put up with these parents. They didn't sound very, flexible.

"I'll meet you there," I promised.

According to the beautiful, artsy web site, The Homeless Prevention League does very good and innovative work. The HPL developed the innovative idea that instead of homeless encampments or large group homes, they would provide RVs able to accommodate four to eight people (all the same gender and propensity) and move said RV around the community so that no one neighbor could cry "NIMBY" and claim the homeless, er, homes, were a blight on his neighborhood. Most of us in the business have asked the Homeless Prevention League, at one time or another, for a schedule of the RV parking – mostly for MLS photos or to make sure an RV isn't parked next to a property when we're holding an open house. The staff at the Homeless Prevention League has never, in recent memory, been that forthcoming with information. All the staff members said the same thing: "placement of the RVs is random."

According to their site, HPL owns about 35 RVs in all. A big operation.

I heard Patricia greet Katherine, as the door chime rang. I wandered out to the foyer.

Katherine limped into the office and waved at Patricia

before the office manager could even open her mouth.

"I am exhausted. That woman is the devil incarnate. How does she keep clients if she is so demanding?" Katherine dragged her briefcase as if it held two computers and seventeen escrow envelopes, not the one, sleek, red laptop.

"How did your session with your personal trainer go?" Rosemary popped out of her office and smirked at Katherine.

Katherine glared at her. "You said it was super slow."

"That sounds benign," I offered.

"It may have been slow, but after minute three, I thought I was going to die! My legs hurt so bad, I could barely get out of the Beemer."

Rosemary grinned, "It's good for you."

"Maybe not," Patricia piped up. "Josh said that slow is good for you and all, and it builds long term muscle mass, but I read in *O Magazine* that you need to work out really fast for quick weight loss."

"Bursts of energy," Rosemary nodded wisely. "It's supposed to be good for your heart rate."

"You're suppose to mix up your routine, but your core program is extremely important," Patricia countered.

Katherine paused and considered her briefcase. "I'm going to slowly lie down."

"No one said it would be easy," Rosemary said. Her tone was a bit too sanctimonious, even for her.

Katherine rolled her eyes and limped back out the front door.

"I knew she couldn't do it," Rosemary crowed.

"Isn't Joanna a client of yours?" Patricia asked.

"What does that have to do with it?"

"Oh, nothing." Patricia turned her attention back to her computer screen. The daily postings from the news (she prefers the awful and grotesque) kept her riveted.

"Did you hear about the winery worker who died while he was cleaning the bottom of one of those huge, stainless steel tanks?" She leaned closer to her monitor. "Damn, there's no picture."

If I had more time and energy, I'd be really worried about Patricia.

Chapter 5

That afternoon, I let Ben back into the house. He stopped in the living room and took it all in.

"I'm going to take care of this mess today," I quickly reassured him. Either he wasn't worried about the mess, or he was so accustom to the state of the house, he no longer saw it.

"She painted," he said.

"I insisted."

He nodded, "Good for you. She painted the walls in this dark burgundy when we first decorated the house."

The idea of them decorating a house together gave me a sudden pang. How did she get to be so lucky? Who was she?

"She toned it down to lilac by the time I came on the scene," I said.

"She considered herself very artistic." He glanced up at the bedroom, then at me.

I nodded. I hired cleaning professionals of the more haz-mat variety, they had wrought a miracle with the walls and ceiling. The carpet was replaced by Wednesday afternoon. Everything else, the spread, mattress and all the clothing and shoes Beverly had left scattered around the bedroom floor, had to be thrown away.

I had no idea why Ben was drawn to that room, but that's where he headed, up the stairs.

I trailed behind him on the carpeted steps. The one thing that kept me from falling head over heels for this man was I was certain I'd end up the major breadwinner. He had a handyman business, Rock Solid Service, and he was good at what he did. But my income was higher. My grandmother says I'm crazy. Now my assumptions had been proved wrong. Now what do I do?

"I take it you have plenty of money," I said to his back which was easier than looking him in the eye. This was clearly not a subject of which he was terribly fond, otherwise he'd flaunt it as much as every other rich guy I came across, or God help me, dated.

He slowed on the stairs, but he didn't turn around to face me. "Does it matter?"

"Only that I don't have to support you," I replied to his stiff back.

He nodded and continued to walk to, yes, the master bedroom. I followed him. He turned slowly around the bedroom taking in the bare walls and the new bed spread and pillows. (We couldn't get everything out.)

"Where did you put the art?" he asked.

"What art?" I replied.

"You didn't see any art when you viewed the house?"

"Not the first time," I said. "I have the photos. They're on the web if you want to confirm." I had replaced the photos of the downstairs, but kept the photo of the unsullied master bedroom. And there was no art on the walls.

"No, no," his voice was quiet, hurt. "She must have sold the art. Why did she sell the art?" He said it more to himself than to me.

"How much art?" I asked.

He frowned at the walls, as if they had eaten up his investments. "We, she, had a pretty good collection. We bought much of it together."

"Better to buy jewelry," I said. "Take it with you."

I wasn't good at art. The two of us met over art and the controversy it produced. Who knew art was controversial? I'm of the school where art should be pleasant and match the living room furniture. I'm not on very sure footing when it came to a discussion about post-modern, modern or pre-post-modern painting.

Now, jewelry I understand. Carrie told me about the Romanoffs. She learned about them at one of her JC lectures. That family took all their jewelry and hid it in their clothes before their escape. Precious stones are easy to transport. All that jewelry did the royal family no good in the end. I'm merely pointing out that a few rings are easier to pack than a 5 foot by 10 foot canvas.

"She had jewelry, too,"

I stepped to the free-standing jewelry box, something

Beverley probably bought through the Horchow Collection. The box was packed with baubles, all in a jumble, the same as the living room, the same as her bedroom. Most of her stuff was faux, but good faux, faux that still ran into the thousands for each piece.

Ben glanced into the box, "She certainly believed in being good to herself."

"Or her boyfriends did," I said automatically.

Ben winced, "I suppose she would get gifts from them."

I resisted picking up a piece or two.

"Do you know any of her girlfriends?" I asked.

"I didn't see anyone at the funeral who could have been a girlfriend, who had that girlfriend look. Of course, they wouldn't seek me out, would they? "

"Maybe she earned it," I defended her jewelry, if only to protect the age-old contract women have with men. Diamonds are a girl's best friend.

"Maybe," Ben stared at the empty walls. "All gone, as if they didn't matter."

"Did she have any siblings?" I walked across the room to the closet. Had the cleaning team worked this area over, so I wouldn't be surprised? I held my breath and opened the door.

The closet was one of those walk-in styles. It was the size of Carrie's apartment. And packed with clothes, so many clothes the poles sagged and more clothes were lumped up under the racks. Three pyramids of shoes were piled in the middle of the floor.

"No, Beverley was an only child."

I heard him, but I was too distracted by the abundance before me.

"What about her parents? Would they want this?" I asked.

"They want nothing," Ben confirmed, "I'll give them that much. They are farmers; I think artichokes. They were angry that Beverley made such a big deal out of my trust fund and about how she needed alimony. They weren't too supportive of her decisions."

I picked my way through the tossed garments and separated one dress from the next and wiggled it out. It was a Gucci: silk, wild pattern, the real thing. I pulled out another designer dress, then another. All were in size eight, sometimes six. I looked more closely; some dresses still had the store tags. We could return them. But that would be a little bizarre. Donate them to the Hospice store? To the homeless? Look stylish as you beg for money? No.

I kicked over a pair of Christian Louboutin shoes. These were black pumps with sharp, weapon-like heels, and brand-new. The bright red soles, the Louboutin signature, were unmarked.

I held a shoe up to the light. Oh, to buy something this beautiful and not even wear it once. What a shame.

Ben moved restlessly outside the door. I reluctantly dropped the exquisite shoes. The closet was a riot of color: red, leopard, stripes, black, aubergine. The outfits wedged into the closet were all perfect for this season. I pulled out a severe St. John suit, very chairwoman of the board. I found a sheared, mink jacket, dyed bright blue. It was politically incorrect, but it was lush to the touch. I ran my hand over the fabrics, elegant party dresses, some beaded, some smooth and diaphanous; all were perfect for Christmas.

I carefully backed away from all the temptation. It was a good thing I wasn't Beverley's size, or I'd be all over the holiday action on those racks.

"Had enough?" Ben asked.

"She must use another closet," I said.

"For what? That one is stuffed."

I gave him a withering look but declined to comment. I marched to the guest room – this was clearly used as a catch all. I recognized some of the tables from the living room. Random furniture and more clothes were piled around a double bed, decorated with a spread she bought in Target. I slid open the flat doors to the closet.

The space was empty, not a sandal, not a pair of white pants, not a single linen suit in sight. It was completely empty.

"She was going somewhere, she was going somewhere warm," I announced.

"What?" Ben had followed me.

"See? No summer clothes."

"Maybe she packed them away. It is winter," he pointed out,

and in his world, that argument was completely rational. However, when it comes to our wardrobes, women are not always rational. Could the closet be the window to a woman's soul?

"God, look at all this crap." He looked around as if finally remembering his life here.

"We never did decorate this room. It was a guest room, but we had no guests."

"No friends? A gorgeous, gregarious guy like you?"

"Not so gregarious." He shook his head. "I had a lot of friends in college, but once I married Beverley . . . ." he trailed off. He pushed some magazines off the edge of the bed and sat down rubbing his face.

He changed his name and sequestered himself with his grandmother. That's a long time to nurse pain. It was like the scene in *Lilo and Stitch,* when Stitch realizes he doesn't have a family, when he reads the story of the ugly duckling.

I almost cried as I remembered that scene, it always makes me cry.

Ben gathered himself. "You're right. She kept her off season clothes in this room."

"And your clothes?" I prompted.

"The other room. I kept them in the room I used for a study."

"Of course," The woman couldn't even share her closet. My, my. I was looking better every minute. Thank you, Beverley.

Ben rubbed his shaven chin absently, as if stroking a phantom beard. He could be; we haven't been together that long. I wondered how he'd look with a beard.

"Beverley never operated alone; it wasn't in her nature. She always had someone with her. She loved, needed, to have people around. She loved being loved."

"You loved her?"

"Yes," he rose and moved restlessly back to the master bedroom. I followed him, there was nothing more to see in the guest room.

He ran his hand over the surface of the dresser. "Yes, I did. But I couldn't now tell you why or even how. She needed me. I knew that, I enjoyed it."

She had cleared off the surface of the two chests of drawers, per my request. In fact, it was one of the few cleaning jobs she accomplished. Beverley covered her bureaus with silver framed photographs and personal photos distract buyers from the house, people tend to concentrate on the pictures of cute babies or wedding photos from the early 1970s, and forget to look at the wainscoting or the double hung windows. The photos were all gone.

"It's nice to be needed," I offered.

He opened the top dresser drawer and pulled out a dozen small, framed pictures.

"Yeah, but I wasn't the last to be needed."

He sorted through the photos as if he were dealing out a stack of cards. The frames clicked together in the silent room.

"A different guy in each one. Cruise, benefit, cruise, benefit, benefit. Cruise. She loved cruises didn't she?"

"Do you love cruises?" I asked him. Did he miss her? Even after all these years? Or was being upset normal? Did he kill her? Oh, that's ridiculous.

"No, I vacation in the Sierra Foothills." He lifted his head and offered me a ghost of a smile. I smiled back. We "vacationed" in the Sierra foothills this last September. It took us weeks to recover from our time off.

"It was all about dressing up and showing off for her. She needed to be seen. Thus, the men." He tossed the pictures back into the drawer. I heard glass crack but didn't point it out to Ben. It didn't matter.

"Did the police have any ideas?" What I really meant was did they share anything with him? I looked around the room. The new carpet was soft and cushy under my feet; new padding, always buy the best. I hired painters transform the walls from Steven King to Danielle Steel. Everything was white and pristine. We call this "move in ready".

The police never said if they found the murder weapon and not much was being said about the cause of death, at all. It was still being called an accident. I shuddered.

"The clothes bother you," he observed.

"So much," I mused.

"What exactly does that mean?"

"Sometimes, women need to shop because of the feedback they get. You are very important when you're spending money, and your importance increases with the amount you spend. Even the store owner pays attention, if you spend enough. For the price of a good dress, shoes and a coat, you can be fawned over all day. You've seen the movie *Pretty Woman?* It's like that. A woman gets feedback, love, in a way."

My gaze wandered to half a dozen cashmere sweaters stuffed on a shelf by the bed. "Lots of attention."

"It's how they get affection, too?" he did not sound convinced.

"Sure, it's also how we nurture ourselves, by buying beautiful things, wrapping ourselves in luxury. Like that." I glanced up at him.

He stared at me, uncomprehendingly.

"It's like buying fine wine." Not a glimmer of understanding in his face. I tried again.

"It's like buying new power tools."

His expression cleared, "oh, okay, I see."

The shear volume of stuff flowed from bedroom closet to the kitchen. Beverley stashed an incomprehensible amount of new goods in every cupboard (I spent a paragraph in the MLS on the storage in the kitchen). Piles of holiday plates for every holiday were crammed into the pantry. A huge industrial grade mixer in pink for awareness sat on the panty floor. New looking Calphalon pots and pans swayed from a hanging rack above the range.

I found blenders, another mixer, a regular sized Cuisinart mixer, a small Cuisinart blender, and the mini Cuisinart chopper displayed on a lower shelf in graduated sizes, they resembled the babushka dolls Katherine brought back from one of her trips to Russia. A shiny espresso machine and matching coffee grinder gleamed on the granite counter. Every item represented the best of its breed. This was not a woman who was sitting at home watching the shopping channel. I've been in those homes. Shopping Channel crap never stays put; it has a propensity to spill out of cupboards and storage bins, as if the sale items missed the spotlight of their most recent television appearance and need to always be admired.

Beverley had the taste and the cahones to buy everything that was pricey and "valuable." Yet the coveted items were not neatly put away, or even used. It was if she opened the packages and abandoned the prize right where it was first unwrapped.

I was reluctant to open the garage door, and I was right to be cautious, no heavy objects fell on me, but that didn't mean they couldn't have. Carelessly stacked boxes, furniture, tables, more chairs, and loose collections of free gifts from name brand cosmetic promotions swayed precariously from the breeze I created by opening the door. The stacks and stacks of boxes were so high that a sneeze would topple them onto the late model Mercedes wedged between the living room chairs and stacks of papers and periodicals.

"I'll never shop again," I said out loud.

"Then our work here is done," Ben said, with the first real smile I'd seen all day.

But the questions still lingered, as well they may. Ben rummaged through the paper and packaging strewn kitchen, randomly opening cupboards and closing them without much regard.

"Why sell the art? Why mortgage the house?" It was a rhetorical question, I knew he didn't expect me to answer.

"Drugs?" I suggested.

"Maybe, but she didn't die of an overdose."

"No, she did not. Blackmail?" I offered up, anyway.

"But why? It would be very, very difficult to really black mail a person now-a-days. A scandal wouldn't necessarily decrease your stock in society. It would probably elevate you to notorious, always a desirable status in this culture."

He opened the high cupboard over the stove, a popular place for liquor that is not often used, as was the case with Beverley. He pulled down an ancient bottle of Kahlua coffee liquor and a huge bottle of industrial grade vodka, half full.

"A scandal barely makes the local paper. No one really cares after the first conversation, and nothing stays on the front page for very long." He held up both contents to the light. "I swear these were here when I moved in."

"Not much of a drinker?"

"At least not alone."

I nodded. He was right.

"So why did she sell?" I asked him. I thought it was obvious, but he had to come to his own conclusion. I was in no position to denigrate a recently dead client.

"A quick get away? Liquidate all the stuff and leave the country?" He dumped the liquor down the sink and tossed the empty bottles into the recycling.

He put his hands on his hips and glared at the door leading to the garage. "Should I clean that up before we show the house?"

He looked tense, and I had learned quickly that he was a man of action, taking his stress or energy and channeling it into outward focused activities. His expression told me he was ready to tackle something big, some huge distracting project, and in every home, that meant cleaning the garage. It meant tossing out things that had some good left in them, tossing out all those things you may need some day. I meant chaos.

"Do you think she was planning to escape to some place warm?" I asked. I edged closer to the door connecting the kitchen and garage to protect the contents from his well meaning administrations.

He raised his eyebrows. "Remind me not to underestimate you in the future. That's a good possibility. I'll call the bank."

"They won't tell you anything."

"Yes, they will. I'm still on her accounts."

"That makes you appear even more suspicious" For instance, he told me he hadn't stopped by to sign the listing papers, but his signature was there on the agreement.

"It does, doesn't it?" He agreed, matter-of-factly.

I narrowed my eyes. "Have you been talking to the police?"

He sat down at the kitchen table, it wobbled when his elbow hit it. It was not the best quality. Maybe she was a patron of the shopping network after all.

"I already talked to the police. They were kind enough to inform me that I'm their number one suspect. Don't leave town, person of interest, and all that."

"Loved ones usually are."

"Or screwed over ones." He ran his hands through his hair, but at least there was no glue to make his hair stand on end.

"I'll have to disclose the death and the murder when I show the house. At this rate, I'll get a reputation," I pointed out.

"Undeserved."

"Who do you think did it?"

He rubbed his face and smoothed his hair. "My first guess is something out of the *Orient Express,* and everyone did it. Every one of those guys in the pictures probably gave her something; jewelry, gifts, at the very least, dinner. And what did they get? Nothing."

I disagree, they probably got something, was I the one to bring that up? Besides, I was too distracted by the idea of each man taking . . .

"You think each took their own little, piece," I said.

"Sit down."

I sat down and tasted my hazelnut latte for the second time this morning. But I couldn't sit still for long.

"We could start with all those pictures, and ask the men who dated her."

He gave me a pained – a very pained – look.

"Okay," I drummed my fingers on the table. I needed to do something, besides the difficult and daunting task of marketing "Murder Mansion". The clothes, I could do something about the clothes. The Homeless Prevention League would be the best option, since Beverley supported it. I'd take over a car-full on my way back from the Broker's Open tomorrow morning.

I wandered over to the kitchen counter.

I rifled through her paper work in the kitchen; most important paper work starts in the kitchen. I found the listing agreement in a basket next to the LAN line phone. I flipped to page six.

"You signed the listing agreement," I pointed out.

"Did not," he contradicted mildly.

"Did so. Is this your signature?" I brought it over to him.

He glanced at the page. "No, but it's good enough, Benjamin

M. Weiss."

"What does the M stand for?"

"Manly."

I did not take the bait. "She said you'd be happy to sign."

"I'm sure she did, and I'm sure this wasn't the first time. All those loans against the house? I probably happily signed for those, too. She was clever."

"Apparently not that clever," I pointed out.

"The police said she liquidated everything, all her accounts, and obviously, she sold the art. I wonder to whom?"

I reviewed the listing price. "How am I going to explain the murder?" I said out loud.

"Accident?"

"They said that in the papers."

He nodded. "That detective? The one who raced up the stairs?"

"Yes, I thought he was the coroner or something."

"Doesn't matter. At the station, the detective told me they didn't want to release the details of the murder, so the confessions would be easy to cull out. Apparently, there are a number of people happy to confess to murders."

"Gets them on TV." I confirmed.

"Exactly, and when they don't get on TV?"

"It must piss them off," I concluded, "but wouldn't that be dangerous?"

"What, pissing off a psychopathic murderer? The police don't think he'll strike again, and they went to great lengths to tell me they thought this was personal."

"About as personal as you can get," I agreed. "Listen, what about reducing the price?" I suggested tentatively.

"Of course. How much do we need to sell it for?"

"Not too low, I want to give you a bit of wiggle room," I suggested.

"Drop it to the bare bone minimum, enough to cover the commissions and the loans if that's possible."

I calculated, "it's possible." I glanced up at him. "Thanks."

"I always pay people for their work," he said, seriously.

Chapter 6

Thursday was not shaping up into a fun-filled day. On the other hand, I could maintain the illusion that I had business and was busy.

It was raining, not unusual, and not because it will contribute to the general atmosphere of gloom and despair for the day. It just rains here in the winter – or the rainy season as we are now calling the wet months of December, January and February. To make the 8:30 MLS (Multiple Listing Service) and Broker's meeting, I had to get out of bed earlier than my usual time. There was no Ben to comfort me or cajole me or otherwise entertain me in the dark morning, which left me feeling flat and uninspired.

I groped around in the shower for my shampoo and banged my elbow. Because it mattered, my hair didn't cooperate, and I couldn't find my favorite Charles Jordan boots, and was forced to settle for my second favorite pair of Anne Klein boots, which were brown not black, which necessitated a whole new whole outfit. To add insult to injury, the skirt that matched the boots didn't fit, and I had to come up with yet a third option.

I hit every red light from my house up to the Hyatt and had to circle the parking lot twice before finding a space big enough, so the doors of the Lexus wouldn't get dinged.

A two-story Christmas tree festooned with enormous red bows that gradually decreased in size as they reached the top of the tree decorated the Hyatt hotel lobby. A red draped angel with a tiny gold trumpet hovered over the fake pine tree. It was pretty enough to make me pause. I admired it for a second or two before turning to the greeter. She nodded, as I approached the table with the River's Bend Realtor Association Sign prominently displayed.

I pulled out my wallet. I had no cash. The cost for breakfast is eight dollars, I only had two, one dollar bills.

"Will you take a check?" I asked her.

"Allison," Mary Beth (from CPS) looked at me with pity in her eyes. "You are aware the hotel asked us to take only cash. If you ever came to a Board Meeting you'd know that."

"I'm on the Board? I'll have to owe you," I threatened. My hand hit my phone as I rummaged around for a pen to write an I.O.U, I pulled it out and turned the ringer to vibrate.

She looked at me. I looked at her and tried not to tug at my skirt because this one was fitting pretty snuggly as well.

"Oh, promise not to eat anything," she grumbled.

I took a breath right before I walked in. I surveyed the crowd for a friendly face, found none, and slunk to a table. I grabbed a cup of hot coffee on my way. No matter how long I work in this business, there is something very intimidating about the weekly MLS meetings. I feel I was a theater major stepping into cheerleading camp. This, from a former cheerleader.

I missed the opening announcements. Agents were now grabbing the mobile microphone to announce community holiday fairs, the coat drive, and where we could drop off new un-wrapped toys for Toys for Tots. A new Farmer's Insurance agent was introduced. She stood, licked her shiny, glossy lips, and proceeded to waste three minutes describing how she saved this hapless Realtor money with her fabulous insurance services and she, Heather, can do the same for any of us.

"I've been serving Sonoma County for years," she cooed into the microphone, and repeated her phone number twice.

I squinted at her glossy lips. I recognized her. Oh my goodness, it was Heather. She was one of those bright young things who seems to have great potential the first week on staff, but ends up a bad deal by the second week. Heather worked for our office for only one month. It turned out she was not very good finding her way around River's Bend. I think she even got lost driving to her own house. As for years in the business, the only years Heather had already racked up, was tenure in the glee club.

I wished any and all Heather's insurance clients the best of luck. When Heather finally sat down, the group applauded politely, but unenthusiastically.

I nodded to two other Realtors and they nodded back. I glanced at, but did not make eye contact with, the third member of my table. He was a self-proclaimed member of the River's Bend Sign Elimination Committee For the Betterment of River's

Bend. Rosemary nick-named this group the *Sign Nazis* because of their draconian, and often illegal, sign removal. Self appointed, this group pretends they work for our local listing resource and as such they feel justified to take down any For Sale or directional sign that they themselves, deem unsightly. There were not many of us who had not lost a sign or two to this group because the sign wasn't in the "right" place. It can get expensive. The *Sign Nazis* don't return your signs; they throw them away. I focused on my coffee and did not look up again.

The meeting moved quickly forward; announcements, buyer's needs, pocket listings, new listings not on tour.

I raised my hand, and the microphone and its handler made her way over to me.

"Hi, Allison Little, New Century Realty."

"Allison, is this another house of death?" A cheerful voice called from the back of the room.

"REO? Or is it really a DOA?" Called another.

"Did you find another dead body?" That was from Heather, joining in the fun. I was momentarily distracted, as I considered how to take revenge for that comment.

"Are you now exclusive to accidents?" Another rude question.

I opened my mouth, then closed it.

"Allison Little, New Century Realty," I repeated. "I have a new listing, not on tour." I glared at the tables daring anyone to interrupt me. The group finally obliged. "It's in the Villas. Priced." I searched the room for the last agent who spoke. He should talk; his listing has been on and off the market for a year now.

"To sell."

"Did you get the body out yet?" Called out Pete, from a competitive office.

"It's a great property and a great buy," I parroted. Stay on message, I knew that. You'd be surprised how difficult that is when all you want to do is lash out at people.

I stood and endured two more witticisms and sat down. My coffee was cold. I couldn't leave until we finished up with the tour sheets and the group all left to tour the open homes we had interest in or had clients for. It would look bad, even cowardly, if I slunk out now, and I already looked bad.

I knew what was on tour, and I wasn't in the mood to view the five measly homes on tour that morning. The holidays take a toll on home sales, always. No one wants to sell during the holidays, and no one wants to buy (but come on, a new house for a Christmas gift? A memorable gift, no?)

The rain had not let up by the time I hurried to the end of the parking lot. I didn't pause to chat with any of my detractors; it was enough that I avoided eye contact with any and all Realtors plus the Committee for Betterment guy. He would probably rush to my listing to determine if my sign met their random criteria.

I got lost hunting down the Homeless Prevention League offices. The GPS voice had to recalculate many times, as I made U turns around and between one of the many business parks that blur the edges of River's Bend proper.

Driving during the holiday season in River's Bend is not pleasant. I understand why the onset of Christmas Day inspires frantic consumer activity, but I don't understand the frantic driving. I love to shop, please understand, but it's a sport best exercised by those of us who have trained for years, perfecting our craft and increasing our credit limits to astronomical amounts, not by weekend warriors who write out of town checks and forget their IDs.

In my family, we draw names for gifts. This year, I picked the same sister-in-law I chose last year. Debbie, married to my oldest brother, Richard, was remarkably unimpressed by my gift last year, I would need to come up with something new and interesting, if I had any enthusiasm left. All families are annoying in their own way.

After half an hour of driving in circles searching for the Homeless Prevention offices, the GPS voice was finally satisfied, and I found myself in a parking lot that was a wasteland of asphalt.

The Homeless Prevention League could probably park their homeless shelter RVs right in front of the business park, and no one would really notice. I wonder if the board of directors ever thought of that.

The rain increased as I dragged the box of clothes from the back of the car. I couldn't manage the box of clothes and an umbrella simultaneously, so I balanced the stuffed box as best I could and dashed to the HPL offices that I thought were located to the right of the complex. No. I dashed down one courtyard, only to discover that the numbers stopped one digit short of my destination, so I scrambled back up through the courtyard, down a second courtyard, past a broken fountain, filling with rain water, and to the very back of the complex where I found the discretely marked office door. By then, my hair was lost to the ravage of rain, and wind. And it was only eleven in the morning.

I backed into the glass door, holding the now very damp box of clothing with both hands.

"Oh," a woman was just descending the stairs, as I set down the box on the floor.

"You're making a donation." Her voice was high, on the barely tolerable side of grating. She was dressed in tight jeans decorated with studs and embroidery, and high heel boots. Her outfit was of good quality, but I couldn't identify the designer. She wore an incongruous holiday sweater decorated with penguins of the more cartoon variety.

"Yes," I confirmed. I tried to fluff my hair back up again, but the rain soaked me.

The woman looked at me, as I tried to save myself. She marched over to the box, her high heels clicking in the silence of the empty building.

"Oh, these must be from Beverley," she said, before I could even explain.

"I recognize the dress. Are you donating the shoes as well?" She craned her neck around looking for the bag of shoes that should, of course, accompany the clothing.

"I could, I suppose."

"Do," she nodded, vigorously. "That will make it easier to sell the clothes."

"Sell? Don't you give them away or something?" I asked. Judging from the roll of her heavily lined eyes, I made an incredibly naive comment.

"What would a homeless woman do with silk?" She

demanded. "They need blankets and food." She thrust out a slender hip and eyed me, as if I were a total fashion moron, which I am not.

"We sell them to the *Just As Good Store*, and they mark up the goods for more than they paid and sell them to someone who can really use them. For women," she eyed me, taking in my soaking hair, bedraggled trench coat, and second favorite boots, "who want a bargain. We both get what we need, cash for more important things."

She gathered up the clothes and whisked them off to the back of the narrow office.

I looked around a bit. The stairs looked to lead to more offices. To my right was a small office, to my left, another identical, tiny, office space. Scarred, clearly used furniture buckled under the weight of the old, full-sized computer monitors. The staff was probably running on old Windows systems. Did non-profit programs exist to help the helpers and people who work administration in the non-profit? Clearly, there should be some kind of help.

I should mention that to Carrie. She understands this side of life much better than I do.

"There," the woman returned. She must have calculated the financial boon the clothes could bring, because she was much friendlier. She offered me a big smile in exchange for my donation.

"Bring in the shoes tomorrow," she instructed.

"Oh," I was a bit taken aback.

"What size?"

"What size what?" I was too distracted by her dramatic make-up which was appropriate for evening, but in the cold light of morning emphasized the tired lines fanning from her eyes.

"What size are the shoes?" she repeated patiently.

"Oh, ten."

"Pity."

"Tell me about it." I didn't have much to say after that. How's business? So, what's your ROI? Nothing came to mind, and she certainly didn't invite more conversation now that she had her donation.

I pushed open the door, and it didn't move. I pulled it back towards me – a gross violation of California fire codes. It wasn't until I was safely back in my car that I remembered I needed a receipt for Ben's taxes. I did not want to go back out in the rain.

I'd get it tomorrow. When I brought back the damn shoes.

The day did not improve, once I returned to my own office.

Inez, our manager sat stiffly at the head of the conference table. She was perfectly in tuned with the season, her red, wool suit matched her long red nails. I always admired her perfect manicure. She started the meeting at exactly 12:00.

"It has come to our attention that we've had a series of potentially dangerous incidences, and you all need to be aware of them." Inez began doggedly, to an audience of three.

Rosemary and Katherine drifted in at 12:15 PM, each carrying a small lined bags with, I figured, their own diet focused lunch. Katherine was still limping a bit, but Rosemary looked hungrier.

So far, in the misery race, it was a tie.

Patricia walked in carrying a pink bakery box and set it on the conference table. Tom, another agent with no last name, carried in two large soda bottles and plastic cups.

The sandwiches, it turned out, were either vegetarian or chicken salad.

It's December. Where's the hot pastrami and roast beef? Or, if your holiday movie of choice is *How the Grinch Stole Christmas*, Roast Beast.

Where was my Roast Beast?

"The situation needs to be addressed," Inez continued as I gingerly chose the chicken. "First off, you are no longer to hold an open house alone."

Rosemary and Katherine groaned out loud, so I didn't have to. I bit into the chicken salad to keep from voicing any opinion.

"We've had two incidents of agents attacked or in harm's way. We simply can't afford it." Inez picked at her vegetarian sandwich, her long nails were painted a holiday red.

"I have three open houses this Sunday. I can barely find one person for each house, let alone double them up." Katherine protested.

Only three? That is slow for Katherine. She usually has more homes on the market than that.

"I have two houses open this weekend." Rosemary agreed. "What am I suppose to do, run back and forth?"

"We have agents who need the work and the contacts." Inez was not a woman easily derailed. She stared down her two, ahem, largest producers. They blinked first.

"I'll get my husband to sit with me," Rosemary muttered.

"I'll call a friend," Katherine acquiesced.

They both started accusingly at me. I was still distracted by my puny sandwich and wishes for roast beast.

"Me?" I squeaked. "I have to find someone to stay in the house of death for Sunday, top that."

"This is your fault." They chorused. At last, something they agree upon - my perfidy.

Joan taught me that word.

"It's not my fault that she died in her own house," I protested.

"The papers say it was an accident," Inez said firmly. "And I am making sure that during this holiday season, there are no more accidents."

Inez glared at us. We meekly agreed, but not in so many words.

"Am I being clear?" Inez repeated, she did not move a muscle.

"Yes," we grumbled.

"Good, now eat your sandwiches."

It was not my fault. I happened to find a dead body after I listed a house, but that was in Marin, different county. This last body was just a fluke, could happen to anyone. Shouldn't happen again.

"It better not happen, again," Rosemary muttered, effectively reading my mind. "Or we'll be completely shut down."

Chapter 7

The HPL dinner immediately followed Beverley's funeral. And I suppose at this late date, the League couldn't just cancel the annual dinner, these events are important for donor appreciation, or so Carrie tells me. I began my day at the Hyatt, with an embarrassing breakfast meeting. I could finish my day in the same ballroom, feasting on dried chicken filet. Full circle of fun.

I stared at my closet and felt, uninspired, not to mention a little full around the waist. Bland chicken salad must have expansive qualities. After much consideration, I finally pulled out something purple. I wasn't really ready for the evening, but once I saw Ben, I had nothing on him.

The accumulation of the funeral, facing all Beverley's financial maneuverings and losing his art must have caught up with him. At first, he assured me it was no problem, he was sad, but there was no problem. However, from the additional lines on his face, and his haunted look, he was clearly losing sleep. It was very much a problem.

"I don't think I can take much more of this," he said under his breath.

"Come on, one more night." I tucked my arm under his and led him into the crowd, milling around the closed ballroom doors.

"Everyone talked about her, but I don't think anyone really liked her or understood her. Maybe, I didn't either."

"I'm sure you did, otherwise, how would you know they didn't?" I squeezed his arm. The only thing I could do was support him. Obsessing about the past was not going to help me, or him, at all.

"I'll be right here with you," I assured him.

And it was a good thing.

Ben was spotted as soon as we stepped into the cocktail reception area.

"Mr. Weiss?" The formidable, and infamous (based on Carrie's impersonations over the years), Martha Anderson bore down on Ben like a cruise liner hitting four knots.

"You are so kind to attend our little soirée after your tragic loss," she bellowed. Her voice was loud and projected so well, half the guests in the lobby paused to hear what she would say next. Her voice was a result of practice, rather than being naturally loud.

Ben allowed her to take his hand and shake it vigorously. As if that contact wasn't enough, she pulled him into a bear hug. He almost disappeared. I thought my breasts were big, but hers had their own zip code.

"It's Ben Stone actually," he managed to say when she released him.

"Ah, that's right. I met your grandmother. Lovely woman, lovely. She's a Geary, I understand, quite a philanthropist in her own right?"

"She supports the arts mostly." Ben smoothed his hair, tousled after the affectionate ambush. "We all have our pet projects."

"Ah, well, then let me tell you a bit about what we do. After all, I couldn't very well speak of the HPL during poor Beverley's funeral? It was such a tragedy."

"She was so young," I put in.

"Yes," Mrs. Anderson echoed, seriously. She looked at me, apparently did not find what she was looking for, and thus dismissed me and continued to address her remarks exclusively to Ben.

"Well, we do so much good. Were you aware that we maintain and support over thirty movable shelters that house over seventy of the chronically homeless? We are located in seven counties. Because of our work, many of our clients are able to move on to jobs and subsidized apartments of their own. We have quite a track record of success, one of the best in the country."

She beamed at Ben, then as a gesture of good will, smiled at me.

Ben was mute.

"That's wonderful," I interceded.

She waited for Ben to produce some sound of understanding, or an indication of how impressed he was with her facts, anything, really.

Ben actually looked a little dazed. Maybe he lost some oxygen in that hug.

"Mr. Stone is so overwhelmed right now, what with the funeral and the holidays. You can imagine." I drawled out the end word, for emphasis. I took his arm and gave him a little shake, so he'd look more alive.

"Oh, of course." Mrs. Anderson took a step back as if to give Ben the physical as well as emotional space he would need to make an informed philanthropic decision.

"He is taking everything into consideration," I told her. I did not tell her that as he helped extract me from his truck, he commented that he had half a mind to donate $10,000 to the charity with the best graphics on a dinner menu. He wasn't feeling too focused right now.

I do not blame him in the least, particularly since he was an arts guy, and Beverley's philanthropic works focused on health and human services. Those two endeavors were very different.

We were left alone for a minute, but only for a minute. I sipped my wine and looked over the crowd.

"Most of these people are from the funeral," Ben finally said. Oh, he lives! He moves! I kept my opinions to myself.

"Patrick said he'd be here with Carrie." Ben knew Patrick only casually/ I knew more about Patrick because of what Carrie told me, but that did not matter. Ben needed an ally, and Patrick was his man.

"I'm not very good with direct service charities," he muttered. "My mother worked with the homeless when I was a kid. She discovered a couple of her clients were rather good artists and she made a good commission promoting their art. She plowed most of it back into the shelter, but she stopped volunteering there and switched to supporting the arts. I'm more comfortable with the arts."

"You could save people,"

"I do too much saving as it is," he said, absently. "Beverley was one of them, and you saw how successful that was."

A man in his mid thirties, tall and lanky with a mild manner about him, headed   towards us. He held a tray, which was an encouraging sign.

"It was an accident, remember? You weren't there, remember?" I said through my smile. "And by the way, you don't have to save me," I said confidently. I lie, he's already saved me, twice. We are not even.

"Not in the same way, no," he agreed. "I think I'll stick to art." He glanced at my cleavage, anything I wear produces cleavage, I don't have to try that hard.

"I think I'll stick with you," he added after a second or two.

"I couldn't help seeing you were talking with Martha." The man greeted both of us. "She's our membership chair. Shrimp?" The man was nice looking in an academic kind of way, but thin. He made Norton, my music professor client, look like our former state governor on a particularly bulked up day.

I glanced at the pretty shrimp he offered, and took one.

"Yes, we were." Ben took a turn carrying the sophisticated conversation load.

"She was telling us about the shelters. Are you familiar with their work?" I asked.

"Familiar?" The thin man balked for a moment, then glanced down at the shrimp, as if shrimp tails forecast the future or the present.

"Oh, well, yes. Sorry. I'm not a waiter, well, I'm acting the part of a waiter for tonight. Allow me to introduce myself. I'm Harold Meyer, Vice President for Development for the HPL."

"Yet, you're serving shrimp." I had to point it out, in case he had forgotten he was shelping a large tray of curled crustaceans. He also carried a handful of cocktail napkins. I took one, emblazoned with the Hyatt logo.

"More cost effective for an event such as this. The staff pitches in to save the organization money," his voice conveyed a little conviction, but not enough. At least, I wasn't convinced. I didn't think he was either, but he put up a good front.

He took my silence as agreement and took advantage of the opportunity to address the former Mr. Weiss, presumably because Dame Anderson already warmed him up. Ben, not Harold.

"So, did Mrs. Anderson tell you about the thirty two

movable shelters we maintain to great success and with very little overhead?"

"Yes," Ben said weakly. Oh, man, he was a sitting duck. I have never seen the will sucked right out of him before. This Vice President wasn't even that impressive, I've fended off worse at Chamber mixers.

Harold nodded, encouraged that Ben already was so well informed. "We have a vigorous and devoted staff. We accomplish a great deal considering our narrow margins. Ninety cents of every dollar goes to direct service, which is better than the industry standard. Our donors demand efficiency, so we have three paid staff members: the President and CEO, and a staff of two." He nodded to a man in his late fifties standing across the room from us.

The president possessed all his hair. It was white and elegantly brushed back from his high forehead. He wore a custom made tuxedo and was accompanied by a custom made blonde, the same blonde who took Beverley's old clothes earlier this morning. Tonight she was swathed in a vintage Bob Mackie made during his sequin period. It was completely inappropriate for Sonoma County, but it looked great on her.

"He looks very, efficient." With his looks, the CEO could be a symphony conductor, or an elegant actor who only takes character parts.

"The woman with him is his secretary, but she only works part time," Harold explained. "We don't pay her nearly enough for everything she does."

"I don't imagine you do," I said neutrally. Perhaps, she was a cost effective perk, although she did not look cost effective. From her blond highlights, I'd guess that she was not cost effective in the least. I'd ask Carrie what she knew.

"And our only other paid staff is Anne, over there."

"Serving the baked brie?" I asked. I love baked brie.

Anne was cute in a mousy, why-Miss-Magillicudy- I- had – no- idea –you – were – so - beautiful –without – your - glasses kind of way. She was small boned and not very pre-possessing, but then again, she was attending a formal dinner dressed in a rented tuxedo, and serving food. How confident could the girl be?

"You're bottom line is all about efficiency?" I repeated.

"Yes, we also use one of our own recipients of our services to serve as our key note speaker for this event. It saves some cash as well, and, of course, we have corporate sponsorship for the dinner."

Cooper Milk was one of the sponsors listed on poster board displayed on a stand at the entrance to the hotel, as was Flex Paint and Safeway.

"And what did Beverley Weiss do for you?" Come on, you wanted to find out, too. I just said it out loud.

Ben blinked. I gave him a shrimp and he obediently ate it.

"She delivered blankets and food to the moveable shelters and counseled the clients. She was convinced they weren't reaching their full potential and was bent on helping them." Harold handed Ben a napkin.

"Sometimes, she even found jobs for them, part time and temporary, of course. A couple of clients were good at home repairs. I think she hired them for that kind of thing." He looked at me, seriously. I suspected that he was the kind of man who was always serious; everything was serious. I have found, recently, that the only thing in life that should be taken seriously is death. The rest is pretty trivial. I was not going to point that out to a serious man with a serious mission: serving shrimp.

"She was quite a volunteer," I offered.

"She was excellent in the field," he said, cryptically. I took another shrimp, hoping I'd spoil my dinner. If the organization was operating on a tight budget, dinner would be chicken.

"It was lovely to meet you; enjoy the dinner." The vice president in charge of shrimp gave me his card and marched away, bearing the hors d'ouvres to the masses.

"Good in the field," I repeated.

"Doesn't that mean she was a pain in the ass in the office?" Ben roused himself.

"That's what it usually means," I popped the last shrimp in my mouth and chewed thoughtfully.

"She wasn't perfect, but you'll think so, after tonight," he remarked.

I swallowed. "If she was perfect, you'd still be together."

"Maybe."

I wondered what the residents of the HPL shelter units thought of Beverley's charity? What kind of jobs does a homeless person prefer? Where did she send them to work? This was not her only project by a long shot. Ben said he had been contacted by no less than a dozen non-profits in the county, from the Girl Scouts to the Food Bank, all of whom delicately inquired about Beverley's will.

Carrie once told me that you have to ask or you get nothing, which is what Beverley left of all these good hard working people, nothing. All her assets reverted back to Ben, which did not make Ben look very good to the police.

Ben, in turn, planned to donate to each of the organizations that Beverly helped. It was only a matter of how much. I was chagrinned to learn that he also planned to donate his own money to a couple of the art based charities to celebrate never having to pay alimony again.

"So," I took his inert arm and steered him away from the core of the crowd, "you already gave to the De Young. Planning on more?"

"Yes, Beverley and I are founding members of the Lost Art Museum, I'm donating to them as well."

"Founding members for the Lost Art Museum? Please, tell me someone thought that was ironic."

He smiled, a little. "Yes, the donor levels are Founder, Pathfinder, Explorer, Map Reader, that kind of thing."

"I didn't think he had it in him."

"The director, Fischer? He doesn't; my mother suggested it."

"Why do I think your mother is some kind of superhero?"

"She is, on her own tightly controlled planet. She is the Little Prince; she lives in her own world, and so, is the queen. Since you asked, there's an event at the Lost Art Museum. I thought we'd go, and I could ask if anyone came across pieces of Beverley's collection."

The word *pieces* was a good one. I paused for a moment to swallow my shrimp again. I remember the last time the Executive

Director of the Lost Art Museum and I spent time together was during a particularly difficult period that involved controversial art, my own difficult clients, and the Executive Director's poor - now late - father. That didn't end well, either.

"Come, we can look at our panel again," Ben cajoled.

"And the new bathrooms you paid for."

He nodded.

"Sure, send me the invitation," I acquiesced.

I realized, that since we first met, I spent too many nights worrying about whether or not I could afford Ben. Despite my grandmother Prue's insistence that I should only marry for love (that's another story), I was still wary. Discovering that Ben could support himself left me feeling awkward and embarrassed about my own doubts. Did I secretly want him to need me, financially? Was that my only contribution to the relationship? Nope, I was also excellent at getting him into trouble.

Carrie and Patrick arrived. Carrie, bless her heart, managed to look much better than the President/CEO's secretary to at about 1/100 of the cost. Carrie wore the same red dress she wore to seduce Patrick. Judging from the way Patrick held her arm and casually pulled her close as they talked, the dress was still working.

Carrie accepted a flute of sparkling wine and smiled winningly at the President and CEO who hurried over to greet Patrick, who, in turn, nodded solemnly and looked official.

Patrick Sullivan, born into money, behaves similarly to the princes of England. He understands his place; he understands his job, and he doesn't relax until he is far from the public eye. Carrie assures me Patrick really is great fun. She reported that he accurately mimics the full Steven Martin *Wild and Crazy Guy* DVD. He even owns a banjo and a fake arrow that he wears on his head in the evening.

I should ask him to recite my favorite scene from *Picasso at the Lapin Agile*.

Plus, Patrick looked good in his tuxedo.

Ben blew in my ear, "hey."

His color was a bit better. When a fundraising volunteer gets too close, Ben retreats. I wondered if he contracted hives during the PBS pledge week. Maybe, he left town.

"Having fun yet?" I asked.

"How much should I give them?"

"Let's wait until after the dinner; you still need to critic the menu."

"Patrick." Ben reached around me and shook Patrick's hand. Ben, we may add here, was not wearing a tuxedo; he wore an old suit, not so old that the general population would notice, but it was old enough so that I noticed, and people such as Martha Anderson and the secretary draped in sequins, would notice. I sensed this was an old habit. I wonder if his attitude bothered Beverley, who focused on making an entrance, while Ben clearly enjoyed playing the role of awkward escort; wrong suite, wrong shoes. Passive aggressive.

I hadn't the heart to point out that the old suit gambit only made every woman in the room want to take him home and reform him, or at least make him change, and watch him do it.

We fell comfortably behind Patrick and Carrie's wake. They moved together as if they were already a royal couple. Carrie's dark hair contrasted dramatically against the red dress. Even in her high heels, her head barely reached Patrick's shoulder. She looked delicious. Without her rival, Carrie had clearly come into her own. Since she began her career in River's Bend as a secretary for the Senior Center, this must be sweet indeed.

Ben leaned into me, "They work well together."

Carrie approached the spangley, part-time secretary. In contrast to Carrie's simple beauty, the secretary looked contrived. She smiled carefully at Carrie but stayed focused on Patrick, the main man.

Mistake. Carrie told me time and time again, the women often have the last say in donations, especially when it came to large amounts. Even if the husband is the CEO of a large corporation, it's the wife who often controls the funds. Carrie smiled easily at the secretary, confident that she had the upper hand. But, for how long?

I moved restlessly away from the scene and glanced at the now open doors to the ballroom.

Ben sensed my move, "Good, let's sit down."

"You should be working the room and making new contacts," I mocked him. Actually, I should have been in the mood to make new contacts. In my business, every event, every chamber mixer, every party is the right opportunity for relationship marketing, for connecting, for making sure people know, love, and trust you. Sorry, know, LIKE, and trust you.

I wasn't feeling trustworthy. I was not feeling likable. A waiter directed us to one of the head tables, and I plopped down in front of my place card. We were seated with Carrie, Patrick and a nice young man representing Flex Paint, the big donor table. Not that the donors here tonight were large people, they just had large amounts of money. I enjoyed thinking about the idea of a big donor. Donors should all be the same size as Martha Anderson, how delicious.

"And what do you do?" I leaned over, flashed my own considerable assets and managed to render the Flex VP mute for a full fifteen seconds.

Sometimes, I'm good; sometimes I'm bad.

"We donate the paint for all the mobile homeless shelters," he explained after his long pause. He grabbed his water and drank. I offered to pour him wine from the bottle at the table. He gratefully accepted.

Carrie and Patrick arrived at the table, and we exchanged a flurry of polite greetings. The salads arrived, not served by the staff of the Homeless Prevention League, thank goodness.

Carrie twisted the wine bottle on the table and noted the vintner. "They donate to us as well," she glanced around. "I wonder if there's more."

Our cocktail waiter, Vice President in charge of shrimp, Harold, joined us along with the other staff member, the young woman.

Carrie smiled at the woman and rose to give her a hug. "You look adorable in a tux," Carrie said warmly. "How have you been?"

The young woman glanced at Patrick, then over at our Flex Paint representative. "Oh, we are devastated by Beverley's death, of course; she was so young."

Ben and I murmured something appropriate. I think I said,

"so tragic". At least, I hoped it was appropriate. I poured wine for the rest of the table and gestured to the nice professional waiter for more.

The young woman's name was Anne. I thought it was fairly appalling that the two of them had to act the role of servants at a formal event, but I'm not conversant with the various methods of charities. Perhaps all staff members at a non-profit are treated like servants.

We worked our way through the house salad and were allowed to swallow a couple bites of our main course, dried chicken with white sauce, before the President and CEO commanded our attention. I was working up enough enthusiasm to talk to the Flex Paint gentleman, and he was getting up enough nerve to look me in the eyes, so I was disappointed.

The President and CEO, Steven Baker, graciously acknowledged the major donors, who were called up in alphabetical order, to accept a tall, acrylic statue (in the shape of a flame) from the hands of the secretary who simpered like a low-rent Vanna White. She pushed an appreciation award into Patrick's unwilling hands, he nodded to her and hurried back to his seat. He set it down and stared at it, balefully.

"Maybe, they should give you a bottle of donated wine instead," Carrie suggested. She patted Patrick's arm sympathetically.

Ben grinned.

The President then delivered a lengthy tribute to Beverley, listing among other attributes: her work with the homeless, her ability to find them work and things to do, her visits to their shelters, and her work on the board.

As with anyone who had recently left us, the positive attributes were conflated, and any flaws were excised. Still, I shifted in my seat and played with the butter knife. Great, he had a perfect ex-wife; that always gives the current girlfriend confidence.

"As you are aware, we have an opening on the board," the President said jovially.

Patrick glanced at Carrie, but she was politely focused on President and CEO Steven Baker. She is a good audience.

Finally, after canonizing Beverley Weiss and her many achievements, the President invited Ben to come and accept a larger size glass flame award to commemorate Beverley's work with the League.

"Bigger than yours," he whispered to Patrick on his way back to his seat.

Patrick smiled, "Sucks for you."

"And now, as we have in previous dinners, it's my pleasure to introduce Professor Marcel Von Drake. He has been our program speaker for five years now, and you always ask him back. The Professor is one of our HPL Shelter residents, and he is grateful for your continued support. He is here to tell his story. Professor?"

The professor looked the part of an aging academic, he was round and portly and barely fit into the rented tux someone had tucked around his body. But he did carry an aura of authority, as the man with all the answers. Not what I'd expect from a homeless person. I believe that was the point.

Judging from his speech, the professor had an ax to grind with most of the civilized world He did complain with panache, I will give him that.

Patrick shifted in his seat as the man spoke. He poured more wine into first Carrie's glass, then his own. He gestured with the bottle toward the other tablemates, but they shook their heads, entranced with the vibrant message the speaker delivered.

"I can't believe he's not working in some college," Carrie whispered.

"He was with a very small, liberal arts college," Anne confirmed. "He had to leave; there was some scandal, so he can't get a job anywhere. That's part of his challenges."

"He is an awfully good speaker. I wonder if he'd come to our Rotary meeting?" Our Flex man said.

At first, I thought Flex was the name of a paint store, - for houses (of course I would think that). I learned Flex Industries actually makes coatings for optics, very high end. That's all the information I have because the awards and lectures interrupted my conversation with the Flex man.

Carrie sipped at her full wine glass and continued to politely listen to the lecture, or rant.

Patrick leaned over to me and whispered, "Maybe, he wasn't too stable, or rather he's not too stable."

"How can you tell?"

"I heard a lecture on the psychopathic mind last year."

"Good heavens, why?"

"We support a mental hospital in San Francisco," he replied shortly.

The professor did have style. He threw out his hands, bellowed, and ranted against society; he accused us all of being shallow and of not paying enough attention to the pain and suffering all around us. He clearly hadn't attended Thanksgiving with my family; I feel I experienced enough pain and suffering for a whole year.

The professor made a segue into the invisibility of the common man and how it takes so much to get noticed, and that is all anyone really wants; to be noticed.

"Okay," Harold leaned over to Anne and whispered something in her ear. She leaned into him for a second longer than necessary, but he didn't seem to notice. She nodded and moved quickly from the table, dragging the tablecloth and upsetting her wine, but Harold caught the cloth just in time and righted the glass. Anne staggered over something, recovered and made her way down the parameter of the ballroom.

Harold picked up the offending object. It was one of largest purses I have ever seen, brown vinyl, and riddled with zippers and flaps. He set it carefully on her chair.

Anne snuck down against the wall and edged behind the speaker.

"Fifteen minutes of fame. Everyone will have fifteen minutes of fame. There are whole magazines devoted to exploiting and celebrating everything that is mundane."

Anne tapped him on the shoulder, while deftly plucking the wireless microphone from his fist. It looked to be a practiced move.

"Thank you so much, Professor," she said into the microphone. "We are so fortunate to be able to help you in your time of need."

He grumbled something in response, but her hand covered the mike, and it didn't pick up. Clever girl. I felt a bit more respect for her, even though she was dressed as a penguin.

Chapter 8

Friday morning, Ben and I met again at what I now thought of as his house. For the record, we each went our separate ways after dinner. It wasn't because I was focused on being good so Santa Baby will come down the chimney tonight. I didn't imagine that after hearing all those accolades about his ex-wife, Ben was much in the mood to make ME happy. And I wasn't in the mood to BE happy.

He drove me home and agreed to rendezvous back at the Silverpoint property in the morning. I wanted to pull out as many of Beverley's clothes, and shoes, mustn't forget the shoes, before the open house on Sunday, not to mention all the rest of the stuff. I loathed the necessity of sorting it, but it would be criminal to throw away the tons of papers and magazines without looking through it, wouldn't it?

I wanted the house to look and feel as clean as I could make it. I was already laboring under the cloud of the murder or "accident" as it was being called, so I needed to make the house as appealing as possible. That cloud, the murder cloud, followed me wherever I went. Oh, and the other cloud, with Ben's mother name on it. Two clouds.

"Mom will be at the Lost Art Open House, Saturday," Ben reminded me.

"Great," I said. Let's add that to my day. It had been twenty-four hours since I announced the Silverpoint property at the Broker's meeting. It was the lowest price – by far – in the Villas. The photos were beautiful; the price was excellent, yet I hadn't received a single call. Not even a call to mercilessly tease me about mysterious accidents at all my listings. People always make sweeping generalizations. In all my years as a real estate agent, there were only two dead bodies in my listings. The other time, I was representing the buyers, which was totally different.

Ben arrived, armed with boxes of black garbage bags. The sky was overcast, blocking any residual warmth from the already low winter sun. It was a good day to be depressed.

He sighed and squinted up the stairs. "Where do you want

me to start?"

"I want you to get as much paper, toiletries, stuff, magazines, more stuff, crap, mail, files, dirty dishes, and Styrofoam food containers out of the house as you possibly can. I am in no way responsible for what you throw away, you are." I glared at him with my best impersonation of Katherine in her lecturing mode. "Throw everything you can away. No storing it, no going through it. No saving for later, when you have more time. This," I gestured to the burdened living area, filled with a tornado of diet drink cans and fast food bags, "needs to go. Now."

"Wow, you're pretty bossy." He held up an empty bag and waved it as a flag of surrender, "but you're right."

"Thank you." I left him to his work. I didn't ask if he was the cleaner in the relationship and if he was the one who picked up all the time. I imagine if he were, it would get old fast. But I didn't ask.

I had time in the afternoon to make a run to the HPL offices before they closed for the weekend. At least on this trip, I didn't get lost on the way.

"We'll take good care of this." Anne took the bags of clothes and shoes from me. There was no sign of the secretary.

Harold, the shrimp man, stared moodily into his computer monitor. A small Christmas tree decorated with colored lights and five or six plastic hearts from the Volunteer Center's Giving Tree program was tucked in the corner next to the door.

I found my favorite boots and a skirt that fit much better, which proves that there is a difference between a $100 garment and a designer $350 garment (on sale). I was feeling a bit better than yesterday.

"I was told that you sell it to the Just as Good Store, and they mark it up and sell it for more at the store."

"Sell it?" Anne looked down at the boxes of clothes and shoes. "We give them the clothes. We don't do much with clothes directly, unless I hear of something specific from one of our residents, they are trending towards male and so these," she lifted one of the boxes and set it close to the stairs leading up to the second floor of office suites, "will go straight over to the Just as Good Store."

"Oh, my mistake," I said quickly. She gave me an odd look, so to cover up my gaff, I started talking, "You must work pretty hard here; do you do everything for the organization?"

"Pretty much. I'm the marketing director, sales, donor relations, and chief bottle washer." She allowed herself an ironic smile. "Our membership is handled by Martha Anderson; she does a lot of work for us at no charge."

"That must be very helpful."

"Yes, well." Anne looked a little vague around the edges with that comment, but she was allowed, I suppose. Carrie never talks about the donors or the volunteers for the Senior Center; it wasn't proper protocol for staff to discuss volunteers.

Harold snorted, but that was the extent of his editorial contribution.

I smiled back at Anne. "You must be pretty talented to do all those different things."

It wasn't much of a compliment, but Anne stood a little taller and preened a bit. Clearly, no one gave this poor woman enough attention. I was dying to tell her to do something – anything – with her hair, but I refrained. I would not make a snarky comment to this girl, because I sensed she couldn't handle the banter. I left her alone.

"I was impressed with the way you handled your speaker the other night. Does he sometimes gets out of hand?"

"Sometimes?" She repeated.

Harold snorted again.

"He can be a bit of trouble," Anne glanced at Harold, but spoke directly to me. "But despite that, he's our homeless poster boy. I don't have the whole story as to why he became homeless in the first place. He never said."

"Our female board members love him, and he is quite an asset for our cause." Harold's voice came out of the gloom. Anne looked relieved at his interruption.

"I understand that charm is not the issue. A person has to be pretty competitive and cut throat to make it at a university," I said, thinking of some of the stories my friend, Joan, told me over the years. Her hair raising renditions of the political maneuvering at her college made me glad I was involved in a business, by comparison, was simple and innocent. For instance, I find real dead bodies in my homes, while Joan claims the university is filled with the dead, but they all still walk the earth, and many teach undergraduate classes. Sometimes, I don't understand Joan at all.

"Did he ever work at a university?" I asked, thinking maybe Joan could tell me something.

"Maybe," Harold offered from the dark recesses of his office. His narrow face was thrown into relief by the virtual glow of his computer screen. He typed as he spoke, the sound of the keys accompanied his short comment.

"Maybe," Anne echoed. "It's difficult to get a straight answer out of him, but he speaks well, and that's all we need, someone who doesn't "look" like a homeless person, but is one. Do you know how hard that is to find?"

Not as hard as it used to be. Our office was handling more and more clients who were on the verge of losing their homes, and we were losing agents to part time or even other full time jobs. They too, were losing their homes. People were even moving in with their parents.

It will take an earthquake of 8.6 magnitude and a complete leveling of every building in Sonoma County plus a big, big tsunami obliterating the coast line before I would consider moving in with my parents. At that point, I'd simply drive to Claim Jump and move in with my grandmother.

"So, the professor is the poster boy," I concluded.

"Literally," she gestured to a big poster in various shades of blue, one color processing, but it appeared to have at least three colors because of the shading and degrees of that one blue ink. There he was, the smiling professor, not in a tux, but a baggy suit, looking a bit sad. He could act, too. Talented guy.

"For years," she said, immediately, but then calculated more closely. "I think it began about three years ago. It was my idea to dress him in a tux for the awards banquet. The donors went wild."

She smiled, not at me, but at the memory of a triumph, and from her expression, I realized she didn't have many from which to choose. "Even Chris Connor was impressed. She wrote a nice blurb in her *Goings On* column, and she is never impressed about anything we do."

"That's for sure," Harold said.

The local paper, in general, and the columnist Chris Conner in particular, wasn't really anyone's friend. I didn't blame the reporters, but the bad news piled onto bad news was becoming more than a little frustrating, which is why the lack of bad news about Beverley was so puzzling. Who did I know at the paper? Anyone? Would Ben?

"You get it," Anne nodded.

"I do get it," I said. "The only time the River's Bend press even considered covering real estate was the month most of the major real estate offices stopped buying advertising. Only then, did the editors realize that trash talking headlines about real estate and diminished ad revenues from real estate companies were causally linked. By then, it was too late for both our businesses."

"The only time we make it in the paper is when there's a scandal or something. The good news is never published."

"Which doesn't really help." Harold acknowledged.

Anne looked at him for a bit and nodded. "Beverley's death got us a little bit of attention, at least some good?" She directed her question to Harold, who did not look up.

Come on, I thought, at least look at the girl, a little mascara, better posture, and she'd be pretty.

"I heard the accident was kind of gruesome." Anne finally said in the absence of her colleague's response.

Sure, but not from me. I smiled my go ahead, make the counter offer, smile. "Who told you it was gruesome?"

I knew it wasn't even on the Internet because Patricia was trolling for any change in information and under orders to report what she found. Why was this so effectively covered up?

"I don't know," Anne shrugged. "I heard. Maybe last night. There was a lot of talk, rumors, that kind of thing." She said vaguely.

Somehow, the word got out, not to the point of showing up in blogs or in the paper, not even the intrepid girl reporter, Chris Conner, had reported the rumors. It was a small rumor. Maybe,

Beverley's death wasn't all that important? That was a depressing thought. If someone with Beverley's credentials wasn't big news, then what hope did the rest of us have?

"Is Patrick Sullivan really dating Carrie Eliot?" Anne asked me, but in a way I knew she wasn't really asking, only talking out loud.

"I think so." I confirmed non-commitally, as if that's possible.

"I never thought his sisters would let him out of their sight. They are very tight, that family. There was some tragedy, makes them hyper aware of each other, protective."

"Death?" I guessed, since death was on my mind.

"No, no, I don't think death. Something. Anyway, not a big deal. Carrie is pretty nice, not a bad match for Patrick Sullivan. He's been single for a long time." Worry lines creased Anne's mouth and between her eyes. Her skin was dull but nothing a couple sessions with a good facialist wouldn't solve, or she could meet with my Mary Kay Consultant. That may be more cost effective. Anne was younger than me but looked ten years older. I felt depressed on her behalf.

"So, I hear," I said. Good, there wasn't a rumor about the Sullivan family. I did not want Carrie walking into something she couldn't handle. She was swimming in pretty deep water as it was, but so far, doing fine. She's a good swimmer, but I was still worried.

Anne brightened on cue. "Thank you again for the donations. They will do a great deal of good in the community. I have to get back to work."

I was properly dismissed. I remembered to pull open the front door and glanced back as I exited. Anne placed both hands on her battered desk and bent her head, looking as if she was completely defeated. What did she know? More than she was saying.

I checked in with Ben and he promised to take out as much junk from the property as he could, but he had work to do Saturday. At last count, he stuffed 100 garbage bags with, as he put it, poetically, more shit than anyone has a right to acquire.

I think anger is a stage of grief.

Chapter 9

The best thing about Friday was my weekly drink with Carrie, and even though Ben was manfully executing garbage runs, and even though I probably should be helping, I didn't want to forego my time with my best friend.

Tonight, we met at the wine bar down town: low lights, soft couches and lovely Cabs and Merlots by the glass.

"So are you going to do it?" I twirled a dense red Malbec (usually an Argentinian grape, but this was from California) in my glass.

Carrie had this year's Nouveau Beaujolais. She was still dressed in her work clothes; slacks and a bright turquoise sweater that highlighted her clear, young skin and brunette highlights in her hair. She and Anne were contemporaries, yet Carrie looked so much better. Clean living? The love of a best friend? I'm going to assume it's because Carrie has such an excellent best friend.

"Do you think it's a conflict of interest for a staff person from one organization to serve on the board of another?"

"Could be, are there rules for that kind of thing?" There are huge, massive, paper intensive rules and disclosures in my business, attorneys hover over real estate transactions as if each sale represented a complacent, slow moving, cash cow. I thought non-profits would be staffed and boarded, so to speak, by sensible people who only wanted the best for the underserved in the community.

"Is that the way to talk about them? The underserved?" I asked out loud.

"That's a good word. Direct Services is the over reaching term. A little passive, but hey, it is what it is." She sipped her wine. "I don't think there's a rule. I'm worried that it will be odd, not an acceptable thing to do."

"Why doesn't Patrick sit on the board then?"

"Can't, the meetings are on the first Wednesday of the month, and he has an obligation in the City on that day."

"Of course."

"Hey," she shot me a warning glance. Carrie was doing everything right to keep Patrick by her side, including wooing Patrick's sisters who, since she attended a lecture of Greek mythology, she calls the Furies.

I've never met either woman. I have nothing to say about them. I have my own sister-in-law problems.

"Sorry. My mother called me today," I confided.

"You did remember to behave at Thanksgiving didn't you? You said Richard and Allen weren't drinking too much."

"I've already forgotten about Thanksgiving. It was fine. Debbie called mom and complained that I picked her name again for the family gift exchange and she did not, and I'm quoting directly here, want another crappy gift card."

"How full of Christmas spirit she is," Carrie commented. Carrie deals with neglect and pain on a large scale, which, in my world, makes her the perfect foil for my sister-in-law to whom everything is given, and so, nothing is good enough.

"I have to come up with something wonderful." I concluded.

"Still keeping the limit at fifty dollars? Get her a bottle of rum and a Johnny Depp DVD, Yo Ho Ho and call it good." Carrie said, dismissively.

"That's a little cold, even for you."

She took a breath. "I spent an hour listening to Roberta Brown complain that her children never visit, they are particularly scarce between Thanksgiving and New Years."

"You don't visit your parents either," I pointed out.

"That's different," she countered. She tossed her head back and drained her wine glass. "Roberta's cancer is back, and it doesn't look good."

"Do the kids know?"

"Would it make a difference if they did? They don't care now, and I don't think cancer and imminent death is going to galvanize them to action."

I gestured to Steve, our usual waiter, for more wine. Carrie's parents are a long story, not relevant to the current situation. I changed the subject.

"Are you going to exchange gifts with Patrick's family?" I thought of that challenge. Carrie lives carefully on her salary as an administration assistant at the Senior Center. When we go out, I pick up the tab; she's worth it. Apparently, Mr. Sullivan feels the same.

"No, Patrick won't hear of it. He wants me to make him something, something sentimental."

"That's sweet. So are you going to join this board?"

"There's an introductory board meeting next week. I'm going to attend and check it out, what's the harm?"

"How do you feel about that?" I did my best impression of a psychologist, which wasn't very good. I don't see shrinks much. For special events, like the holidays, I self medicate. It works out fine.

"I have no idea. Patrick's really pushing for me to join, and a few board meetings beats the personal trainer."

"Anything and everything is better than the personal trainer. What was his name?"

"James," Carrie smiled, looking as smug as I had ever seen her. The personal trainer idea was a fast and quickly deleted part of her life. Patrick thought it would be great if they both got in shape. Carrie was not so sure, and after her first session, she was really sure it wasn't for her.

So, she stuffed herself into the smallest, most uplifting outfit she could find - and I bet she found it on sale - and distracted poor James, the personal trainer, so thoroughly that he dropped a barbell on Patrick.

End of sessions.

"Why this push to help the Homeless Prevention League anyway?"

Steve brought our wine and whisked Carrie's empty glass away.

"Patrick's dad was an early supporter. He helped purchase the RVs when the idea was first presented. Apparently during the first year, Cooper Milk also allowed one of the RVs to park around their facilities, but the residents complained they were too far away from down town. I understand that Harold and the President thought of the idea of moving the RVs around."

"Why?"

"So that the homeless aren't living really next to anyone for very long." She gave me a look. "Charity doesn't begin at home at all, it's best when it's far away and removed."

I thought about that. "I wonder why Beverley's parents aren't more involved." I mused. Were they the ones suppressing the information about Beverly's death? Did they have that much power? If the accident report was the official report, they knew less than me.

"What is there to be involved in? I think they accepted the idea of accident, it put Beverley in the poor victim position, her mother seemed comfortable with that."

"As opposed to Beverley the woman, who was running away to a warm country with an unknown man?"

"Yes." Carrie finished her first glass of wine and started in on the second.

"Who told Beverley's parents it was an accident? The police?"

She shrugged. "At the funeral that's what was said, an accident. A pretty horrible one from the look of it."

"Closed casket?"

She nodded.

Saturday, I returned to the scene of the crime so to speak, and pick up even more stuff, a preliminary for the fun evening at the Lost Art museum – and meeting Ben's mother.

Most of the crappy, paper, garbage, was gone. The guest rooms were empty now, and the garage was only slightly more packed, I was very happy Ben had not tackled the garage.

"Hey," Ben strode into the house then slowed down with every step.

"Hey," I trotted down from the master bedroom.

"I finished a job early and came by for more abuse," he glanced around at the living, but smiled as I approached.

"You're in a better mood." I kissed his cheek.

He shrugged and headed up the stairs. "May as well."

"Come up, we can finish with the rest of the clothes and what's left in the office."

"Should we give all of this away?" Ben straightened his shoulder and walked into the master bedroom as if walking to a firing squad. How much time had he really spent in this room? He eyed the largest chest of drawers. It was stuffed full of sweaters, lingerie with no built in support, and a few pairs of expensive pantyhose.

"I can take it all to the Homeless Prevention League," I offered. "I took all those boxes yesterday and a box the day before."

"And I noticed it didn't make much of a dent." He peered into the closet and shook his head. "As much as you can cart away would be good. How about all that kitchen stuff?"

"You may want a couple of things or how about your grandmother?"

"Emily? She'd not really a stuff person."

"In that big house? I think she is." I countered.

"The house is pretty massive, isn't it? She bought it out of spite, to show my mother that a person could live luxuriously and well out in the country and you don't have to live in the city to be happy."

"That is a rather expensive way to make a point isn't it?"

Ben shrugged, "My family makes very big, expensive points."

I waited for a whole second.

"The family money originally came from the Geary side, my grandmother's father. Silver."

I waited.

He fidgeted, drew his finger across the top of the dresser, then surrendered. "The family always felt themselves to be "new money" so there was pressure to behave and be civilized and cultured, and act the part of the upper middle class. Anyway, my grandmother wasn't one to follow along with the newly conceived family tradition of decorum and social norms, so she promptly fell in love with a newspaper man – Stone, although that may not have been his real name. Stone sounded good on a by-line."

Ben scratched his head, losing track of his narrative and clearly losing interest in the story. His eyes wandered around the empty master bedroom, with all the garbage and strew clothing gone, there wasn't really anything to rest his gaze on and I knew that was part of his discomfiture.

"She married him," he continued after a deep breath. "The Geary family members recovered and built the house in Pacific Heights for her as a wedding gift. Stone was killed covering the labor riots. Grandma never married again. We all lived in the house together for years even after mom married and my brother was born. Mom appreciated the address: it gave her immediate prestige. When I was about five, grandma and mom had a falling out and grandma moved. I spent as much time with her up here as I could. You see, we're used to each other."

"Did your father, Weiss, have money?"

"Oh, yeah, mom met him at prep school. He had a boat load of money and the boat to keep it in. Dad grew up in Sea Cliff, we kept that house as well. My brother lives in the Sea Cliff house."

I did some mental calculations, superficial of course, because money doesn't buy happiness, but it buys lovely containers in which to put the happiness in should you stumble across any.

"Why didn't you get the Sea Cliff house?"

"Well, Donald, my brother, works in the City, so it seemed fair. Besides, I don't care for fog."

I understood some of the problems in his first marriage. Beverley cared about money, position and status, Ben did not. That must have made her crazy.

"So, the jewelry? The photos?" I pointed to the drawer where he had tossed away the photos a few days before. I was not sure quite what to make of the suddenly pedigreed Mr. Stone, Weiss, Geary in descending order. Where Carrie had purposefully and deliberately followed her goals and found the obviously rich and clearly organized perfect man, I found Ben in the yellow pages.

I'm an old fashion girl.

"The jewelry. Could we sell it on eBay?" Ben suggested.

I shook my head. "Nieces? Your nieces?" I suggested. Now that he was away from the marauding philanthropists and contemplating an evening with questionable art, he looked much more relaxed, even while standing in his old house.

"I don't have any, Donald has two boys, wow," he perked up. "That pissed mom off, she wanted cute little granddaughters to take to tea at the Sheraton Palace. She got more boys instead.

She gets mad all over again, every holiday."

"Why did she expect anything different?"

"She didn't take genetics in school."

I flipped open the top of the jewelry case.

"Really, take a couple of things, for your nieces." he encouraged. He walked over and stared into the case. "I could never tell the fakes from the real thing." He murmured.

I glanced at him, and waited for the obvious conclusion, but he didn't offer it and I wasn't interested in grinding him down about his past.

I stared at the mix of shiny stuff a little longer before I admitted that he was right. Big gaudy jewelry would be perfect for my two nieces as well as for the constantly disappointed Debbie. The chains and pendants glittered invitingly.

"Come on, make a choice. Or take a handful." He encouraged.

"It seems odd." My hand hovered over a cuff bracelet covered with bright, large gemstones. I wanted it for me.

"Better you than anyone else."

I picked out a set of bracelets for Debbie, lines of red, green and white square cut stones in a channel setting – if they were real, it would be far and above the gift limit of $50. If they were fake, they were still over the limit.

I chose out a set of bracelets for one niece. I took dangly earrings and a necklace for the other niece. From the bottom drawer I pulled two silver cuffs that resembled a twisted cable, along with a matching necklace with a large blue center stone. I held them up.

"They could be David Yurman, or forty dollar knock offs. Either way, can I take them?"

He gestured, "take more, with any luck they're real."

I smiled. "You said you didn't care about that."

"I don't, but for you, I hope they are real."

I regarded the full drawers of glittery stuff - pirate treasure.

"Why didn't they take anything?" I asked out loud.

"Good question." he followed my train of thought. "The police asked me that. They dusted for prints on that," He nodded at the jewelry stand. "But they found nothing, only Beverley's prints."

"Doesn't that seem odd?"

"The murder didn't take her computer, and her purse was untouched, from what I understand, the police don't have a clue, and if they did, they are not sharing."

"We'll check the purse in a minute." I had to carry my own ill-gotten gains down to my own purse. I remembered her purse was downstairs.

"Do you need a Cuisinart?" He asked, it was not as random a question as you may think.

"I would if I cooked. Give it to your grandmother."

"I would if she cooked."

What was I hoping to find in Beverley's large, quilted, chain draped Chanel bag? The bag was an attractive model, spacious with a more discrete double C logo than I initially would give Beverley credit for, I was hoping the matching wallet would be stuffed with foreign currency so I could immediately trace where she was headed.

No such luck.

From the wallet, I pulled out three visa cards, and two master cards, Nordstrom, Macy's and Exxon. No library card.

Ben whistled as I handed him the credit cards. "This is substantial."

"She may have used the free checks from one account to switch balances to another, it gives you an extra month or so of no payments."

"But it cost twenty nine percent interest." He protested automatically.

"Yes it does, but if you are abandoning the whole thing, what does it matter?"

"True. Where was she going?"

"And with whom?" I countered.

He leaned against the granite counter and shut his eyes for a minute. Speed meditation, I do it every morning.

"I can't think of anyone," he repeated out loud.

I waited, mostly because this technique of not talking was really working. Ben was opening right up.

"I didn't pay enough attention to her. She'd call, sure, ask for money, ask for an advance on her alimony amount. Ask. But we never talked. She never asked me, how's your family? How's your business?"

"Maybe she knew your family hated her and she didn't want to ask," I said helpfully.

"Okay, that is true. Still, I hoped for better communication. Something more congenial."

I started to say something else comforting, but my phone rang, and out of habit I lunged for it.

It was Owen, he had found another condo on Craig's List, this, he was certain, had potential.

Ben waved at me and headed back upstairs, the pull of that master bedroom was disturbing, I'd have to work at keeping him out of the house all together. Better for him.

I patiently listened to Owen's glowing report on a condo that I was pretty sure Owen had seen last spring but had rejected – the shingles looked loose? The stairs weren't even? (He carries a level with him where ever he goes). I couldn't remember why he had rejected the place the first time around.

"Sure," I promised, of course I promised. "I'll meet you in an hour and we'll take a look."

I brought the Chanel purse upstairs to put in one of the drawers, We didn't need to give it away yet.

"Would they tell you where she was going?" I said, meaning the police.

"It may not matter." He absently smoothed the new bedspread.

"But what if she was leaving with someone, and that someone was her murderer?" I asked, but that idea didn't make sense.

"No," distracted, Ben pulled out the framed photos and laid them out on the dresser surface. "I'm still the main suspect."

All together there were twelve framed photos. They were originally scattered around the bedroom and I belatedly wished I could have seen them in situ. Would the photos next to her bed be of the men she loved the best? Or was currently seeing? Now we couldn't tell.

Ben squinted at one and then another. Two were of the

same man, three were of another man, the rest were singles; Beverley posed with every one of them.

"Did she have a regular relationship?" I asked, but if what he said was true, then Ben would have been the last person she'd confide in. Did anyone besides members of various non-profit boards attended her funeral? Or was it packed with acquaintances rather than friends?

He picked up a framed photograph, then the next. "She loved men, needed them."

I leaned over his shoulder. Beverley wore a different dress in each photo, although about five of photographs looked to be from the same cruise, the background was the same, the seats in the dining room were the same.

"She was all about the show." Ben gazed at the pictures. "She kept her weight down because she was worried about how she looked in photographs." He held one up. "How do I look? She asked me that all the time. That's why I now go for more," he squinted at me, "solid women."

"Should we see him?" I gestured to one of the pictures ignoring the back-handed compliment.

"Probably all of them." His hand shook and the frame dropped on the dresser with a loud clatter. He crossed his arms and frowned at the collection. "I only recognize one person."

I picked through the collection and pulled out the two of the same man.

"I recognize this one, but I can't place him." I took them and studied them. Beverley wore a red silk dress that showed off her small breasts to as much advantage as a woman her size could reasonably manage. The man was dressed in a tuxedo. He was a red head, unusual in a man. Beverly's hair was dark in the photo, it almost blended into the background. Both photos were taken on cruises. A little gold was barely visible under the frame.

"They date these." I said. I pulled off the frame back and pried out the photo. "See? This was taken last year. And this one," I pulled out the other of the red haired man. "Was taken, two years ago. Well, that doesn't help."

"'But this does. Recognize him?" Ben held up three frames in one hand, they were all 3 by 5. In fact, not one of the men merited an 8 by 10.

I looked at the one with the background of the Hilton ballroom. The man cast his arm around Beverley's boney shoulders, but the arm seemed to hover over her as if there was a force field between her skin and his arm.

"God, not him!" My outburst was spontaneous.

"Do you think she dated him?" Ben asked.

The man in the photo was Peter Klausen O'Reilly the Third. And he was not Ben Stone's (Rock Solid Service) favorite person, for various reasons, not the least of which was that Peter Klausen O'Reilley the Third was an attorney. Most divorced men are not found of attorneys, Ben among them. I flat out dislike the whole species.

Ben squinted and stepped closer. "It's entirely possible," he took the picture from me and scrutinized the happy couple.

"But he's so terrible." I said.

Ben nodded. "But you have to admit, they would make a perfect pair. He handled her side of the divorce."

"Who handled yours?"

"Some kid from Charlie Concron's office. He did a fair job, at least he was intimidating."

"From Charlie Concron's office." I repeated. Concron was a notorious attorney in San Francisco, and it wasn't because he dressed well. His office staff defended rather heinous criminals, and won. But Concron could possibly be an old family friend. I suspect that Ben's background was far more illustrious than he let on.

Ben studied the photo. "This was a while ago, it could have been – judging from the way he gingerly holding her – at the end of the affair."

He grinned. "There wasn't much O'Reilly could do. He got her possession of the house, but she couldn't afford to buy me out, and in fact, didn't really want to. She got $6,000 a month in alimony, not enough of course, but she managed to squeak by."

I thought of her shoes, squeak by was right. There was no way she was paying for those clothes and shoes and jewelry on a mere $6,000 a month. Which was probably where the missing art came in.

I did not express that idea out loud. "Was she the friend?"

"What friend?"

"When we first met and you and O'Reilly were so rude to each other, and you explained it was because he screwed with a friend of yours - was Beverley the friend?"

"No, but that's a great guess. Beverley wasn't a friend."

"The woman you married was not your friend?"

"It's complicated."

"I should say so."

But I didn't pursue it.

***

"Why didn't you pursue it?" Carrie demanded when I called her from my car to update her on the Ben situation.

"It's complicated," I repeated.

"It's always complicated when they don't want to explain something," she said sarcastically.

"I honestly don't have an answer, and here is my client. I'll call you back." It was the first break Mr. Owen Spenser had ever given me.

Misty rain is not ideal for viewing condos, they look bare and small in the overcast dim light, I was 100 percent certain we had seen this condo before, but since Owen Spenser was determined to buy at the very bottom of the market, and because he re-discovered this one on Craig's List, it had the patina of a bargain. The rain was not a deterrent.

"It's pretty cheap," he told me. Owen not Craig. Owen is a comfortably average looking single man who teaches math at the local Junior School. I think both my nephews had him as a teacher. I never felt threatened by Owen, which in the light of the warnings currently posted over my email from the Realtor Association about the inadvisability of women agents showing homes alone, was a comforting thing. Sometimes an empty condo can feel as isolated as a country house in the middle of a five-acre parcel.

All the admonishments from the office finally penetrated my sometimes thick skull. I looked up as I opened the door to the empty building. The only human I saw, was one man strolling in the opposite direction, he didn't look interested in me. Good.

"Many of the condos in town are pretty cheap." I confirmed to Owen. I pushed open the door so Owen could precede me.

"And," I continued, out of habit, "it has windows and a view out to the field and a full kitchen, including a new stove." I had to glance down at my MLS print out. New Stove was a feature. When there isn't much to say about a property, agents resort to listing the relative age of appliances.

Owen wandered to the upstairs leaving me alone in the kitchen. I peered out the window, but saw nothing and no one.

Owen's footsteps were heavy on the stairs. "The closet poles aren't perfectly balanced. That's too bad."

Last time he viewed this property he was concerned with the slope of the patio and whether it drained properly. I did not bring this up again, he seemed to not notice this time.

I looked at the gloom outside, the sky had gradually faded into dark and hung heavily over the field that was considered a "view out the kitchen window."

"What are your plans for the holidays?" I asked Owen; at least a conversation would keep the noise level up and dissipate some of the stony silence.

"My daughter will have us all over." He said. "You?"

"We're having dinner at my sister- in-law's." I said it as if it was a yearly occurrence. But it was not.

I took a deep breath. Owen seemed neither disappointed nor enthusiastic. Actually that was progress. Owen Spenser was a man always in balance; each side of the equation equaled the other, nice for math, terrible for decisions. It took him fifteen minutes to debate between ordering a latte or a cappuccino when I offer to buy coffee. Over the last six months, I have learned not to hold out for a sudden decision from him. Even if he claims he's interested in buying, I do not rush to the office to fill out the purchase agreement.

"Maybe it could work," he carefully placed his feet on the stair treads either because he may fall, or to not disturb the carpet nap. He put his hands on his hips and scanned the empty living room again.

"I'll let you go so you can think about it," I announced as cheerfully as I could. "Go home, call a couple of your friends, and give me a call, you have my number, and I'll always pick up your call."

He nodded, "That's a good idea, I'll talk to my friends, it's difficult to leave my old place, but my rent's increasing in January, so I don't have much time."

"So you say."

"I'll get back to you," he said vaguely. He always promises to get back to me, but never on the same listing.

"You have the flyer and the link," I pointed out.

At this point, after working with someone for months, showing the property, always meeting them on time, bringing options to the table, the client usually disappears, never returning calls and never acknowledging email. Usually, it makes me mad, in Owens's case, I was hoping for that very phenomena. But no, he keeps calling, and stupid me, I keep showing up.

I drove by the walking man and give him a jaunty wave, here I am, your friendly Realtor, trying to keep your condo development from lapsing into one too many rental units. He should be grateful. He eyed me as if he wasn't.

Chapter 10

In deference to the holidays and to the event in question, Ben borrowed Emily's car Saturday night. It was a more luxurious ride than his truck.

"You look nice," he greeted me at my door and escorted me to the car.

"Thanks." I wore my own pair of Laboutrox pumps and a diaphanous green and purple dress in a swirling, vaguely floral design that was quite vogue this season. It also had the advantage of hiding my flaws and emphasizing my excellent ankles.

Ben was dressed in a much better suit than what he wore to the Homeless Prevention League dinner.

"So," I settled into the leather car seat and checked my lipstick so I wouldn't have to look directly at Ben. "Your mother will be there?"

"Don't worry about my mother."

"No, sorry, that's not possible. You met my mother, she thinks you're a God with a drill. She loves you. Now, I have to live up to your stellar reputation."

"You don't have to live up to anything," he assured me.

But I wasn't on steady footing with Emily yet, so I didn't have that back up, just in case his mother hated me. And since I'm a working girl from Novato, rather than the fabulous, skinny – skinny is important – socialite, that Beverley was, I didn't think I stood much of a chance of impressing his mother.

What bothered me the most was that this bothered me at all. I loved Ben, I was possibly in love with Ben, so why care about what his family members thought? We were grown ups, family shouldn't matter.

But it mattered hugely to me. When my own grandmother fell in love with Ben, it was along the lines of receiving a papal blessing – and we aren't even Catholic.

"Do you think Catholics have a better Christmas than the rest of us?" I said out loud.

"I think Muslims have a better Christmas than the rest of us,"

Ben commented, then continued, "Really, you don't have to prove anything. Mother is usually more concerned about herself and the impression she's making on everyone else in the room, than she is about connecting with another human being."

Startled, I glanced at him, but his face was impassive. Was he aware of what he just said? Was he talking about his mother or his ex- wife? God, no wonder he was all tied up into knots about all this.

"I'll be good," I promised.

He relaxed a bit, but his hands still gripped the steering wheel as if he was wrestling with a loaded truck with no shocks on the back roads of Claim Jump, not a luxury sedan on the freeway headed through Marin.

"You're always good," he assured me.

The Lost Art Museum collection was housed in a brand new building. The new museum hovered on the edge of the Tenderloin making a brave stand against poverty and the brutal outside world.

The building had a faintly Frank Lloyd Wright air about it. It was built of natural dry stacked stone and oriented around a central sweeping staircase. It was described in the *Chronicle* as the twin to the Guggenheim in New York.

Ben dropped me off at the entrance, but I didn't go right in. I hovered by the front door waiting for him to come back from parking the car. I didn't want to walk very far in my heels, but I also didn't want to walk into the party by myself. I twisted my own bracelets as I waited. I wanted to wear one of the large pieces I acquired from Beverley, but I didn't want one of the guests, or God forbid, Ben's mother, to recognize it. That would be too embarrassing.

Ben dashed across the street. "You could have gone inside."

"Where did you park?"

"Over at the club, it's easier than parking on the street, and Pablo takes care of the car."

"The club," I repeated.

"Bohemian Club," Ben said easily and guided me into the museum.

I had no time for a response, because we were inside and I

had to focus on the party prospects. The guests were directed to the second floor. We trailed up the curved stairs and admired what I could only assume were the less controversial pieces of the collection as a whole.

"It looked like that," Ben pointed to a black and blue painting that reminded me of a riot in the making.

"What does what look like?"

"The painting I bought when I was young, it was one of my first "real art pieces". I really loved it. Beverley sold that as well." He looked around for a plaque to check the name of the artist, but none of the paintings decorating the curved stairs were labeled.

A tree made of dowels and paper snowflakes marked the entrance of the main hall. Large white paper snowflakes hung from the ceiling and twisted slowly in the warm air.

"There they are," Ben pointed to an older couple. "My parents, Mrs. and Mr. Ben Weiss Senior."

"You're a junior?"

Ben nodded. "See the problem? I was not sorry to give up the junior crap by taking the Stone name."

"Oh my, yes." I agreed. I stopped and observed the power couple in awe. Gloria and Ben Senior flowed through the crowd with much the same panache as I had observed with Carrie and Patrick. But these two were, of course, far more practiced and skilled. Not only were they born doing this kind of gig, they enjoyed it. They would circulate and manage to greet every important guest without appearing to know the guest was important. They would be practiced at expressing astonishment when they discovered the nice young man they had spoken with for an hour was really the featured artist, how fortunate!

My friend Joan, who has a number of degrees in literature, would say Ben's parents were characters straight out of *The Age of Innocence*. I remembered because Joan gave me a colorful lecture about Edith Wharton and her society. She also gave me a copy of the book.

Anyway, this party was all about the old guard mingling with the up and coming artists and collectors, I felt privileged to be here.

"Why are we here again?" I whispered to Ben. He liberated two flutes of sparkling wine and handed one to me.

"I want to discover to whom my ex sold our art."

"What makes you think people here will have that information?"

He raised his glass in the direction of an enormous painting of a suffering Jesus. I recognized it. My first encounter with this particular Jesus was in a house in Marin. The painting was originally part of a collection of "dangerous" art that was indeed dangerous in that possessing it got the owner killed. The angry Jesus painting didn't get the poor man killed; another painting did. The museum had that painting as well. I looked around, but didn't see it.

"I can't believe he'd display that," I referred to angry Jesus. "Shouldn't that one have stayed lost?"

An elderly couple paused at the painting in question and gestured excitedly between each other.

"Answer your question?" Ben asked.

"I am constantly amazed," I admitted.

"That's why we're here," he grabbed my arm and propelled me into the center of the crowd.

"Ben." A small gentleman, about 80 years old, dressed in a blazer and khaki slacks hailed Ben.

"I wanted to thank you for finally releasing that Kahlo. It looks great in my collection."

"One of her self portraits, I assume." Ben commented.

"Well," the man was a bit startled. "You signed the sales receipt, it's the one with her pet monkey."

"Of course it was. Did I say anything about why I wanted to sell such an interesting piece?" Ben asked carefully.

"No, Beverley said you needed to clean house. I'm thrilled of course."

"Did I get a good price?" Ben's tone was mild. I was impressed. He was far more stirred up when we were discussing "feelings" than he was now, over real money.

"Hell, yes, $200,000 is more than generous." The man said.

I sucked in my breath, but Ben seemed unperturbed.

"Did you want it back?" The man asked.

Ben shook his head. "No, no. You enjoy it, take your turn."

The elderly man looked relieved and moved forward to grab more stuffed mushrooms.

"That much?" I took a swig of sparking wine to steady my nerves. $200,000 would buy a lot of shoes. If a girl was planning to get away to a country that say, didn't set much store by shoes, a girl could make that $200,000 alone go for a couple years, at least. Maybe Beverley did have a good plan.

"I was lucky, I had found some interesting work when I was young. That's how I met Fischer, we were scouring the same flea markets, looking to pick up what had been rejected in the past."

"And is desirable now," I put in.

"That's how it's played. My parents are collectors, so I learned early."

"My Dad taught me how to golf," I said.

He smiled. "I do love that about you. The whole thing with my family gets a bit unreal at times."

"Did you collect everything in that kind of category?"

"You mean the expensive category? No, there were some works I collected for fun. The one I was really fond of was similar to the painting we saw on the stairs. Mine was a weird swirling piece that looked quite similar. I bought it because the color spoke to me, it cost about $2,500 at the time. So it's probably not worth much more than that now. I could ask around," he mused.

"It doesn't matter how much it's worth if you like it," I pointed out.

"True," he agreed. "It was back when we were first married." He gave me a wan smile, "Our marriage was so short, I suppose the whole marriage could be categorized as *when we were first married*"

"Why didn't you take your favorite painting with you?"

He lifted his shoulders. "I wanted to get out, completely escape. At the time I wasn't really thinking about the paintings. They were attached to the wall, the walls were part of that house. She was in the house." He shuddered, a macabre rendition of the nursery rhyme, the House that Jack Built.

I never got as far as moving in with a lover, so I didn'dt

really understand. But I'd see him through this, he was important.

"Ben, darling," the voice startled me out of my fond reverie.

Ex-wives hacked up in the bedroom, Rosemary on a diet; I could handle a great deal. I'm even a bit bullet-proof. But that voice cut through the crowd like a silver letter opener, it cut so quickly and invisibly you couldn't even see the slice at the top of the envelope, or through your ego. The crowd fell away as if they were so much shredded paper. I had no defense against silver letter openers.

"Darling, how lovely to see you." Ben's mother was so thin she reminded me of a preying mantis, the kind that eat their mates after sex. I looked around for Ben's father, but he was not in evidence – has she eaten him?

"Mother," Ben weakly responded.

His mother was dressed in a crimson cocktail dress, sleeveless to display not exactly muscled arms, but arms that held their own against any sleeveless dress clad woman in the room. She wasn't necessarily perfect, her face has clearly expressed disapproval one too many times. And she was too classy for a face lift.

"Gloria," Ben turned and took my hand, holding it, not gently, as if I was a precious flower, but more with the force of a vise made by Acme. He was the coyote about to plummet off the cliff and apparently I was the only thing keeping him from falling.

It was kind of sweet.

"This is my girlfriend, Allison Little."

The words girlfriend warmed my heart, but not enough to weather Gloria's sudden cold expression.

I know, I know, but you don't have to make those faces when you meet me. I am aware my name is somewhat of a misnomer. In all my advertising, it's only my head shot, no more.

"Allison," she extended her hand and gripped mine almost as hard as Ben, I was a bridge suspended between the two, mother and son. It was not a metaphor that bore further consideration.

"How nice to meet you, Gloria," I said.

"How nice to meet you, Allison," she responded tonelessly. I had a flash of how she and Beverley behaved. Ben must have learned to stay completely clear of the fray.

We released hands and then stood in silence. I took a breath ready to plunge into some kind of inane conversation about the weather, the museum, lost art in general, but she beat me to it by ignoring me completely.

"Ben, honey, there's a leak in the upstairs powder room, can you take a look at it?"

"Right now?"

"No silly, this week," she waved her hand in the same gesture Beverley used to dismiss everything she didn't want to address or deal with. "Sometimes, anytime. Come over when you can, yes?"

"Of course, have you seen dad?" Ben asked.

"Oh, your father." She glanced around as if she may have set the man down next to the mushrooms, but he wasn't resting on the buffet table. "Well," her eyes fluttered over my face, "lovely to meet you."

I bent my head in a royal gesture of acknowledgement.

"See?" Ben whispered as his mother floated away. "She makes your mother look like a laugh riot, all warm, fuzzy and cuddly with her loving family."

"I am not ready to nominate my mother for sainthood." I said, and would have said more but I was interrupted.

"Ben and Allison." The Executive Director, Doctor Fischer, enveloped us in the obligatory friendly hug of more than acquaintances. We gingerly hugged back. Ben patted Fischer on the back twice and released him as quickly as he could.

"Thank you for coming," Fischer bought a number of canvasses from one of my clients and now owned one that was enormously controversial and thus, popular. But he still wasn't sure about us – how well could we keep the secret about his father? Well, we had no reason to expose the sad history of Mr. Fischer's father's past and his attempt to right what he saw as a long festering wrong. No reason at all.

I tried to smile but I was still recovering from Ben's mother.

"My pleasure," Ben was more relaxed in this environment and I noticed that he didn't shrink from the Fischer or from the occasional woman who recognized him from years past.

"It's a lovely building," I said.

"Yes, we're very proud. Did you see the panel? I may have a lead on the second."

"I thought the other two were destroyed?" I said. The panel in question was one I happen to find hidden in a house in Marin. The painting that got the owner killed. It's a long story, but this work, by an artist named Guerra, did end up being saved and displayed.

"No, apparently there are two more, maybe other curators didn't have the heart to destroy good art, either." He paused awkwardly, "you two have plans for the holidays?"

"Family," we said simultaneously.

"My mother hosts Christmas dinner," Ben explained. Fischer automatically sought out Ben's mother.

"We usually have dinner at the Club," I supplied, as if he asked.

"Well," Fischer tugged at his French shirt cuffs and glanced around the room.

"We were just heading to the buffet table," Ben said helpfully, giving Fischer way to escape. He did not want to insult us by leaving our conversation so soon, but he had many other donors to attend to.

"Excellent, we have lovely donated food." He left with relief and we headed towards to the food to make good on our comment.

Ben took about three steps with me, but was distracted by another patron. I left them to their conversation and continued to head towards the food. I had met his mother, I had done my part, now it's Miller Time.

I stuffed three slices of Mascheo cheese into my mouth, poured more wine from the bar – at least it was Kendall Jackson, rather than Charles Shaw and wandered into the crowd. Most of the guests were milling in the main space, admiring or pretending to admire, the work.

I poked my head into the women's rest room. Ben had apparently not only designed and installed the new bathrooms he also donated the materials. I wondered how Ben managed to do the work without engaging the Plumbers Union and all the other unions in this town, but I supposed it didn't really matter. I admired the block of undulating sinks with the shallow basins that flowed into one another. The unused water washed behind the sink into a kind of waterfall, instead of down a pedestrian drain. Very elegant and museum-like.

I walked back toward the stairs again. A freestanding poster had been shoved to one side; I passed it by.

I did manage to find our "lost" panel. It looked more impressive here in a gallery setting than where I found it, hidden behind sheet rock in a little used powder room. The colors were bright, the woman painted at the center of the panel was clear and her skin was beautifully rich brown. She clutched a long stream of water in one hand, choking it off, and in the other hand was a bundle of wheat, held so tightly the artist had made the lower half of the wheat black, as if there were no more oxygen or water molecules in the state left for growing any food.

Political? Very, that's why in the thirties, the painting was considered too controversial for display, and so, lost. The painting's original fate was to be destroyed.

Dr. Fisher was lecturing; I joined the group. "The WPA did a great deal of good, hiring artists and writers to do what they do best. But some of the results weren't exactly what the government officials had in mind. Much of what was originally created and paid for, was hidden. That's what we are trying to recover, the lost art, most of the work from that time period of course, but anything else that's been hidden or rejected because the artists needed or felt compelled, to reveal the truth."

"Isn't that biting the hand that fed you?" A young girl asked.

"That's the risk with artists," he acknowledged.

"It looks like a cross between Diego Rivera and Frida Kahlo." Someone said.

"Yes, it does, but they did not collaborate." Fischer said with confidence.

"And it's not as personal like Kahlo, it's more political," offered another guest.

"I've seen aa modern artist who has this same kind of style," a handsome man with dark, swept back hair, and dark blue eyes, commented.

"But he's not dead," someone pointed out.

"Still, I think one of his work went for something close to $100,000 at a gallery opening I attended. Huge works, quite impressive, but really, nothing I'd hang in my living room."

"I know what you mean," I said under my breath.

He glanced at me and favored me with a blindingly polished smile. It tugged at my memory. I smiled back because I always smile at handsome men.

"I think we may have one of those," said Fischer. He directed his group to the next painting. I hung behind.

"I'm Roland Bentley," the handsome man introduced himself as the group broke ranks and wandered towards the next enormous canvass.

"Allison Little, New Century Realty."

"And are you interested in art?" Roland asked.

"Only where it ends up," I answered truthfully. "I'm here with Ben Stone." I glanced over the crowd to find the infamous Ben Stone.

"Ben Stone, wasn't he married to Beverley Weiss?" Roland said immediately.

"You knew her?" I searched a bit harder for Ben, he'd want to meet this man. Then I realized that maybe, maybe, he did not want to meet former boyfriends and lovers of his ex-wife. I hadn't considered that.

"Can I buy you a drink?" I asked.

He laughed, "or shall we head to the open bar?"

"We could do that, too."

Roland turned out to be as helpful as he was handsome. We poured ourselves more wine and repaired to a quiet bulge in the wall of the gallery, there didn't seem to be a single ninety degree angle anywhere.

"I was acquainted with Beverley, we even dated for a month or so. We met at one of the fundraisers here, or rather at the old museum. Anyway, she was fun, but really needy. I couldn't give her enough."

"Gifts?" I guessed.

"That," he agreed, "but also myself, she even resented my

work, she wanted my attention 24/7. And what she needed if I wasn't there, were more gifts to remind her of me."

"Then why did you keep coming back?" I asked reasonably.

"I didn't."

Ben walked up behind me. "Hello, I'm Ben Stone."

"Roland Bentley."

The two shook hands.

"She had a picture of you in her bedroom." Ben said. That's where I had seen him, in one of those banquet, happy at the table, photos.

"Really? After all this time? I'm flattered." He didn't look sad or particularly upset over losing Beverley. But he hadn't heard she was dead. Apparently they had dated for only a short time, a long time ago. All that was left of the relationship were the necklaces and bracelets for her, a perpetual visa bill payment for him.

I couldn't ask the next question that came to mind. What was it about Beverley that prompted such largess on the part of her beaus? Not even Ben was showering me with gifts – ice cream and wine to be sure, but that was a direct exchange for a happy Allison and thus more sex and thus a happy Ben.

Oh.

"It's been interesting to meet you," Roland shook my hand, shook Ben's hand.

"And you," we echoed.

"That was good." Ben watched the man move only five steps before he was stopped by more guests.

"Thanks, I recognized him, couldn't place him, so I stopped him to talk anyway. Any luck for you?"

He sighed. "I found a couple of people who heard about the sales of our art and they gave me some names, but most of the buyers are either on vacation or golfing in a warmer place that this. I may not get to them until after the holidays."

"It's not difficult to know why Beverley sold the paintings, she was leaving town for good, taking all her cash and traveling to some out of the way place."

"With whom?"

"Not O'Reilly, he was still in town, not this Roland Bentley, perhaps that other man who merited two photos instead of one?"

Chapter 11

I asked Ben to hang out with me during my open house. I was mindful of Inez's wrath if I didn't at least try to get someone to protect me from the serial killer. I left a message with Carrie to that effect as well. Carrie declined, she had an afternoon silent auction and brunch to attend with Patrick. Ben had to fix his mother's bathroom. My only orders were to make the calls, say the words and then look innocent when Inez asked – did you get someone to stay with you?

I would say something fatuous about how nothing bad happens in the Villas; it's too snooty, overpriced and filled with careful people who hire Mexican immigrants to remove three leaves from the lawn using a gas powered blower, but obviously something bad DID happen in the Villas and I was here from 1:00 to 4:00 to fend off the crowds of curious sensation seekers – Come see the Murder House - look under the bed for the weapon, smell the minty clean guest bath (it still smelled of Scope mouthwash even after the cleaning team worked through, my bad) and otherwise make completely nuisances of themselves.

But, just when I through prurient interest would drive the day, the momentum was lost. Not single person stopped by in the first two hours.

I suppose the driving rain didn't help much.

Perhaps I was giving off bad vibes, a common mantra from both Rosemary and Katherine, who, it may well be noted, weren't exactly bundles of positive energy themselves of late. Dieting, especially during the season of eggnog and homemade fudge, is really futile and makes a girl cranky.

It took a great deal of self-restraint on my part to not tackle clearing out another stuffed closet. Ben had thrown out bags of papers and junk, and then, to clear out the rooms, shoved everything else into the closets.

I wanted to pull it all out and get ride of more.

But that doesn't look good during an open house when the whole home has to look perfect.

So I resisted the urge to clean and clear. I flipped through old *Vogue* and *Baazar* magazines, played a few games of solitaire on my phone and watched the rain fall into the deck immediately off the dining room.

As usual, I called my grandmother at 2:00 PM.

"How is your new house of death?"

"Dead," I said. I thought I saw a shadow of movement on the front walk. I stood and continued to talk as I checked the door to make sure it was not locked.

"Is Debbie still bent on an old fashion home made Christmas?" Prue tends to get to the heart of things rather quickly. She says she's too old for bullshit, but I work with many people older than she who love bullshit. I think Prue came this way.

"Yeah, she's tired of the Club, says it's too impersonal."

"It is too impersonal,' Prue asserted. "We had a good time celebrating here at my house."

"Until Richard found the liquor cabinet," I pointed out.

"True."

"And Allen found the matches."

"Ah, there is that," she admitted. "The change in venue should be interesting," she offered brightly.

"I take it you're not interested in participating in the grand experiment?"

"The atomic bomb was a grand experiment. And I didn't need to attend the detonation, I'll read about it later."

Detonation was not a great word to describe our upcoming holiday experiment. Debbie was stubbornly oblivious to Richard's drinking, and as a result never fully appreciated my mother's attempts to control what sometimes could be a volatile situation buy always meeting in public spaces. I really wanted my grandmother with us, but she was adamant about her living her own life. This independence, coupled with she and my mother's thinly veiled animosity, increased exponentially with each passing day of Advent.

I dropped the subject. We chatted about the new person on the Claim Jump City Council, Prue has lost by a handful of votes to a woman named of all things, Debbie. Grandma was still mad.

Lucky Masters, one of the more prominent developers in town, was offering homeowners rebuilding packages after the fall forest fire. All he needed was approval by the County Planning Commission.

"The project would give a lot of people jobs," Prue concluded. "Raul offered to set up web cams in the trees to monitor construction. But even that idea didn't appease this Debbie, she's dead set against Lucky's proposal. Can't say I really blame her, no one trusts Lucky."

Raul was a video artist. I often visited his web cam trained on grandma's street, you know, to check on things. And the idea of setting up a web cam wouldn't be that outrageous, Lucky Masters was known to cut corners in his buildings. So far no one had proved anything, so there was nothing more to say on that subject.

I assured grandma that Ben was fine, because she always asks, and we signed off.

I finally had a visitor at 3:30 PM.

"Hello?" A man opened the front door and poked his head in.

I struggled up from the one couch left in the living room. "Hello, come on in!"

He stepped in and slid off his rubber clogs.

His long grey hair was bound back in a ponytail with a rubber band from the morning paper. He wore a faded tee shirt that originally hailed from an upper end store but, judging from its condition, it had been worn once, and rejected as no longer cool and consigned to the second hand shop.

An out of date tee shirt seemed to be a fine wardrobe statement for this sixty year old.

He smiled. His teeth were dark, stained.

"Hi, just looking – I saw this on the Internet - Craig's list."

"Yes," I agreed because he had seen it there, Patricia placed it for me and kept up the listing.

He stepped into the foyer, hands on his narrow hips- he was too skinny – I would guess the speed/meth/coke diet, but I didn't want to judge.

"What an amazing price! It this accurate? What's wrong with

it?" He surveyed the front room.

"Nothing," I said immediately. The pest report was clear, the roof was new, Ben really did take care of his things, and his ex-wife's house was no exception.

I was suddenly aware of all Inez's warnings – which is unusual for me. My visitor did not look like a neighbor. He did not look as if he was from around here at all. He actually looked more like a transient. I edged away from him and closer to the front door.

"There must be something wrong to merit such a low price for this area." He turned and walked towards the kitchen. I followed him, because that's what I do.

"All the appliances are top of the line," I said.

He opened the cupboards, I held my breath willing the contents to stay put. We still hadn't cleared out the cupboards. He studied the flooring.

"Is the floor hardwood?"

"Yes, " I confirmed.

"Bamboo is more sustainable," he said.

"This was built before the bamboo craze," I pointed out. Because how environmental was it to rip out perfectly good wood floors in order to replace them with "better" floors? Not at all. Maybe part of being green is to make due with what you already have.

He rubbed his hand over the counter tops and the cabinets. I hovered in the kitchen doorway. He wandered around the lower floor and I followed him, not trusting him much. But upstairs I allowed him to enter each room while I stood in the hallway. Don't let yourself be boxed in a room with no escape except past the creepy (but with buying potential) visitor.

He exited the master bedroom. "Didn't I read something about this house?"

"Yes," I said straight out. "There was a death here. Umm, recently." The saying goes: the only buyer who sues is a surprised buyer. Disclose everything, and in this house, Beverley's death would need to be disclosed over and over. But at this point, it was being reported as an accidental death, not a violent crime. So I was happy to go along with that myth.

He nodded, "I thought so."

"Is that a problem?" I tried to keep my voice from squeaking because he unnerved me. He could have climbed straight down from the ridge above Claim Jump, where the reprobates, drug dealers and aging hippies escape from reality on a regular basis and grow the means to do so. It was not a reassuring picture.

He had nothing, but I'm not an idiot, he may have a relative who did have something and wanted him - desperately wanted him - off their living room couch.

I understood.

"No worries. I can get a cleanser here to take care of the bad energy."

He strode all over the house once again. He checked the carpet and opened every closet. Not a good idea, at this point, you can't really see the actual closet. But to his credit, he didn't complain about all the stuff and junk smashed behind every door.

He paced the size of the rooms and mulled over the garage space, seeing, he assured me, past all the boxes and furniture jumbled in the two-car space.

He didn't finger items, and he only glanced into the bathroom medicine cabinets. So he wasn't a thief. Then again, I wasn't giving him much opportunity.

"Thank you for stopping by," I said as he moved towards the front door.

"Here's my card," he pulled out a bent card from the back pocket of his paint splattered jeans.

I glanced at the card. He had an address in the west county - out of cell range. But, he did have a web site, and an email address, a comforting sign of his commitment to civilization. I appreciated that.

Bo Freedman. I read. His web site was BFDeal.com

"BF?" I said out loud.

"As in Big Fucking fill in the blank," he said calmly.

"Of course," I took a breath to steady my voice. "Well, Mr. Freedman, you've seen the place, do you have an agent?" I asked half-heartedly. Why, why do I get the weird ones?

"I do not."

"Of course not. I can help you on both sides if you want.

Give me a call."

He glanced up and squinted at the living room walls.

"Didn't those use to be purple?"

"Yes, how did you know?"

"I can see it. That's good to paint it a neutral color, purple wouldn't have worked in here. Well, thank you."

"You're welcome."

He could see the purple through the new paint? I squinted up at the offending walls myself. I could see nothing but beige, precisely as I had ordered.

* * *

"You will never believe this," Patricia announced as I walked into the office Monday morning.

I had an appointment with Peter Klausen O'Reilley the Third, the odd Bo Freeman was the only potential client and he was odd and I had no clue what to buy Ben for Christmas.

"Believe what?" I stupidly asked.

"They found a body in the creek. A homeless woman. Wow, it was exactly like the one they found a couple months ago? You remember, they never did find her feet."

I stopped dead, (bad choice of words), missing feet?

"Patricia," I said,

"Okay, okay, I'll stop talking about it." Patricia, our office manager has a touch of Goth about her. Her favorite contact sport is to discover gruesome murders or odd accidents and share the details with the rest of the office. Sometimes it's funny, occasionally it's bizarre, today she actually imparted information I could use.

"When? When did they find this body?" I asked. I moved closer to Patricia's station. I heard Rosemary raise her voice but then it dropped down to a low mummer.

Patricia glanced back at her computer monitor. "Yesterday afternoon. They're calling it the holiday murderer, they found the other body around Labor Day, and now it's like Christmas, holiday murders, see?"

"And why is this body different? Than any other murder I mean?"

"Oh," Patricia said happily, "it was all cut up. Pieces everywhere. I read a blog that said all the officers on the call got sick, ruined all the possible clues. The one over the summer was easier to find. They found most of the pieces, they weren't scattered so far from the original body."

I swayed but grabbed the desk in time.

"I didn't say not to use any means of extra help," Rosemary voice raised to a level easily heard all around the lobby.

"You didn't say it would work, you lost fifteen pounds last week," Katherine fired back.

"Water weight!" Rosemary countered.

"It says here that the police won't comment," Patricia continued, unperturbed by the shouting in the adjacent office. "I'd comment. There's a man running around town with a chainsaw, cutting up women into tiny pieces."

I leaned into the edge of the desk and swallowed multiple times. "How did they figure out the weapon was a chain saw?"

Patricia tossed her hair back and squinted at the computer. "It doesn't really say, I'm guessing, but that would make a lot of noise wouldn't it?"

"Yes, yes it would," I agreed. The high counter separating Patricia from the more or less innocent clients and strangers, dug under my breasts, but it helped steady me.

"Maybe, they used something else," she said enthusiastically.

Ben spent the night at my house last night. It hadn't been a great evening. I was unnerved because I had spent a whole afternoon doing nothing except entertaining that strange Bo Freeman who, of course, was just looking. Ben was unnerved because he had spent the whole afternoon fixing things for his mother with whom he did not see eye to eye – on anything.

So what do I do? Yes, I bring up our relationship with one of those tedious and often unnecessary We Have To Talk episodes initiated by yours truly in a fit of openness and desire to express our true inner feelings.

This is how it went:

Me: And why, why aren't we out in the world? Why aren't we dating officially?

Ben: To protect you. Beverley can be quite vindictive.

Me: But you're divorced.

Ben: That wouldn't stop her. I'm sorry, it probably looked pretty bad to you, as if I was hiding something.

Me: And you weren't?

Ben: Maybe I still am.

Me: God. Maybe you still are? You're still protecting me when the house has clearly already fallen on the witch? Why now, when we have parties, and events and this, this, situation. And why now?

Too late, he remembered that the way to my emotional center is directly through my stomach, and calming mixtures of cheese and fried bread always do the trick.

To forestall any more sharing, he quickly whisked me out of the house and to the nearest Italian restaurant. I felt we were finally on a real date. Together, in public no less.

After two glasses of cab/ merlot blend, he apologized.

After three slices of cheese, covered bruschetta, I apologized.

He promised to take me out more often.

I promised not to make him share his feelings again until Valentine's Day.

He agreed that would be fine.

"Are you okay?" Patricia asked me, in a moment of unprecedented solicitousness.

"I think I'll get more coffee." I avoided offices and headed to the break room for a relatively fresh cup of coffee, it wasn't Starbucks, but it would do the job. A holiday murderer. Come on, the Thanksgiving killing of Beverley had to come up in the papers; the story was too good, and frankly, too easy. This was not good news for an already paranoid real estate office. I shrank back and watched Rosemary march down the hall to Inez's office as if she were doing her aerobic exercise for the day.

From the immediate responses, Inez was clearly in no mood to respond reasonably to Rosemary's demands. Rosemary and Inez argued over Rosemary's open house so loudly we could hear it all the way in the lobby. And Inez's office is a very long walk from the front desk.

"If you can't get two people in there for the afternoon, you'll have to cancel them," Inez said curtly.

"Cancel them? Do you have any idea what you're saying?" Rosemary shrieked. She must not be eating enough emotionally calming fats and carbs, just spiky green things. I had no idea what kind of tincture Rosemary was taking to make her lose fifteen pounds in a hurry, but knowing Rosemary, it wasn't on the FDA approval list. She was sounding a little shrill.

Katherine lurked back into lobby, obviously listening in on the altercation.

"I have people." She told me gleefully. "I pay my friends to hang out at my open houses. There's not much going on right now, I don't understand why she's so worked up."

"No, it's not in keeping with the holiday spirit," We heard Inez say dryly, "but in this case, money is not everything."

"Holiday spirit!" My sellers won't have a freaking holiday if I don't sell their house. I have to hold it open!"

Which is not entirely true, open houses are of dubious value in the sales process, but that wasn't Rosemary's point.

"There was another murder this morning," Inez said stonily. "Get someone to stay with you."

Even if Rosemary was bullet proof (and I suspected she was), Inez was clearly worried that one of her own would be next. I thought of Mr. Bo Freeman, a potential client and a potential murderer? How big of a stretch was it for him to return to the scene of his crime? Don't people do it all the time? Well, none of the nefarious characters I've ever met, but it could happen. I decided to keep this Mr. Freeman to myself, for the time being.

Debbie Little, my sister-in-law, the one you've been hearing about, called and I knew enough not to ignore her. What a toss up, meet with an attorney or talk to my sister-in- law? It was not a great beginning to the week.

"We are having a themed Christmas," Debbie informed me as soon as she figured out who I was. She doesn't have caller ID; she must enjoy the surprise.

"Themed?" I asked.

I couldn't simultaneously sit quietly and listen to Debbie talk. I wandered from my office to the lobby, where all the action in our office usually takes place. Patricia was fishing out the holiday tree from its box and Rosemary was helping by holding down the box flaps.

"I saw it on TV, it's a nostalgia theme. You're suppose to bring something from your childhood that represents something you loved about Christmas."

I would love a trip elsewhere. "Does that include my Barbie?" I asked, playing directly into her already low opinion of me.

"No, no, things to EAT and the gifts are not nostalgic, those need to be new and recently bought."

I waited to hear her suggest where the recently purchased gifts need to be from, but she stopped herself in time.

"Jell-O salad? That kind of thing?" I asked. I thought the holidays were nostalgic regardless. From the time they married, Debbie had always promoted Christmas as her favorite holiday, but except for her big party, she didn't get much of a chance to inflict her version of holiday cheer on the rest of us. My mother kept tight control of family events, keeping Richard away from the bar, Allen from too much of any one activity, the grandchildren in line. There was a lot to it. And now we were shaking it up. For no good reason that I could determine. But, I don't have kids.

"Mary is already bringing the Jell-O salad and your mother is bringing the vegetable dish."

Onions in cream. I already knew what dish mother would bring. She tried to foist it off on us every year for about two centuries until Richard, in an unfortunate fit of honesty, told my mother what he really thought about her cooking. And Debbie gave mom an opening to resurrect the damn dish. She was so clueless, had she not listened Richard's stories, had she ignored Allen's?

Guess not, we can willfully ignore any fact if we work hard enough.

"So, do you have a suggestion?" I asked carefully.

"Well, since you don't cook," she said it with disdain but I hardly notice anymore. "You can bring the favorite rolls that your brother talks about, I have no idea why he wants them, they are not even homemade."

"That's what made them special," I said automatically. "I'd be happy to bring the rolls and the butter."

"I have butter," she snapped.

She had low fat margarine. I'd bring real, Cooper produced, butter and people could choose. I would also bring olives so my nieces and nephews could slide one black olive on each finger and run around the house, another family holiday tradition that was difficult to do at the country club restaurant. Well, that part may be fun.

"I'd be happy to bring the rolls, I know exactly what kind to buy."

* * *

Ben and I arranged to meet with Peter Klausen O'Reilly the Third right after my usual Monday meeting at the office. Ben doesn't have an office and so did not need to submit to office meetings of any kind, at any time. Pretty smart.

The rain had let up and fluffy clouds decorated the blue sky. Bright light washed out the Christmas decorations in the store windows, the tree lights in the parks barely held their own against the sun.

Peter Klausen O'Reilley, the Third leased an office in one of the newer office buildings that spread out from the boarders of River's Bend like high tide. We took the elevator and hummed along with Rudolf the Red Nose Reindeer, the orchestra version. Peter's office door was decorated with an elaborate wreath from Williams-Sonoma, the pleasant scent of cinnamon greeted us as we marched through the double glass doors.

O'Reilly greeted us as if we were old friends. Which we were not, but what the hell, it was the season of good will towards men. Rudolf will do that to you. O'Reilley led us into his private office, and we sat facing him over a huge mahogany colored desk.

"She," O'Reilly started. He rested his forearms on the desk and leaned towards us. I wasn't sure if he was sincere or faking sincerity. Maybe it didn't matter in this case.

Ben looked at him and O'Reilly looked at Ben.

"She didn't confide all that much in me after the, " he paused, like a person pauses before blurting out the word cancer to someone undergoing radiation therapy, "divorce."

We all sat in silence and contemplated that which is divorce.

"She wasn't really happy with me of course," O'Reilly admitted. I appreciated his honesty.

"Of course," Ben smiled for the first time. "You traveled to the Caribbean with her?"

"How did you? Oh, of course, the photos. She loved taking photos. That trip she must have taken seventeen photos with every man she could find on the ship. She insisted it wasn't about US, you understand, but she wanted to have fun, and taking all these photos was fun. Expensive too."

"You paid for her photos with other men?" I asked.

O'Reilly gave me a look. "Did you ever meet Beverley?"

I shook my head.

"Kept her away?" O'Reilly glanced at Ben and then turned his attention back to me.

"Yeah, Beverley never knew," Ben confirmed.

"That was smart of you."

"What does that mean?" I couldn't help asking.

"She wasn't all that secure," O'Reilly said. "And she didn't take kindly to competition."

"But they were divorced," that I was arguing with an attorney shows how embroiled I was in this Beverley situation.

"Yeah," Ben looked far away focusing on something beyond the painted wall of O'Reilly's office. "You and she were an item for how long?"

"Long enough," O'Reilly said. He looked at me. "She had this knack. You were the only man in the world, the king. Only you could help her, only you were perfect enough for her. Even with all those photos, I was the only one who could make it happen: pay for the photos, pay extra for the gourmet dinners, make her happy. Only I could find her key card. I can't really explain it."

"She could be completely dependent, yet she was always so fascinating,' Ben acknowledged.

I was no longer part of this conversation.

"She made you feel so important," Ben said dreamily.

"How?" I asked. I wanted the bullet points, Power Point slides. .

O'Reilly pushed back in his chair, "yeah."

"Yeah," Ben repeated.

I hate men.

Ben recovered first. "So who do you think could do such a thing?"

"Do, wasn't it an accident?" O'Reilly sat forward with a bang.

I swallowed, remembering the scene.   Ben regarded O'Reilly.

"No," he said finally. "She was murdered." I gave him some credit, Ben could have taken advantage of the situation and strung O'Reilly along, but he didn't. He disliked O'Reilly - and I think there's a list of grievances - yet he didn't go for the cheap shot. And I admired him for it.

O'Reilly turned a paler shade, much paler than his usual light complexion. "I had no idea. Why didn't the papers say anything? Why wasn't it on the Internet?"

"She's not all that significant," I pointed out, a bit churlishly I admit, but honestly, she apparently was the first girl in history to make men feel important. It was annoying.

"Murder," O'Reilly twisted his hands. ""Shit. I heard she had a number of boyfriends after me. But no one she royally pissed off. She didn't marry any of them."

"No, but when she wanted something . . . "

O'Reilly nodded. "She wanted it now. It could have been a frustrated lover, but I don't see it."

"I don't either."

"Thanks for telling me, in private," O'Reilly said. He stood and pushed out his hand. Ben took it.

"By the way," Ben said casually, "Cassandra is back in town."

O'Reilly froze. Ben kept his grip on the other man's hand.

There was the cheap shot.

"She is?" O'Reilly gulped. "Here in town?"

"No, she's north. She's taken over her parent's vineyard."

Ben released O'Reilly's hand.

"Ah, yes," O'Reilly said, as if he knew all along that was her plan. He absently rubbed his knuckles.

"Well, thank you for the information." Ben said.

"Or lack of it," O'Reilly acknowledged ruefully. The comment about this Cassandra, she of the new winery, Ben's new partner, another woman of mystery, seemed to have completely derailed O'Reilly. He didn't even point out that Ben was the reasonable first suspect in the murder of his ex-wife.

Chapter 12

The holidays raged around me as I went about my business. I worked from home in order to stay off the streets, and out of the office. The rancor between Rosemary and Katherine escalated to such a pitch that I wondered if you can lose weight simply by staying angry. Except with that kind of diet program, you'd lose everything else as well. You'd be thin and lonely.

By Wednesday evening, I was thrilled to hear from Carrie and take a break from my own thoughts to listen to hers.

"I need to talk about this, and you're the only person I can tell," she said succinctly over the phone.

"We can meet at our wine bar," I offered.

"No, I'll come to your place."

"I don't want to be overheard." She explained when she arrived, flopping down on my soft cushioned couch. I served her a Viognier in a Reidel chardonnay glass. I drank a north coast syrah in my Reidel, yes, Syrah glass.

Ben insists that the wine tastes the same, regardless of the glass. He once told me an Opus One would taste exactly the same when drunk from a jelly glass as it would from a burgundy glass, which is how they drink wine in France, and THOSE easily fit in the dishwasher. The jelly glasses. But I am not giving up my hobby, and he has not produced a bottle of Opus One (the retail value is rather high) to demonstrate his point. Besides, an obsession for specific items, assiduously circulated among my immediate relatives, often garners good Christmas gifts.

"This is nice." Carrie sipped the white. It was a little fruity for winter for me, I'm a big, bold girl. When it comes to wine.

I sank into my favorite chair, covered in beautiful, green leather with a matching foot rest. It is my TV watching, premium ice cream eating, sanctuary. "You attended the first board meeting for the Homeless Prevention League, how did it go?"

"We met at a restaurant, there wasn't room to meet at the offices, which I thought was a little short sighted on the part of the board who approved the office lease. Anyway, we met at Ralph's, are you familiar with that fifties themed place?"

"Not terribly elegant," I agreed.

"Better than the pizza place, or the pub," she said with some disgust. "This is suppose to be important and official; serious business."

"You've always treated the board seriously at the Senior Center," I put in. I sipped my wine and watched the night darken from black to impregnable. It was only six o'clock. At this rate I'll be ready for bed by seven.

"That's right, our board members at the Senior Center take themselves very seriously, I practically have to bow and courtesy as I hand them their perfect, hand stapled agendas on a silver serving platter."

The image reminded me of the HPL staff, serving shrimp to the donors and guests. I shifted and folded my bare feet under me.

"No staff served you?" This time.

"No, they aren't invited to the board meeting. Only official board members attend, and the president. And CEO." she added, as if schooled in the title. "He's a handsome man of course, quite commanding and," she frowned, thinking of the afternoon.

"And?" I prompted.

She drank more wine and twirled what remained in her glass, which is what these glasses are built to do. Come on, think of wine as a contact sport, many rules, yet so easy to win.

"I'm new," Carrie explained, "I didn't want to jump in and say, well, I've been here fifteen minutes and I have all the answers to all your problems because I read the brochure, and so this is what you must do."

"But don't all non-profits have systems in common? So you probably do know what to do."

"Yes," Carrie backed down at bit. "I do. The HPL has created a number of counter intuitive systems, which I don't approve of, by the way. For instance, only the President knows all the pieces of how the organization fits together, the rest of us are left with half a picture. The financials we received at this meeting were incomplete, but no one seemed to notice. I asked for a schedule of the RVs locations, but apparently, there is a rule that the staff doesn't disclose the Mobile Shelters' locations, not even to board members."

"Sounds pretty secretive," I confirmed.

"They treat their information as a need to know situation," Carrie said with disgust. She wrinkled her cute nose and took another swig of her wine.

"Then this Martha Anderson."

"She of the tragedy of it all," I interrupted.

"Yes, the *tragedy* of it all. During the meeting, Martha Anderson was all over me. When I asked a simple question about the financial statements for October, she gave me, me! This lecture all about how the shelter has this proud tradition of frugality, and helping the most people for the least amount of money - by the way, they've only been a 501 (C) 3 since 1989 so it's not all that venerable - and she shook her finger, and told me that I should have FAITH in the staff and their systems, otherwise, I shouldn't be on the board." Carrie leaned back in the couch exhausted.

"That's a little harsh."

"I thought so, I brought up the same questions our board members ask at the Senior Center. The same questions I asked at Forgotten Felines. The same questions that any new board member asks at any non-profit. You are right, they're not all that different."

"Kittens and homeless people?"

"They are both lost and no one cares," Carrie gave me a severe look.

"Don't make that face too often; you will freeze into a Martha Anderson look-alike."

"Gross." Carrie massaged her features to make sure nothing was sticking. "But I have considerable background in non-profit operations, and Martha Anderson treats me like a bimbo girlfriend. She scowled again despite my warning.

"Who is this Martha Anderson?"

"Remember Anderson Savings and Loan?"

"She's the Anderson part of that title?"

"Her family started it, they sold it middle of last year. Martha is now focused on doing good in the community, no matter what it costs."

"Maybe that would have been Beverley's fate, as well," I suggested.

Carried considered that idea, "maybe her death was a blessing, if that was her future. But there was something about Beverley that would have prevented her from growing up to be Martha. Beverley didn't have her own money for one, and you have to back up your assertions with cash, if you want to be a bully in the long term."

I grinned at her.

"What?"

"You really do get it, don't you? Patrick was right to ask you to do this."

"We'll see," she still looked doubtful, Carrie is one of those women who doesn't know her own strengths, that's why I enjoy seeing her stand up for what she believes in, even when she believes I should diet.

"Tomorrow, the staff is taking me, and a couple of other board members, I don't remember their names, and of course Martha, on a tour of the shelters. We're only viewing the ones here, not the East Bay, or anything."

"They operate in the East Bay?"

"All over," Carrie assured me. "They have about fifty shelters. No, maybe thirty."

"I thought Martha said thirty two."

"Then, that's the number. They do well on their budget, as least the part I looked at. They keep the web site all in house, and all the fundraising and advertising in house. It's a pretty tight ship."

"It's been my experience that sometimes you should pay for outside help."

"Sure, if you're a for-profit company. Non-profits around here can't afford anything extra. And speaking of which," she poured herself more white wine. "Do you want to come to Cooper Milk party?"

"When?"

"Tomorrow."

I ran through the social calendar easily stored in my head. The only thing I had planned was a date with my favorite chair and holiday cartoons. "I'd love to, but how on earth are you justifying my attendance?"

"I thought it would be good for your business, and Patrick said to bring a friend, since he'll be busy. So I'm asking you."

"Won't his sisters be company?"

She drank more wine. "They are getting better, in that they aren't as openly hostile, but it's hard," she acknowledged. "They are very protective of Patrick."

"That explains why he's been single for so long." I thought about what Anne said.

"It's not only them, he got a little jaded over the years; so many local girls offered," she rolled her eyes. "Well, you can imagine."

"I can."

"I happened to hit him at the right time."

"Maybe, you're the right person," I said encouragingly.

"Maybe," she leaned forward. "Come with me, I'd feel better if you were there."

"Can I wear my velvet outfit again?"

"Wear leopard print spandex, if you want, I don't care. It's at the St. Marie winery this year."

"Do you think anyone would have a lead there on Beverley's killer?"

Carrie considered that for a moment, "The story is still that it was an accident, but I'll ask around."

"Be careful."

"Oh for heaven's sake, what can possibly happen to me?"

The Cooper Milk Co-op, with its history of humble beginnings, and strong reputation for giving back to the community, actually throws quite a party. Most of the residents of Sonoma County read about the holiday soiree, it's covered in the River's Bend Press, far less are invited. I was looking forward to checking it out.

I picked up Carrie in case she wanted to go home with Patrick. For fun, I wore one of my great-grandmother's minks. The mink coats are mine because my grandmother Prue wouldn't be caught dead in dead animal fur and my mother likes her furs, more fresh. I wear them to look like I come from old money.

Speaking of ill-gotten fur, I had a surprise for Carrie.

"Here," I pulled out Beverley's sheared blue chinchilla jacket, and tossed it into Carrie's lap.

It was too big for Carrie's tiny frame, but I knew the color would make Carrie look fabulous.

"What is this?"

"I'm fairly certain it's not made of kitten fur, so you're okay."

"It's so luxurious," she stroked the jacket fur all the way to the party.

And indeed, as we strolled to first open terrace of the St Marie winery, Carrie tossed the fur over her narrow shoulders and looked magnificent. I was happy to contribute to her new "it girl" status. She wore a slinky, jersey black dress she bought at Ross about four seasons ago, and clutched a glittery purse. The mink was the perfect, final touch.

"What is that?" I gestured to her hand. The walkway to the front of the winery was lined with luminaries, paper bags glowing from candles placed inside. The homemade glowing lanterns are a tradition from back when California was Mexican. The winery itself was built in the Spanish style, so it all fit. You don't have to live in a winery to display the luminaries, some tract homes around River's Bend sport walk ways lined with small, glowing paper bags at Christmas.

Carrie lifted her purse to show me. "A Judith Lieber bag, Patrick's sister Kathleen loaned it to me. We're getting along better, as of today."

She grinned, because when it came to Patrick's sisters, small, incremental steps towards making things better was really a huge triumph.

She offered up the shiny, hard bag, covered in colored crystals and shaped like . . .

"It looks like a bunch of asparagus," I stopped walking to look at it more closely. "It is a bunch of asparagus, you are carrying around a purse that looks like food."

"It is not food, it is a designer bag," Carrie was as stiff as her hand-sized purse.

It was pretty, and shiny, even in the soft glow of the luminaries, the green crystals glittered, but I could help think: elegance on a stick.

"Does Judith make one in the shape of a hamburger?"

"Now you're being silly," she snatched the bag away from me, and marched through the entrance.

I followed her past the gift store, roped off for the evening, and back outside to another courtyard. Space heaters kept the temperature pleasant.

"I'll greet a few people here, and then we can move to the caves." Carrie gestured with the asparagus and I followed.

She seemed more confident tonight. Maybe, she was feeling more as if she belonged. I usually don't have a problem finding her in a crowd, but with the bright blue mink jacket, she was a petite beacon in the night. I had opted for black myself, after I realized that I'd be in the dark for most of the party. I not only could blend in, if I spill, no one can tell.

A waiter cruised by with a plate of hors d'ouvres. I picked up a real stem of asparagus, wrapped in prosciutto; it looked like Carrie's purse.

Carrie greeted a few people, introduced me, but we didn't stay to chat. We moved quickly to the main event: dinner in the caves.

The point of wine caves is to have the perfect environment, which means the perfect temperature, to store barrels of wines. These caves were natural, so natural that the mold grew thick and black on the walls. It's not as gross as it sounds, but don't lean against it.

Fairy lights strung throughout the caves gave off a warm glow. Candelabras filled with flickering candles were positioned along long wood dining tables. Instead of decorating the niches cut into the wall every few yards, with traditional greenery, or a tree, the arches were filled with winter white floral arrangements set on empty wine casks. The Sullivan's not only knew how to throw a party, they knew how to throw a classy party.

"You look fabulous." Patrick finally extracted himself from someone, it could well have been a former mayor, I wasn't sure, and hugged Carrie.

"That's an interesting piece," he rubbed the mink and Carrie's arm.

"Allison loaned it to me, isn't it fun?"

He kissed her, hard enough so she'd have to reapply her lipstick, an enviable problem. "You look great in anything."

"Thanks for coming Allison," he finally noticed me, and put out his hand. I shook it politely. Our problem, Patrick's and mine, is that we hear far too much about each other. Carrie talks to me about Patrick, and I'm sure she has described some of our exploits to Patrick, but the two of us haven't exchanged much information directly. As a result, we end up keeping our face-to-face exchanges formal, and polite.

"Can I take her away?" he asked, conscious I was here to make sure Carrie wouldn't be alone in the first place.

"But of course." A waiter carrying a tray of sparkling wine carefully walked by and I grabbed a glass, "go, talk amongst your selves."

I, in turn, wandered around the party appreciating the mixture of the very best of River's Bend society and production line workers, from the milk processing plant. Cooper Milk did all the manufacturing right here in town. Pretty much have to, that's the way milk is.

Because of the thick natural walls of the cave, sound didn't bounce around much, so the party atmosphere had an intimate feel, and it was easier to ease drop on other conversations. I wandered past tiny knots of guests (there wasn't a lot of room in the caves) and munched on another delectable treat, something wrapped in filo pastry, and drank more wine.

"I heard her house is for sale."

I paused immediately outside a little indent at the wall.

Another voice, male, joined in, "I heard this wasn't the first time she found a body in one of her listings."

"I don't think that first one was her fault."

"Doesn't matter, she's bad luck."

Bad luck? My stomach clenched. I was not bad luck. I carefully backed away from the voices. I swallowed down more sparking drink and tried to calm myself. I knew it was about me, and normally I'm thrilled when the conversation is about me, but not tonight. I needed more listings, hell, we all did. But a label like bad luck could tank my career.

I looked around for a friendly face, but I couldn't even spot Carrie in the dark halls. The black mold looked more ominous than a few minutes ago. I couldn't breath very well. I hustled outside to the cool air. A waiter passed by with a tray of fresh sparkling wine. I stopped him and set my glass on his tray.

"Can you tell Patrick Sullivan Allison had to leave?"

He nodded, and I escaped.

I hunkered down for the remainder of the evening with my *Nightmare Before Christmas* DVD and a pint of Imagine Whirled Peace. Bad luck, my ass.

I decided not to call Ben and harangue him about – well, anything at all. He too, had enough

Saturday morning I slept in because the night did not go well. I was restless and uncomfortable. The extra two hours in bed did not help, I woke feeling ill at ease, cranky and I had bad hair. The only reason I didn't waste the whole day and night with a good book was I had to dress for the New Century Regional Holiday party, at the Hilton. How much dried chicken breast must a girl endure?

So I swung into action and worked desperately to live the life of a diva. It did not go well. Instead of a long bubble bath, I ran out of bubbles and had to shower. The hot water ran out. My hair refused to succumb to the curling iron, which in turn, died a smoking death half way through the process.

I wrapped up my hair in a twist (plan B) and squirted myself in the face with the hair spray because the nozzle was apparently clogged. At least the random spray set my mascara, it was clumping and I had no time to call my Mary Kay consultant for more. I mean, she does house calls, but with fifteen minutes notice?

I squirted the hairspray around my head, shooting the mirror, the bathroom sink, all the towels and some more of my hair. What I really needed was a big can of Aqua Net. I miss my Aqua Net, but it wouldn't do to have some greenly inclined client smelling it on me. Really, people do get so in a twist about these kinds of things. My hair is important, but not worth burning through what's left of the ozone layer.

My first choice, beaded dress, wouldn't fit. If I sat down in it, not only would the beads be uncomfortable, but so would the seams. I tried it on with a stretch Spanx - the new girdle - then with control top pantyhose, then with both, but I couldn't breath. I pulled out the second, back up, velvet and lace skirt and matching jacket. Feeling perverse, I teamed the whole thing with a tightly fitted – yet stretchy – red bustier, you can imagine, and red high heels. So I gained some weight, it was the holidays. Maybe, Rosemary and Katherine could give me tips. No, that was not a good idea. They were on the cranky girl diet. I had no interest in alienating friends and family in order to reduce my waist circumference by an inch.

I slipped on the big David Yurman bracelet from the Beverley Weiss collection, the bracelet covered with large, bright, gemstones. Two of the stones were deep red and matched the shoes and bustier. My hair could stand against a class four hurricane. I was ready for the damn party.

I grabbed the gift for Patricia.

"Hi," Ben looked rested and more like himself, casual, but in control. He wore a designer suit, an upgrade even from the one he wore to the museum party. I felt honored he'd make that effort for me.

"Was I supposed to bring a gift?" He glanced at the decorated bottle bag in my hand.

"No, guests are exempt, only the New Century agents and staff exchange."

I wasn't keen to walk alone into a room filled with people, even people I work with on a daily basis. I think I ran out of small talk. And I wasn't feeling myself, I was too distracted by Ben in the throes of being distracted by his ex-wife. I was immensely that he was even coming with me to the party.

One of the agents, from the north office, admired my bracelet.

"Thank you, it's . . . "

Ben gave me a look, and I immediately changed my story. "David Yurman, it's new." New to me.

"It's fabulous," she breathed as she examined it closely.

During the gift exchange, I gave Patricia two bottles of wine. She was suitably grateful it wasn't something awful, say, a clown statue.

My gift was a necklace made of fake plastic beads that didn't even muster up a glow under the relentless ballroom lighting. In comparison, the faux stones in my bracelet glittered as if they were real.

"I would have loved a Barnes and Noble gift card," I said quietly, but fortunately no one heard me. I wondered if Rosemary and Katherine got diet books. They preach all the time; what you think about, you bring about.

"Really?" said Emily. She was from the Mendocino county office, and sat at our table. She fingered the gift card she received, "I got one that's not even good for music."

"Ah, well, we all have our burdens," Ben said.

Once dinner and the gifts were taken care of, agents began to circulate and talk.

"Well, Allison, at least you have an, interesting listing," one person snickered as he walked past me to the bar.

"Yeah, people must be dying to see the house," said Emily, whom I no longer liked and I hope she hated to read.

Ben squeezed my hand, but that didn't assuage my feelings.

This, from what should be my own people.

"Did you hear about the new category? DOA instead of REO?" Another person, I didn't recognize him, threw that bon mot out as he passed by the table.

I can take as much ribbing as the next woman, but my pantyhose top was cutting into my soft. vulnerable stomach and I needed to pee. Or I thought I did.

I escaped to the ladies room, used the facilities, and thoroughly washed my hands. I applied some hand lotion. I sat down at the vanity table and re-applied my lipstick. I thought I could rest here, in the ladies lounge, for a minute or two, or an hour. I put my head on the marble counter top, and closed my eyes.

"Allison," Ben's voice came from right outside the door. "Are you okay?"

"Yes, I'm fine," I said loudly enough for him to hear.

"Then why are you locked in the bathroom during a holiday party?"

"I'm not locked in, I can leave anytime I want." The counter top was cool on my forehead. I could stay here forever.

"Oh, for heaven's sake!" He pushed the door open and strode in.

"What are you doing in here?" I shrieked. My voice echoed nicely around the tile walls.

"Hey, you have nice bathrooms," he surveyed the lounge with his hands on his hips.

"You should know, you work on them," I shot back, it was kind of nasty and I don't know why I said it, but there it was.

"We all have our Waterloos. Come here." He pulled me to him, wrapped his arms around me, and let me smear clumpy mascara on his jacket.

"It's okay," he said into my hair. "This will work out, we'll figure out what happened to Beverley, we'll sell the house, and we can put all this behind us."

He pulled up from my head. "Hey, how much hair spray did you use tonight?"

"All of it."

"Oh, excuse me," one of the secretaries from the Marin office pushed open the door, then quickly retreated.

"It's okay, I'm a professional bathroom remodeler," Ben assured her. He escorted me out to allow her to come in.

I tried to smile at her, but she was so shocked that I knew by next week, rumors of my unconventional love life would be circulating through all the New Century Offices. Oh hell.

"Here," Ben handed me a red envelope. "Open it."

"Right now?" Ben was steering me back into the fray. Still on the program: desultory ballroom dancing and a dessert buffet of indifferent quality.

I opened the envelope. It was a $20 Book Gift card.

"I traded for you," he explained.

"I love you."

"I love you, too, now let's get out of here."

I felt much better after I stripped off the many layers that had held me hostage, and changed into my forgiving sweats. Once free, I did exactly what I really wanted to do, sink into my favorite chair and watch three back to back episodes of SpongeBob Square pants.

Ben brought in his lap top and worked while I watched TV.

"Uh oh," he said, as the last episode wrapped up.

"What?"

"The authorities think they found the murder weapon. They first linked it to that poor woman the police found in the creek, but they are now linking it to," he scrolled down, "the body they found this summer, and Beverley. Damn, they named her."

"That was bound to happen. What did they find?"

"A reticulating saw, one of those saws with a thin blade suspended between two handles. I use them to cut pipe, thick siding, anything, they are," he paused, "quite sharp."

I hoped he knew where his was located right now. And I wasn't the only one. The call from the police came that evening. Following all the obvious leads, Mr. Stone, was the reasonable request by the authorities.

"I'll look in the morning," Ben assured the caller.

We watched my copy of *Charlie Brown Christmas*, Ben's favorite childhood Christmas movie and *How the Grinch Stole Christmas*; mine.

Chapter 13

While I was mentally preparing for the awful company party (by doing nothing about it), Carrie was on tour with the Homeless Prevention League. Not a great name for a band.

She called Sunday morning to update me.

"They loaded us into this wine tour van, wine glass holders and everything."

"Did they serve wine?" I cradled the phone in a perfect clench that will guarantee me tense neck pain later on.

"Of course not. Only at the end."

I waited, but she was uncharacteristically quiet, "what else?" I pulled out a dish cloth and wandered around the house wiping dust from the surfaces not protected by piles of books.

"Well, we viewed the first RV, or mobile shelter as they call it. It's parked over by the creek."

It's a long creek, the RV wasn't necessarily parked next to the last location of the most recent murder, so I didn't bring it up. Yet.

"That's where the professor lives, the one who spoke at the dinner. He wasn't dressed as well, of course, but he joined us to give us his, the homeless client's, view of the program."

"Did you go into the RV?" I dusted the TV screen and wiped off my leather chair.

"No, we viewed the outside, going in would be a violation of their privacy. The first one, the professor's, was kind of green color, not in bad shape, I wasn't really scrutinizing it. I had to pay attention to Martha, who was talking incessantly about philanthropy in Sonoma County and how the local colleges needed to stop building new concert halls and start educating, that kind of rant. As soon as she mentioned the university, the professor took the microphone, and stood in front of the bus and lectured us on the tragedy of the homeless, and what the HPL was doing to prevent it. All while, we lurched through the Saturday afternoon traffic."

"So, where were the other RVs?"

"Across town. Of course," she said in disgust.

"Why did they give you a tour on one of the busiest shopping days of the year?" I walked upstairs knocking off the dust between the stair rails.

"Tell me about it. It took forever to get to the next location. Once we finally arrived, that RV turned out to be a kind of coppery color, very modern looking, apparently Flex paint, remember him?"

I nodded. Even though she couldn't see me, Carrie always seems to read my expressions, even by phone.

"They paint the RVs for free, which is lovely of them, so the RV isn't really white and sticking out, it sort of blends in with the . . ".

"Weeds?" I supplied.

"It's not that bad. This second one was over across town, by the Grocery Outlet."

"And the third, or are there more?"

"There are more," she confirmed, "But we only had time to see three. The last one was south of town, and the traffic through there is horrific, five miles an hour the whole way. That RV is parked at the edge of the Wal-Mart parking lot. But it didn't look as if it had been there long. We only had time to look at the three RVs. I had to get ready for a family party with Patrick, and Martha had something. Cyndi mentioned she had something to do. The professor of course, really didn't have anything else to do, so he kept lecturing. After we visited the third Mobile Shelter Unit he, the professor, started talking about the quest for the perfect fifteen minutes of fame and what that was worth now-a-days."

I had managed to finish wiping off the all surfaces - not covered in books - in the bedroom by the time she was finished with that last paragraph.

"Didn't he say something similar at the dinner?" I was distracted by the Flex paint, it worked on things other than high tech coating on lenses, that was kind of cool.

"Yes, he did. I think. Patrick was whispering to me at the time, I don't remember the professor's whole speech."

"Did you meet anyone else, besides the professor?"

"No, Cyndi told us that the residents go to the day program

run by the Salvation Army and some do pick up work for board members."

"That seems odd," I referred to the odd jobs for board members and Carrie knew it.

"Beverley did it a lot, hired them for cash. The professor loved that part of the program, and said so. He also appreciated Beverley because she didn't ask what or where the money went. She paid in cash."

"Was he sad that she was gone?"

"He seemed to miss the work."

I tossed the dirty dishtowel onto the laundry pile. "Did you learn anything new?"

"I have to think about it. I'm not sure."

"They found another body in the creek." I had to tell her.

"Like Beverley?" she immediately asked. She's quick, quicker than the local reporters.

I closed my eyes. "Like Beverley," I admitted. "She was cut up, like this poor woman they found. The papers are going to start talking about it. Just be prepared, the news may or may not affect the Homeless League."

"Homeless Prevention League." She corrected me. Then took a breath. "God, Beverley was hacked up? Who would do such a thing?"

"No one has any theories at this point."

My next call was to the elusive Ben Stone. Ben did find his own saw: it was safe on his workshop bench in Marin. The police were pleased to hear that. Ben was pleased to say it. I was just pleased. For the time being, he was more than fine, despite the signature on the listing papers and the claim that he didn't sign anything for Beverley.

Before I had a chance to shower, Bo Freeman called and wanted to make an appointment to see the house again.

"What do you think, can I see it again today?" he asked.

"Today?" I wasn't planning on holding it open, it was too late in the season. But I had nothing else to do this afternoon. Yet, I was honestly unsure about meeting him alone. I wondered if I could do what Beverley did, and hire the professor to be with me during these meetings, maybe he could hang out with me at the next the open house (in January, thank you). His company would be safer than staying alone in that house.

I dismissed the idea immediately as far too paranoid for what I'm all about. I'm all about strength. I'm all about independence. And I had no clue how to contact the professor short of finding the RV in which he lived, and knocking on the door. And wasn't all that easy to do, as Carrie explained.

I called Ben instead. But he was busy. Last minute holiday repairs, fair of course.

The possibilities of a sale won out over personal safety, which shouldn't surprise even a casual acquaintance of mine.

I agreed to meet Bo at 3:00 PM, when there was still some afternoon light left. I didn't tell him that part, of course.

The house, with my sign on the front lawn waving in the damp breeze, looked innocent and completely normal. The Sign Nazis must not search this part of town; I was still good.

I had one directional (those red arrows) sign at the top of the hill, in gross violation of the unwritten rules. When I am caught, I often claim I didn't remember the rules. I've been forgetting the rules for about fifteen years now.

But, all was well with my signs. The house was now radically staged. The downstairs rooms were not only clear of junk. they looked officially uncomfortable and spare. I don't want visitors to feel comfortable; I want them to buy the house.

The living room boasted one built in bookcase that was completely book free. The shelves were filled with big shells from the Caribbean and various awards of the kind inflicted on Ben and Patrick at the Homeless Prevention League dinner. I left the awards where they had been abandoned. They were easy to ignore.

Bo Freeman arrived at the unlocked door exactly on time, not something I expected at all. I had planned to go through the rest of the master closet and box up another set of clothing, maybe even all of it, while I waited for him to appear. A project made the waiting easier.

But here he was.

"Hello," I greeted him as enthusiastically as I could, considering I thought he may be the serial killer. Although in all fairness, he didn't seem familiar with the house. I heard of killers returning to the scene of the crime, but buying it?

He shook my hand. His grip was warm and firm. I relaxed a bit, but couldn't relax completely. The saw, Beverley's body, the bodies in the creek, and no motive at all, not even a speculative motive, which should have been trumpeted on the front page, had me feeling a bit edgy. With no answers, everyone was a suspect. Be careful, watch your back, don't invite strangers into your empty house. As if I've ever listened to that advice.

Mr. Freeman walked the same pattern he followed when he first viewed the house, but in more detail. He didn't say much, which was just as well. I followed him cautiously, as he wound about the house.

He knocked on the walls, peeked out onto the deck outside the kitchen. He asked about run off, view lines, all typical questions. He didn't ask about anything inappropriate, nothing weird, nothing odd. Plus, he did not mention the murder or the bad chi of the house.

"Do you think the seller is willing to negotiate?" He finally asked.

"Do you want me to write an offer?" It was the only thing I could do, as the agent for   both this Mr. Freeman and Ben, otherwise I'm negotiating with myself, and I have too much information, and not enough schizophrenia to pull that off.

"Maybe," he glanced around the living room. By then I had edged him towards the front door. "It's hard to tell if there's enough light," he commented.

"On the longest night of the year? Yes," I confirmed. "But the dining room has lovely view of the mountains." And of more houses built up on those mountains, but I didn't point that out.

"I'll get back to you," he promised.

I hoped not, but I was representing a client, and this is my job. So I smiled with as much enthusiasm as I could muster, and ushered him out the front door.

It was only three thirty. I glanced upstairs, it was in pretty good shape. I could fill a couple more boxes with clothes. I knew where to get the boxes.

The volume of boxes and packing material stuffed into the

two-car garage was daunting. Should I do this all at once? Of course I should. But, I didn't have the heart for it.

I wondered who would get the car? Maybe Beverley's parents could use a new car, so they could drive better at night. Ben said they were very stoic through the funeral, they asked for donations to be sent to the Homeless Prevention League, in lieu of flowers. They did not ask for any of Beverley's things.

Boxes were piled all across the garage floor, blocking the side window. Some stacks teetered precariously in kindergarten versions of skyscrapers that skimmed the rafters. I negotiated my way to those tall towers. I pushed back one or two tentatively, to feel their weight. I pulled down the empty boxes, they would hold the last of the wardrobe from upstairs.

The last box under the third box tower was a sealed Fed Ex box. I pushed against it to feel the weight of it.

It was heavy. Full and ready to ship.

Of course. It's almost the same to ship as it is to pay the extra weight at check-through. Or, so say Rosemary and Katherine, the world travelers of our office. No, they do not travel together.

There was no destination address label stuck to the box, yet.

I tapped the box and considered. Where? The kitchen, was there a drawer? Most of what littered the kitchen was kitchen related equipment. But I knew that people tend to temporarily store important documents in the kitchen first before carrying the documents or the bills upstairs to officially file them. At least, that's what I do.

Did I have permission to rifle though the private papers of the client? No. Did I do it anyway? Yes.

I pulled open a top drawer below the long granite counter. It only held silverware, something else to give away. Every time I walk into this house there's something more to give away. I opened every drawer. The bottom drawer was jammed with paper and only opened about an inch, or two. If a detective in a hurry came across this logistical challenge, he'd probably reject the drawer contents as unimportant, because they weren't easy to retrieve. There were plenty of files in Beverley's second guest room, enough for the police to rifle through and more than enough for Ben to throw away. This kitchen drawer would not be on anyone's radar screen.

I slid a spatula into the drawer and pressed down on the pile. I gently pulled the drawer all the way open.

I heard a noise out on the back deck. I looked up. Nothing. My imagination, it wasn't Bo Freeman stalking me.

I pulled out a five-inch layer of papers. Recent credit card bills, Visa, Master Card, American Express, Beverley had them all. Cable.

The sound of a footfall. I stopped and listened, someone walking around in back? Another looky-loo, confident that the house was vacant? A vagrant? Bo Freeman returning to cage a warm night in an abandoned house.

I stood and cautiously walked to the back door. It was locked, I flipped the dead bolt and the noise reverberated through the door notifying the interloper of my intentions.

I saw a shadow, and decided on the element of surprise.

I banged the door open and shouted, "what!"

"Oh, hi there." An embarrassed Mr. McMurry stood in his rubber clogs and a faded sweat suit at the edge of the deck, on the verge of complete escape.

"Yes?" I inquired, with as much disgust as I could muster, considering how loudly my heart was pounding.

"I was checking the deck, for a friend."

"You could have called," I intoned. "You have my card."

"Err, yes."

"Have you been lurking around here every day?" I asked.

By his expression, I had guessed right.

"Good, keep an eye on the place, will you?" Better to hire your rivals, as they say. Or is it keep your enemies close? Well, at least they can watch the house.

He nodded and quickly ducked out to the front of the house and to the safety of his own yard.

"Give me a heart attack," I made sure to bolt the door and returned to my pile of bills, at least they didn't belong to me. I finally found the Fed Ex receipts in the fourth pile. There were a couple of bills for boxes already shipped and the address labels for the new boxes ready to go, and stored in the garage. But the labels weren't filled out. The billing was addressed to Beverley here in Rivers Bend. The destination was cut off, perhaps saved somewhere else? Shredded? In the landfill?

Damn! I was so close. But, at least I knew her destination was warm, and the clothes were already ahead of her, traveling to where ever.

I had no doubt there was a person on the receiving end, wouldn't they wonder why the clothes arrived before the woman?

I loaded up two of the empty boxes from the garage with armloads of clothing from the upstairs closets.

Carrie called while I was driving home. She was all worked up. I hadn't heard her this agitated since the Humane Society decided to charge for spaying and neutering feral cats.

"Can you believe this? Cyndi called me and actually told me that the RVs were perfectly placed, and I didn't need more than that as confirmation that everything is fine."

"Fine is what you embroider on a pillow," I said. "What promoted a call from the President's secretary?" I stopped, then started, then pulled around the car in front of me who had decided to drive down the suicide lane with the right blinker cheerfully flashing red in the dimming afternoon.

"I asked about the RVs, where they are parked, and if there was a rotation, who knew about it, and wouldn't that be a problem for the residents? Wouldn't it be difficult to get to your job if your homes was always on the move?"

"Did she have an answer?" I dodged two jaywalkers.

"No! And that's not the worst of it. I was also treated to a call from Martha Anderson."

"You shouldn't give out your cell number." I finally made it to the freeway on ramp. The traffic was moving at a sensible clip of seven miles per hour, but at least there were no stray pedestrians in the middle of the road.

"It's on the board member list – those are coveted lists, let me tell you, everyone's home number. Martha Anderson called to warn me about fraternizing with the shelter's clients."

"Are you kidding me?"

"That's what I said!" She shrieked. "Do you know what she

said to me?"

"No, I don't." The choked freeway was decorated with streams of bright red tail-lights, very festive.

"She said," Carrie continued at an unusually high pitch, "You probably don't know this, being so young. But you don't want to get too familiar with the clients."

"Familiar?" I inched forward, and out of the goodness of my heart, let in a monstrous SUV who had been driving for miles on the right hand shoulder to pull ahead of seventeen cars. "What the hell does that mean?"

Normally I hate that, but he'll have his own bad karma to deal with later. During the holidays, Karma turns around pretty quickly.

"I knew what she meant," Carrie said, a bit more calmly. "But it was such an odd warning. Who dates the clients of a non-profit for heaven's sake?"

Since Carrie was determined not to end up poor and on welfare, the very idea of her "marrying down" was ludicrous. But Martha Anderson would not be aware of that.

"She said that there had been instances of some board members spending too much time with some of the clients."

"And that means?"

"Well, she refused to say more than that, she was trying to warn me off and be terribly discreet at the same time. So I had to back Anne into a corner after the tour and get more of the story. Apparently, Beverley and the professor were friendly, he was giving her advice on something, but no one could tell me what."

"That's a little bizarre." The professor didn't strike me as a man with a gold American Express Card. And Beverley only dated men with the ability to pay her way.

"Funny, Anne seemed relieved that I was asking about Beverley." Carrie's voice calmed down a bit.

"She was relieved you were asking about a murder?"

The news had finally hit the papers announcing Beverley's link with the two women in the creek. Yet, all the details reporters revealed were that Beverly's death was similar, no more than that. A picture of restraint, our River's Bend Press. Too bad there isn't a prize for that.

"Yeah, go figure."

When I arrived to work Monday morning, the office was in an uproar because Rosemary was in an uproar, and she needs to share.

"What is going on?" I paused at Patricia's desk, not really wanting to go much further. I heard Rosemary's voice from the parking lot.

"The River's Bend Sign Elimination Committee For the Betterment of River's Bend called. They gave Rosemary a warning," Patricia said. "Hey, another girl was murdered they think it was the same guy who killed the creek women."

"Yes," I acknowledged, there was no point denying the murder.

"What they'd get her for?" I cowered at Patricia's desk. At least the River's Bend Sign Elimination Committee For the Betterment of River's Bend was a safer subject than Beverley's new, upgraded status as the murder victim of a serial killer. Still at large.

"Brookwood," Patricia replied. "That house we saw Monday on tour, it's at the end of that long driveway."

I nodded. Rosemary had placed the *For Sale* sign on the street at the top of the driveway, otherwise, no one would see that the house was for sale. In our industry, that *For Sale* sign is the second most effective marketing tool we have.

"Off the street? They want it off the street, and only in front of the house? Why don't I put it in the back yard for good measure? We wouldn't want to let anyone KNOW the house is for sale!" Rosemary's voice echoed down the hall.

My phone buzzed. "We are on a mission," Carrie said.

"A mission from God?" I was slightly distracted.

"I have an idea," Rosemary continued at full volume. "Why don't I paint For Sale on the side of the house in orange spray paint? That will increase the value of the surrounding neighborhood properties, that will add to River's Bend's God damn betterment."

I could barely make out Inez's conciliatory tones.

"No, not that kind of mission. I want to find those shelters," Carrie said.

"Or chalk the frigging side walk, how about that? *For sale* written up and down the block. Can we get these people on restraint of trade charges?"

"Why?" I asked.

"Because, something is wrong."

"But you just saw them."

"Rosemary," Inez finally made her voice loud enough. "Have you eaten?"

"Did you tell the staff what you want to do?" I asked Carrie.

Carrie didn't even pause, "I asked Cyndi about it, but she was pretty vague. I asked about the other trailers, and she said they are, and I quote, around."

I eyed Rosemary as she stomped through the lobby to her office. I only nodded in Rosemary's direction, it was not wise to engage any of us when we've been hit by the River's Bend Sign Elimination Committee For the Betterment of River's Bend.

"That's it, that's their tightly organized system? Homeless shelters that are - around?" Carrie's voice rose in sarcasm.

Rosemary was bellowing something about placing a directional sign on every block to retaliate. I love those red arrows signs. They show the way to unknown possibilities accessible by a seductive, tree-lined street. I hoped her idea worked, as a blow for justice for all of us.

"That's it? The shelters are "around"? We are going to find them. Are you with me?" Carrie asked.

"I'll pick you up at three," I promised. God knows I've dragged Carrie around on wild chases, and sometimes the chase didn't end all that well, although we survived. According to the Pirate Code of Friendship, it was my turn.

Carrie was ready and standing outside the Senior Center at exactly three o'clock. She hopped into my car, a Lexus with leather seats. Carrie drives a used, slightly battered, Honda with worn seats. I don't even want to sit in her car, let alone be seen climbing out of it. But it works for Carrie in that it's paid for.

"I made a map of where they told me the five RVs are parked."

"Didn't they give you a map?"

Carrie shook her dark head, "no, we weren't given maps, I

told you, I couldn't get the locations or a list or any information at all. And I'm on the board. The web site has vague language about the where abouts – to protect the residents, they claim."

So we drove around, taking the short cuts to the places where Carrie remembered seeing the RVs. According to the papers, especially our own local harbinger of doom – the River's Bend Press - all retail stores were reporting low numbers, shopping is down, things are looking terrible. Judging from the cars zipping in and out of the big box centers, cars making left hand turns into traffic, cars slowing to make right hand turns into the Do Not Enter driveways, the hundreds of drivers out on the streets this afternoon, did not read the River's Bend Press.

"Wow," Carrie gripped the door handle as I braked to let the last left hand turn car go across me, even though my light was green.

"Damn amateurs," I growled.

She ignored my vocalize editorials. "It was to the right, behind the Target store," she directed me to a place next to the creek.

"See? There is it. That's one," she squinted at the RV in the low afternoon light.

"What?"

"I could have swore the one here was a copper color, but this one is greenish."

"The light maybe?" It looked like a regular RV to me. Boxy and top heavy, the greenish color did help it blend in with the high bushes, and thick, un-pruned trees that grew up from the creek bed. The parking lot was half full, probably used for overflow parking.

"Okay, that's the one where we picked up the professor," Carrie said. "So now, let's find the one over by Wal-Mart."

I dutifully pulled back into the fray and we drove, crawled, stopped and swerved down the few blocks to the next site.

"It should be at the end of the parking lot, sort of behind, watch out!"

I avoided a battered VW bus packed with people, and inched my way past the front of the store. Business was so busy, the store probably needed to hire more greeters. A job for the homeless?

"Does Wal-Mart hire the homeless as greeters?"

"No, but I have seniors who are greeters, gives them a reason to get up in the morning."

"Well, we all need that," I agreed.

"Around here," Carrie directed me, from memory and her hand written map.

Carrie confirmed on her map, "here."

We squinted at the site. A worker dragged out a huge can of trash, glanced at us, but didn't stop.

"It was right here," Carrie peered out the windshield. It was getting dark, but a vehicle as large as a RV doesn't fade into the shadows all that easily.

"It's not here," she sat back, defeated.

"Okay, how about the third one?" I suggested. I did not want to linger in the oil stained parking lot.

She directed me north, we had to take the freeway, because it was the fastest way, most of the year.

"Did you take the freeway on the tour?" I asked, stopping and starting.

"Yes, with about as much speed."

But we eventually made it to the final destination. And found: no RV.

Carrie pursed her lips and shook her head. She was transformed into a veteran philanthropist. She grimaced, sat up straighter and pulled out her phone.

"Cyndi, this is Carrie Eliot, one of the Directors?"

"Thank you, yes. I am over here at the Grocery Outlet, and can't find the RV I toured yesterday. Do you have any ideas?"

Carrie listened. "Oh, I see, well, thank you."

"What?"

"They move the trailers right after a tour, so the board members don't accidentally give away the location."

"But the one behind the Target store is still there," I pointed out.

Carrie leaned back in the seat and closed her eyes.

"I understand no one wants to be adjacent to, or close by, something as disturbing as a shelter. We don't care to be reminded how close we are to becoming homeless ourselves," I suggested helpfully.

She nodded, but didn't respond.

Maybe, this market will change a few minds. Maybe we're looking at a few potential homeless as we speak. But that's another, loftier conversation.

"Don't you think this attitude from the staff is a little vague at best, and at worst, wrong?"

"Yes," I responded cautiously. "But is it your battle to fight? The HSL is pretty well respected. Plus, some pretty prominent companies support the cause, including your future in-laws, I may add. It's Christmas, you don't want to bust a non-profit at Christmas, the paper will go nuts. And you don't have anything more than a huge body of previous experience and a bad feeling."

"You don't think I'm qualified to ask questions?" She demanded.

"Don't be defensive, I'll back you on whatever you think. I have no opinion but I don't want you running off in the wrong direction and hurting people when you don't need to."

"Okay, okay. It's difficult, this moving around of shelters. You for instance, you don't want these things next to any of your listings, or in a nice neighborhood, or marring a country road. No one will buy a house next to a homeless shelter, no one will live close to a shelter. It's not as if these are bad people," she shot back.

This is our political line in the sand. She is of the help-the-poor- at-any-cost via a benign government school of thought. And I am of the free market- rising-tide- lifts-all- boats school of thought.

We never agree. We rarely discuss it.

"Frankly, it's easier to sell the site of a murder," I admitted.

"You're right, I get upset on their behalf," she agreed, without rancor, for which I was grateful. I did not want to argue with my best friend.

"Life isn't fair," I confirmed. I pulled away from the parking lot and plunged back into afternoon traffic to take Carrie home.

"Your car heater works," Carrie commented. "That's nice."

"What do you want for Christmas?" I asked her as I pulled up to her driveway. She slid out of the car.

"The usual would be wonderful."

I usually give her a big basket from Harry and David. I fill it full of food she can't afford to buy herself; but loves. I buy the largest basket they have, and add a few more things myself.

Before I went home, I headed up to the Silverpoint property and loaded up another two boxes of clothes and put those in my car. I filled four more garbage bags with junk and papers, and stuffed those into the gray garbage bin, and blue recycling bin. I dragged both bins to the curb.

I planned to drop off the boxes to the Homeless Prevention League in Carrie's name, to take the sting out of her phone conversation with Cyndi. I hoped to pass off the donations directly to Cyndi. Carrie could use some help in the PR department.

When I entered the HPL office first thing the next morning, Cyndi was there to greet me. She wasn't specifically waiting for me; she was simply already at the office. I admired her shoes and she responded warmly with a long narrative of her trip to Nordstrom in the City. River's Bend is too small to support a Nordstrom, not that women such as myself, and Cyndi, wouldn't give our last pair of Anne Klein pumps to convince a store to locate here.

"These are from Carrie," I turned over my boxes. "She asked me to deliver them to you personally, because you know what do with them."

Cyndi nodded and took both boxes and set them on the floor without looking at them. "More from Beverley?" She asked.

I acknowledged that they were. Cyndi sighed and kicked one of the boxes.

"Anything wrong?"

"I wish I felt more badly about her," Cyndi confessed.

That was close to home, I wish I felt more badly about Beverley myself, a rival was gone before I was even aware of her. But since Ben was distracted, and not really himself since Beverley's death, maybe I had been dealing with a rival after all. Her presence in River's Bend had kept me off the streets with Ben.

I was kind of glad she was gone as well. We had that in common, Cyndi and I.

"Did you see her often?"

"Only during the time when she was making a play for the president, Steven," Cyndi snorted.

"Really?" That's often all you have to say; an encouraging word.

"Then again, that didn't make him all that special. She was always bragging about her men, guys with names like Peter and Rod, Roland. She was always going away with them to some place exotic, like those luxury cruises where they have all you can eat buffets. Her latest thing was to get away from River's Bend forever. As if that's possible."

"Apparently it was."

Cyndi ignored my comment. "She thought she was marvelous, hot stuff. She had the house in the Villas and the designer bags and shoes and the gifts from men, and I didn't have any of that, so she acted like she was so much better than me."

"You don't appear to be that badly off," I ventured.

Cyndi made a face. All beautiful, thin women can get away with scrunching up their pert little noses, and pushing out their full lips in a pout. It's meant to convey how horrible their cushy life can really be.

But, despite the stereotype, and Cyndi certainly played to one, there was something more desperate and contrived in her gesture,

"You haven't heard about my situation have you?" She asked.

"You work here as a secretary and own a great vintage Bob Mackie." And you look like Prom Queen Barbie, what is there to know?

"I'm homeless," she said shortly.

I raised my eyebrows, but not much more than that.

"Yeah, hard to believe isn't it?" She countered.

"You certainly don't fit that particularly stereotype." Did she expect me to coo at her and say comforting words: oh, you poor thing what can I do for you? She was confessing to the wrong woman. We started the conversation with Beverley and Cyndi had managed to turn it around to be all about her. I should take lessons, she was really good at making it all about her.

I glanced at my watch, it was past nine, where was the rest of the staff?

"I live here," she made sweeping gesture that encompassed the whole, bleak office. "That's right, I live here. I don't have a car. I don't have a house, not like Beverley. Steven helped me. He felt sorry for me, and let me stay here. And Beverley tried to muscle in, made it seem wrong. She even told Martha Anderson, as if I need her on my ass day and night."

"That must have made you pretty angry," I said. She'd also be frightened, cornered and prone to lash back. Lash out at Beverley?

"I could have killed her!" Cyndi was vehement; her cute face twisted to become down right ugly. "I would have done anything to make her go away. Marcel, that's the professor, said to not worry about it, I'll be fine. But I learned the hard way, that letting things go when people tell you it will all be fine is a bunch of bullshit. It don't end up fine, and no one will help you, not even the police!"

Did I want to ask the obvious question? I did not. We were alone, and despite the fact that I was considerably larger than she, sometimes that doesn't count for much.

"Then her death was kind of a relief?" I asked a more neutral question, trying to diffuse the situation, if I could. God, it was the same as reasoning with a bank employee during a short sale; impossible.

Cyndi's posture shrank as if a balloon deflated. "Yes, for me and maybe even for the Steven, he told me not to worry, too.

"Well, your secret, if it is a secret, is safe with me. I won't tell anyone," I assured her.

"Better not," she growled, but, to my relief, she finally focused on the boxes of clothes. I did not bring up Carrie's name again.

Chapter 14

I didn't hear from Carrie for the rest of the week. I worked on my own life, saw Ben briefly, but he wasn't in the mood to spend the night at my house, and his grandmother still intimidated me, so I didn't suggest his house. The holidays weren't shaping up to be very jolly at all.

I met with Carrie for coffee in the morning, to check on her.

"I've been getting these phone calls," Carrie admitted. She sucked on her skinny latte and looked up at me through her lashes.

"Phone calls?"

"Telling me to lay off the Homeless Prevention League. Stay at the Senior Center. Keep my nose out of their business. But I'm on the board, it is my business." She toyed with her paper cup waiting for my admonishment, but I was feeling more concerned than righteous.

"Shouldn't you report them?" I suggested, careful not to veer off to the righteous and stay on the concerned side of the conversation.

"To whom?" She demanded. "Who would believe me? And who would imagine that something bad would happen at a non-profit, especially during the holidays?"

"Sometimes the holidays bring out the worst in people." I said. "Maybe she knew something about the League. Are they embezzling money? That's a popular activity, people have killed for less. And if you're asking questions, maybe someone thinks you're the problem." I suggested, albeit cautiously.

"That's why it was important to get me, as an outsider, on the board," Carrie said thoughtfully. "Their numbers are dwindling. A couple months ago, they had to ask a volunteer to leave, he was the Financial Committee Chair, helped take in donations. Martha mentioned that some of his work seemed a bit off, the math didn't always come out as they expected."

"What was his name?" I asked, although why I should care was beyond me. But talking with Carrie delayed my return to the office and the loud and cantankerous dieting contest there in.

"Rod something," she said, "Here, I have an old board list."
Carrie dove into her battered brief case, something she had
picked up at the Just as Good Shop, but she carried as if it was an
old favorite she couldn't bear to part with, not a second hand
object she purchased for pennies on the dollar.

"Here," she pulled out a spreadsheet. "The Finance Chair
was Rod Bixby."

The name tugged at my memory. I tried to connect it. I
sipped on my own venti hazelnut latte (with non-fat milk, see?
I'm trying) but the caffeine was not helping.

"Was Beverley aware about the irregularities?" I asked,
trying to fit things together.

"Martha said that she didn't really pay much attention to
details." Carrie drawled out the last word in another excellent
mockery of the philanthropist.

"She apparently showed up for all the parties, did a few
deliveries, that kind of thing. Her excuse was that she was always
so busy?"

"Crazy busy," I repeated absently. Ask any woman in her
thirties how she is, and she will reply, busy, crazy busy.

I assured Carrie it would all be fine, but I encouraged her to
call the police about the phone calls. She in turn, dismissed my
warnings. She finished her latte and rose to go. "So what are
you doing today?"

"I am going to find a mouthwash that is not minty fresh." I
said.

She nodded and left for the Senior Center.

I thought and thought, Rod, Rod.

I did discover a mouthwash that I hoped would not make me
spontaneously gag, then I absently turned my car left and drove
up the hill to the Villas.

Rod, Rod. I pulled in Beverley's former home, opened the
front door and then it clicked. I raced up the stairs to the master
bedroom and dug through the drawer of photos. I pulled out the
three matching ones, or at least matching because they were all
with the same man. The glass was cracked on one picture. There
he was, that bright eyed look and red hair. Where had I seen him?
I had seen him in a huge wedding portrait hanging in the living

room of his former home, the bride, his former, now dead, wife. In these photos, he was with Beverley on one cruise and two dinners.

She was seeing Rod Bixby, and most certainly before he left his wife floating face down in the hot tub. No one could prove Rod was responsible for his wife's demise, it could have been an accident, except the hot tub was closed and locked down from the outside.

His wife was finally discovered, Rod, however, never reappeared. My hands shook as I held the picture, willing his smiling expression to give me more motive and reason.

He was seeing Beverley Weiss. Had he risked returning to the states to kill her? Had Beverley heard about how Rod had dispensed with his little wife (that murder had made it in the papers, but everyone involved was labeled "alleged"). Or was that part of the attraction, the danger, the excitement, running away from everything regardless of the facts, all for love?

Escaping to an exotic island is all well and good except when the money runs out and you need to find work. At that crucial moment, you realize you don't speak the native language as well as you thought, you discover the romantic bamboo cottage leaks, and the new love of your life, snores.

Was Beverley leaving with Rod? And if so, why wasn't he worried? Has she missed their rendezvous time? Why hadn't he called?

I didn't have a clue what to do with this information.

* * *

I distracted myself by staying busy drawing up the disclosures for Beverley's house, trolling for more condos for Owen, and fortunately my friend Joan threw a party to introduce her fiancé Norman to her friends. Since it was my fault that those two were together in the first place, I was a guest of honor.

I adore Joan, I'm not so sure about her new boyfriend, and live-in partner Norton. He is certainly handsome and employed, two of the top criteria for women of Joan's age group (she's a bit older than me). But I still didn't understand the attraction, especially since Norton was one of my most fastidious sellers. For instance, he had insisted, despite two price reductions, that the pastel purple, pink and lemon yellow of his home's interior walls were not detracting or even deflecting offers to buy.

Desperate, I had asked Joan to pose as a feng shui expert to straighten him out, and convince him to paint the interior of his house a nice beige. And she did. And they fell in love.

But Joan throws a good party. She invites the very intellectual and very bohemian of River's Bend. They live in a brand new, granite counter top, white carpeted, condo located at the base of the Villas – all the address, none of the price. Which can be considered intelligent, but not bohemian. So, the atmosphere is sort of middle class Bohemian: the Beatnik vibe, but with central air.

I wandered through the beige rooms (Joan prevailed) and enjoyed olives from Greece, Tambouli from Egypt and fabulous Armenian and Spanish cheeses.

Joan served wine produced by small boutique wineries that only sell through wine clubs. I did not recognize a single label. I wondered if Ben's friend, Cassandra made some of the wine. But hers was a new venture I don't think she has a label yet.

The guests around me were dressed in organic cotton slacks and bright colored shawls woven by women co-ops in Peru. Very Fair Trade. People usually lingered over more esoteric subjects, subjects I didn't understand. But tonight the subject was more pedantic; the recent murders.

I smiled and struggled not to offer any insights, but it was difficult, I could finally sound smart here. But I resisted. Instead I ate cheese, admired the beadwork on a woman's blouse and hunted down my hostess.

Joan was dressed in a pants suit of red cotton and wore soft black cloth slippers with bright beads on the instep. Her short gray hair was spiked straight up, a good look for her.

I hugged Joan, and asked my burning question.

"Oh, honey," she responded. "The current girlfriend always operates under the shadow of the former wife, and sometimes the dead ones are the most difficult - you can't compete with perfection frozen in nostalgia."

"So, what do I do?" I compulsively tossed squares of cheese in my mouth and drained my wine.

"Hang a portrait of her in the hallway, and walk by without looking. Even if you burned down the house, you will never get rid of her - don't try." Joan patted my arm and considered her work done.

But I left from that party no wiser, and no more enlightened, I was full of cheese. On my way home, I called to check in on Carrie and confirm where we'd meet for our Friday drinks.

"Can't this Friday, I have a meeting with Steven, the president at the Homeless Prevention League, after work. He's been avoiding me for a week now, Cyndi keeps saying he's busy, but it's the holidays, no one busy, unless you're the food bank. He is finally going to talk with me. Really, there needs to be more transparency in their operations."

"I've never heard you talk that way that before."

"Is it sexy?"

"Absolutely, you go girl."

I was at loose ends Friday, so I decided to aggravate my loneliness and drove up to Best Buy to pick up the gift cards for my nephews. Once that was finished, I was done with all my shopping. Except for Ben.

The store was packed with families pushing carts filled with whining children and large TVs. Lines were long. I flipped open a paperback book while I stood in line for the cards. Buy the cards, drop them into my purse – easy. But no, for some reason the gift cards set off the door alarm. I had to explain to the two nice security guards how it was possible to exit Best Buy with only gift cards on my person. What? No movie specials – four for only five dollars? No large screen television? No refrigerator? They're on sale.

Not in my purse, no, I explained.

Once the five security guards and I agreed that my lack of purchase volume was not necessarily aberrant behavior, I was allowed to exit the store, with very little dignity intact.

I wonder if I could use that in my advertisements? *I'll give you a little dignity?* No, too non-profit.

Before I left, I handed my business card to the closest ten

people watching the procedure, wished them Happy Holidays, because I'm nothing if not politically correct and drove straight to KFC for a bucket of conciliatory chicken.

I didn't get home until eight o'clock, and ate two pieces of original recipe before it occurred to me that, one, who made the appointment for Carrie and the President of the Homeless Prevention League for a Friday afternoon, and two, why hadn't I heard from Carrie? Meetings on Friday afternoons don't go long, that's why you schedule a meeting on Friday afternoon in the first place.

I checked my phone, but saw no missed calls. By nine o'clock, I had finished the last of the chicken, and was worried. When Patrick called at 10:00, I was already on the verge of driving down and finding the woman myself, he was very helpful, especially since he was about as brittle as I was.

"Have you heard from Carrie? Is she mad at me?"

Oh honey, she will never be mad at you, I thought. But out loud I said, "mad at you? No, why?"

"I think I pressed her too hard to be a responsible board member, and she was pretty upset with me," he admitted.

"Patrick, I think she was actually pretty concerned with the League. She's still with the Senior Center, one scandal at any local non-profit makes it difficult for everyone else. She told me that."

"But I haven't heard from her, and it's Friday night," he whined.

Oh, for heaven's sake. "Okay," I tried to slow him down a bit. "I'll meet you at the Homeless Prevention League offices, that's where she was meeting the President (and CEO). She's not home, because I called a half hour ago."

"I already drove by her place. And I already stopped by the restaurant where we were supposed to meet tonight, three times. This isn't like her, she is never late."

I sucked in my breath. He was right, she is never late. And she would never miss a date with Patrick. She'd rather die. Why did I think that?

We arrived at the HPL parking lot simultaneously. Patrick pulled up in his hellishly expensive BMW convertible, he had the top down and his thick hair was windblown and as wild as his expression.

"There's her car, she's still here.' He looked around the empty parking lot, "where is Steven's car?"

I glanced around, but the parking lot was empty, not even a HPL Shelter unit in evidence. I turned to make a suggestion to Patrick, but he was already running to the offices at an impressive clip. I barely caught up to him as he pulled at the HPL office door. The door didn't move, and front handle came off in his hand.

"Oh, that's nice."

"That's lucky," I pointed out. "It's not locked." I reached around him and pushed open the door.

"Hello!" I called and stepped in, dodging Patrick's reach. He didn't need to protect me. I shrugged him off.

The office was silent. I didn't even hear movement upstairs, where Cyndi apparently lived. To the right and left were the two tiny, staff offices. CPUs glowed in the dim light.

I couldn't see much, but there wasn't much on the first floor to see. The carpet smelled of damp and fungus. I the embedded nicotine smell was strong as I slowly made my way up the stairs. Up stairs was pitch dark, and although I was not having good luck with anything I found at the top of a stairway, I stepped forward anyway. There was one door at the end of the long hallway, two doors on the left wall. I rattled the first one – locked, and marched to the second.

"Carrie?" I called, cautiously. "Cyndi?"

No sound. By now, Patrick was right behind me, breathing on my neck. It was not as sexy as it sounds. "Is she in there?"

"How the hell do I know?" I opened the second door and hit something. I pushed the door with a smack of my fist and opened it all way. And almost stepped on my best friend.

Sirens, questions and Patrick looking so bad the EMTs offered to strap him to a gurney and take him to the hospital, along with his girlfriend. He rallied at that suggestion and opted to drive to the emergency room himself. I took my own car. I couldn't lock the office door on the way out. Too bad.

I muscled through to the hospital admitting desk and asked

for Carrie Eliot's room.

"Are you family?" The nurse eyed me dubously.

"Yes," I said without a moment's hesitation. Don't hesitate, and you are often believed.

She gave me the room number, too busy to quiz me further.

"Excuse me," I pushed aside a disheveled woman hovering by Carrie's room.

Patrick was already in the room, white faced, and as close to her bed as he could get without actually crawling into it.

Carrie was still unconscious. Her long lashes were dark flutters against her pale and bruised skin.

"Who did this to her?" Patrick demanded.

"I don't have a clue," I said honestly. If it was our holiday murderer, Carrie wouldn't be here at all. She'd be spread, oh, I couldn't think of it.

I leaned over and kissed her forehead.

"Allison," Carrie's eyes fluttered open.

I studied her face, black and blue. Her arms were a mess of abstract brown and black marks. A blanket covered the rest of her body, hiding any additional damage, I was grateful.

"Why didn't he kill you?" I asked quietly.

"Maybe I'm not newsworthy enough."

"I don't think so," I disagreed.

"Thanks," she brightened up.

"Carrie." Patrick butted my head like one of the famous happy Cooper milk cows. "Carrie, how are you? Are you hurt? Do you need anything?"

"Patrick," she exhaled, clearly in some pain. "I'm fine. I'm sorry I missed our dinner."

Of course she was fine. She was bandaged up, bruised beyond recognition, probably harboring internal injuries and laying prone in a hospital bed with a half dozen tubes and wires attached to her slender body. Totally meets my definition of fine.

Did she have enough pain medication? If not, I was ready to make a scene a la *Terms of Endearment* to make sure she got some more, now.

"Did you see who did this?" I asked.

She shook her head, a painful gesture. She flinched and

closed her eyes.

"I went to the office," she whispered. "I walked straight in, Anne and Harold were already gone, but I heard someone upstairs, so I figured it was the President, and I went up."

Patrick sucked in his breath and looked desperately for some part of her he could touch, squeeze or kiss. He gingerly picked up her hand and kissed it. My, that boy really had fallen in love. And I knew she loved him, too. Carrie had begun her quest for a man with the intent of looking after herself, but to my great relief, there was more to it than that. Call me romantic. I want people to fall in love for the right reasons.

"I didn't see him. I was hit on the head, then kicked."

Patrick moaned. Carrie squeezed his had reassuringly. "Hard," she admitted, "by very pointed boots or something."

"Or shoes," I said. "You didn't see anything?"

"No, and the person."

"Assailant," I supplied.

"Didn't say anything, just, left me."

My heart twisted in my chest. Who would be at the office after hours? And who would be un-happy with Carrie? Yes, the elusive Miss Cyndi, part time secretary to the President and CEO, and the one person who resided in the office on a full time basis. The woman with pointed toe, designer shoes, the woman who, for once, didn't cut up her victim. It made me dizzy to think about it.

"Stay," I ordered Patrick, "And don't let anyone in."

"Don't worry, Conner will have to stay outside all night."

"Oh, is that who that is?"

He nodded. "She loves to think she's a hard hitting reporter, but she's small time."

I touched Carrie lightly on her shoulder, and stepped out, mostly so I didn't faint right in front of her. That would distress her more than her own condition. Remember, this is a woman who rescues kittens on her days off.

Patrick did not listen to my directive and followed me out. He glared at Chris Conner, now camped out on an uncomfortable chair in the hallway. How she scored a chair was a mystery.

She mumbled something about needing more coffee and

scurried away back down the hall.

"I'm impressed," I said out loud.

"I'm a big advertiser," he replied.

"I thought advertising and editorial were completely separate," I said, innocently.

"Don't kid yourself," he said shortly. For a moment he was the CEO of one of the largest manufacturers in Sonoma County. He stayed upright, and in charge, but as soon as the reporter was out of sight, he sagged against the cold wall.

"What can I do?" He rubbed his hands over his cheeks and buried his face for a moment, to block everything out.

"You're in love with her, aren't you?" If this was real estate, I'd have two forms for him to sign confirming such a relationship.

"This is my fault. I got her into this, I made her join the board. It's my fault." He moaned.

"Give her some credit," I pushed on his chest to make my point. "She's a grown-up, she makes her own decisions."

"Okay, okay." He held up his hands palm out, a gesture of my superior grasp of the intent of his girlfriend. "What can I do to make it up to her?"

"Diamonds are usually a help." I snapped.

"Okay," he nodded.

Chapter 15

"Everyone has an alcoholic the family," Ben pulled off the freeway and began negotiating the maze of cul de sac that made up my brother's neighborhood.

"Really, Allison, think about it. Have you ever head of any family that doesn't have a member who is addicted to something? We always say that alcoholism runs in the family, but if all families have one uncle or a brother, or a nephew who is alcoholic, then it stands to reason that perhaps alcoholism runs in the human race."

Ben was right, but I was still more comfortable around my brother in controlled environments, I try to ignore the situation, but it's difficult to ignore your family during the holidays.

For my sister-in-law, Debbie, the annual Little Party was not just a gathering of friends, it was defiance in the face of my mother's complete control over the family. To me, Debbie is Custer, defending his last stand.

"What would you normally do?" Ben asked.

"We have Christmas at the Club, it's a more controlled there, and mom doesn't pay for an open bar. We pay for our own drinks. It keeps Richard, more or less, on the straight and narrow, a path my mother favors. Take a right."

During the last Claim Jump Christmas Richard accidentally threw three of Allen's gifts - books - into the fire. I don't remember if it was an accident or not, but it certainly was the last straw.

My mother not only keeps the boys away from the bar, but from open flames as well.

"And tonight?" Ben prompted.

We pulled into Richard's neighborhood. Every other yard was stuffed with enormous blow up Santa's riding various vehicles; motorcycles, helicopters, speed boats. They all swayed invitingly in a soft breeze.

"Quite cheerful," Ben nodded to the lawn displays.

Some lawns also hosted plywood cut outs of either the holy family or the Little Mermaid. Some homes were simply strung with lights.

"It's the house with the helicopter Santa."

My brother Richard, indulged in all three forms of holiday decorating. On his lawn a Santa in a helicopter was ready for take off with a few inflated gift boxes at the ready behind Santa's cockpit seat. The three princesses, Ariel, Belle and Cinderella, stood by the driveway, they were illuminated from below. Multiple strands of lights framed the house, the roof and the front door. It was an overwhelming effect. Ben whistled in appreciation.

Because he can't play with fire, Richard is a master with lights. He love colored lights, he loves white lights. He loves icicles and the big old fashion light bulbs now back in fashion. Loves it all. He spends hours perched on the roof, making sure every string is hung perfectly and aligned exactly equidistant to its neighbor. Hours. He made the princess figures himself, from a kit. Richards gauges the success of Christmas by how many new strings of lights he can fit onto his home before blowing a fuse. He considers *National Lampoon's Christmas Vacation* a training film.

"Oh, Allison." Debbie answered the door. The kitchen/family room was already crowded and the party was in full swing; I try for fashionably late.

"You wore that, again." Debbie wrinkled her nose, a gesture, which, much as Cyndi of the Homeless Prevention League, was in its final useful phase. Debbie was once pert, bouncy, and blond. She was one of the last Home Ec majors in our high school. Richard was fully distracted by her, and her novel culinary abilities. And yes, like most Singletons (my mother's side), they produced their first child by age eighteen.

But the marriage seemed to be working out. I wouldn't have the specifics mind you, my brothers are not inclined to sit down and hold deep, heart to heart conversations with me. Although, I'm pretty sure that the propensity for avoidance is not only a quirk of my brother's.

I glanced at Ben, who was dutifully smiling at Debbie.

"This is Ben? It's nice to finally," she glanced at me, her face still squished, "meet you. You've been dating long?"

I held my breath, because I knew what would come next, Debbie would demand an explanation as to why Ben hadn't been introduced to the family earlier? Why are you hiding him from the family Allison? What is wrong with the family? Hmmm? Are you embarrassed because we aren't a sophisticated, and worldly as you?

See? I project so easily, my family doesn't have to say anything at all.

"Not long," Ben lied easily. "And we both have such busy jobs, that this is one of the few times we've able to be together, socially."

That was the confident Ben I knew.

Debbie narrowed her eyes. She had heard of Ben, probably from my mother, and probably over the summer when Ben and I met. But she didn't say anything more.

"Well, come in."

I cautiously stepped over the floor mat at the door, but Ben hit it squarely in the center setting off a loud atonal chorus of Jingle Bells.

"It's a musical welcome mat," Debbie explained over the noise.

Ben did not look at me. I was grateful for that.

"Give the wine to Richard," Debbie instructed. The doorbell rang, she stepped on the mat, setting off the song again, and greeted more party guests.

We moved past dozens of stuffed Santa's from mail order companies around the world. Debbie had collected so many figures that Richard built a shed in the back to house them during the off-season.

Their tree was of National Forest proportions and dominated the living room to the point that no one could really sit in the room.

"Your sister-in-law must love Christmas," Ben whispered.

"Yes," I scanned the crowd, looking for my parents, I wanted to pinpoint where they were so they couldn't sneak up and surprise me. I didn't see my mother.

Richard's bar, like his house, is a thing of beauty, one could say a shrine, but one would not say that out loud. This is a touchy subject. The bar is built into a niche in the family room and features running water, a back splash of gold mottled, mirrored tiles, a bridge hanging from the ceiling that holds every kind of cocktail and highball glass, and a space for Richard to stand behind the bar, so he looks more official.

Nine strands of icicle lights illuminated seventeen different bottles of expensive liquor stacked on the shelves behind Richard. Ben and I had two kinds of wine to choose from: red or white.

Ben politely turned down Richard's offer of an Appletini and took a glass of the white wine, instead. I ordered a vodka martini and Richard shook it up with panache.

Allen wandered over for a refill of something clear from a glass pitcher, and introduced himself to Ben. The three men fell to discussing the construction of the bar, and how Allen helped with advice and a soldering iron. My brothers still love playing with fire. The Fourth of July can be quite dangerous for our family.

I stepped away from the bar, clutched my drink, and ventured into the maw of the party.

"So," said a voice.

I jumped, and almost spilled my martini.

"Mother, merry Christmas," I leaned in to lightly kiss her cheek, and she politely allowed it.

"Merry Christmas," Fran responded, "is Ben here?"

I gestured to where Ben was standing.

"I'll say hello," she announced briskly. "Have you spoken with Claire? She was asking after you."

"I'm sure she was," I muttered. Claire was one of my mother's golf/bridge/garden club cronies and always asks after me because her own daughter, years younger than me, is married, with three adorable fluffy grandbabies, and lives here, in Richard's perfect-for-children-neighborhood. Understandably, Claire's bragging makes my mother crazy. I knew mom expected me to tell Claire all about Ben. And I knew Claire would need to hear it from me, because it is quite possible that out of desperation, somewhere at the 16th tee, my mother was capable of inventing a boyfriend for me.

Mother pointed to the matronly woman dressed in a velvet pantsuit that was a size too small.

My mother was dressed in a St. John twin set in pale blue teamed with pressed white wool slacks. My mother does not own brightly colored holiday sweaters, even though my grandmother finds them at the dollar store, and sends them to Mom every Christmas. The sweaters always disappear right after Christmas morning. I suspect fire.

"Allison," Claire greeted me enthusiastically. I understand from my mother, that Claire's daughter, Jennifer. I think, is, even after three children, quite slender. "How are you? Are you married yet?"

"No," I smiled, and took a large gulp of my drink. "Claire, I am not married yet, but my boyfriend, Ben is right over there."

Claire glanced suspiciously in Ben's direction, not sure if I was telling the truth or not. I followed her gaze. Ben had run his fingers through his blondish hair and it was standing upright, I was sure he had no glue on his fingers. Fortunately, his broad shoulders and stature made up for the wild hair.

"Oh," Claire raised a thin, plucked eyebrow and regarded me with the superiority that is rooted in years of her always winning the blue ribbon at the county fair, and you, always the second place. She may or may not believe the handsome man across the room was my boyfriend, but she had to accept the evidence as presented. Claire had always struck me as a woman who made her own jams. "So, what are your plans?"

"No plans," I said cheerfully, because, suddenly, I did feel cheerful. I finished off my martini. "Have you tried the stuffed mushrooms? They are divine."

She obediently trotted to the buffet line and I escaped back to the comfort of the bar.

"How is your friend? Is she all right?" Mary, my quiet sister-in-law, sidled up. She blinked sympathetically.

"She'll be okay, but she couldn't make it to the party," I explained.

"I think Debbie understood," Mary said unconvincingly. We both knew Debbie; maybe she forgive Carrie for not making the most important event in the Little year, or maybe not.

Ben reached across me for the white wine and nodded to Mary, who smiled back and headed back to stand with Allen. Mary never really got into the swing of the holiday party. But in Mary's case, it was because she was nervous leaving her three boys with a baby sitter. I think it has something to do with their home insurance, and whether it covers injuries sustained by a paid worker. Allen's boys are quite rambunctious. And Richard's girls have moved into the teenage sullen stage. I could hardly wait for Christmas Day.

"This is the dreaded Christmas party." Ben smiled, encompassing the whole room with his happy expression, in case anyone, say, my mother, was staring at us.

"I was asked about our plan," I said.

My mother waved to Ben, and because I was standing close by, me.

We waved back. Ben toasted her with his wine glass. "There is no plan," he confirmed, still scanning the room and grinning like a game-show host.

"That's what I told her."

"Who is that group?"

"The guys wearing the holiday sweaters? Dad's golf group. Debbie tries to invite a least a couple of our own friends, mix up the conversations."

"Where then, are your friends?" He asked.

"In the hospital."

He put his arm around me, and squeezed, "I'm sorry, do the police have anything?"

"They can't even find Cyndi, the most likely witness." Or perpetrator, Cyndi was still my favorite suspect, however, I'm sure the police need more information for an investigation than my observation that the woman routinely wore pointy toe shoes.

Ben drained his wine. Richard handed him a glass of the stuff from the pitcher.

"I'm going in," Ben plunged into the sweater wearing golf group. No man has done more for me.

"So Richard, are we having the pirate gift exchange?" I held out my empty glass, and he filled it from the same pitcher.

"Yeah," he took a swig of his own martini and toasted me

mockingly with his empty glass. "Debbie loves it, and says it's a great holiday centerpiece, gives people something to do."

"How about conversation?" I suggested, but I was speaking to the wrong person, my brother was not in charge here.

"When did it all change?" He said softly.

"Moving Christmas to your house instead of the county club?" I said brightly. I have never held a serious discussion with either brother. I don't think many sisters do. I patted his hand, and drifted to the hors d'ouvres table. I picked at the processed cheese and green olives. Each guest contributed a food item as part of the admission to the party. From the looks of it, not many women had discovered Trader Joe's, (less a food market and more a magical place filled with racks of pre-made hors d'ouvres, the working woman's friend). I snacked on a few of my own contributions; seven lay dip and tapenade, and worked my way down the table.

I ended up next to Suzie Martin, a friend of Debbie's from the Christian Friend's Elementary School years.

The two women probably don't see each other as often as the used to, now that Debbie's girls attend River's Bend High. It's the only decent high school in town and within reasonable walking distance of Richard's neighborhood. Parents in this neighborhood, Richard and Allen among them, were quite smug about their choices. The flats were far more convenient to everything child related. THEY didn't have to drive their children back and forth to school, up and down from the Villas. The self-congratulatory feeling quickly dissipated when Richard discovered teen-age girls do not walk to school, no matter how close the location. Teenage girls are driven.

"Hi Suzie," I greeted the woman and simultaneously reached for the fudge.

"Hi Allison," Suzie gave me a stiff hug. I tried not to get fudge on her Christmas sweater. Her sweater sported reindeer with real jingling bells. She jingled when we embraced.

"So, Allison, how is business?" Suzie asked.

The long story of my business loomed up like the portly ghost of Christmas past. I couldn't even begin to sort it out for myself, let alone cram a murder, an attack, condo searches and the Diet to the Death between Rosemary and Katherine, into a neat thirty-second elevator speech. Besides, I knew what she really wanted to hear was how the value of her own house was holding up in this market. Not well, but I never tell people that, at least not at a party.

"Business is good," I said briefly. I sipped at my drink, it carried the kick of turpentine.

"You? How are you doing?" I finished off the block of fudge in one bite, and reached for another as she took a breath.

"Oh, we are crazy, busy!"

Activity is the social currency here in River's Bend. Those who are busy, or better, crazy busy, are wealthy in activity and worthy of admiration. In deference to the holiday, I put on a pleasant, expectant expression, as if I greatly admired busyness.

Suzie revved up. "You know, we enrolled each child in traveling soccer. We just got back from a game in Fresno. We are painting all the rooms in the house, and are volunteering with the homeless shelters. Mike is coaching a home soccer team, we have the whole family over for the holidays, and my parents are staying for the whole month! Thank goodness they have the RV. My work schedule is just far too busy and the kids have piano, ballet and tutoring and of course the homework is enormous, but we want to make sure the kids will get into the top colleges, Tiffany has taken the early pre- pre SAT and scored a perfect 1600 so we're pretty confident."

"Really?" I said around my mouth full of fudge. I noticed there were bowls of clam dip (a holiday staple at my brother's house which, I thought, probably counted in Debbie's nostalgia theme for Christmas Day) and a large bowl of ruffled potato chips, But after the fudge, it didn't look as appetizing, I picked up a tree shaped frosted cookie.

I took another, tentative sip of my drink, it was better on the second sip.

"You certainly are involved," I said neutrally. Holiday cheer aside, I didn't want to be too admiring, it feeds into the perception that constant, relentless activity is the best lifestyle to have.

Besides, I could tell how she was. She was scrupulously slender, her tanned features were highlighted by her tight grimace of a smile pressed into service for this evening. All that crazy activity had left her brittle and hollow.

"Oh my goodness yes, I barely have a moment to myself." Suzie went on in a self-congratulatory way. She glanced at the table, realized there were no celery or carrot sticks, grimaced and took a sip of her club soda.

"So what else are you doing?" I asked.

"Well, we were just at the Homeless Prevention League, I feel it's important for the kids to see how the other half lives."

"Oh, absolutely."

"It was for Hands Across the County, have you heard of that program?"

I hadn't, but it was easier to nod and move the conversation forward.

"We volunteered to wash the mobile shelters. They were so nice! The staff there even took us around to each shelter, so we wouldn't have to drive in the traffic. Wasn't that nice of them?"

"Oh very," I took another cookie, a bell frosted with red frosting and decorated with those silver balls that are suppose to be bad for you. I think they're made of mercury or something. I was happy to see them on the cookie. I bit into my cookie and encouraged her to continue by nodding my head.

"We traveled to three different locations, that was all we had time for, and we washed the vehicles, they are not really permanent shelters, they are these nice big RVs, like my parent's one. The RVs were donated by Harvest Ford."

"The largest dealer in the county," I confirmed, I didn't really know that to be true, but that's what the TV ads say.

"Anyway, apparently they have these mobile units all over Northern California, something like thirty six of them. We were only working on the ones here, in Sonoma County. But I did think it was pretty odd."

"Odd?" I said out loud. Odd was not a word in Suzie's lexicon. I stopped chewing my cookie so I could hear her better.

"I felt like we were washing the same RV over, and over. Isn't that silly? I guess they're all alike, but it was an odd feeling anyway. Oh well, we try to always support community events like that. Your sister is really lovely that way, so giving, she's always volunteering for something. I can call you for the next one."

"Oh, thank you." I didn't have a really clever rejoinder to that offer. I gave her my business card.

Suzie finished her club soda and I finished my cookie.

"You're life is certainly busy," I said as a way to thanking her for the information. "I better see how Ben is doing."

"Who is Ben?"

I searched the living room, Ben was still with Dad's golf group. It was time to spring him. "Over there," I gestured with my empty glass. "He's my boyfriend."

"Wow. Well." She had little to say, as sober as she was.

I moved past a whole group of women complaining about the soccer coach, and past another group in the throes of plotting an overthrow of the PTA.

"Hi Dad," I walked into the middle of whatever they were discussing, and kissed dad on the cheek. "Hi guys, do you mind if I take Ben away to introduce him around?"

The men toasted me and I pulled a grateful boyfriend from their happy clutches.

"Thanks," he said under his breath. "We spent twenty minutes on golf gadgets and sizing irons or something. One of the guys painted his golf cart with this new Flex paint that changes colors depending on how the sun hit it. Lovely, I did not realize there is a cult of golfers who trick out their golf carts."

"You'd be surprised. Someday we'll see low rider carts with rap music playing and fuzzy dice dangling from the rear view mirror."

He looked at me, and took my drink, smelled it, and returned it.

"You are making no sense at all."

"Fine then, stay with me to make sure I'm okay, I'm heading back for the fudge."

* * *

I don't image it's often that the weekend staff on small daily paper gets the scoop, but the skeleton staff of the River's Bend Press did. Chris Conner didn't get the scoop on Carrie's situation, but that was nothing compared to the big prize. Steven, the handsome and apparently irresistible, President and CEO of the Homeless Prevention League, had skipped town. As a lovely parting gift to himself, he took a little over a million dollars directly from the coffers of the Homeless Prevention League.

And the only person who knew anything was missing.

Chapter 16

This seems to be a theme at the League; volunteer for the board, take a few things, all the cash, for instance, then skip town. Is that what Cyndi had done as well? I hoped so, because if you didn't skip town, the other choice for a Homeless Prevention League volunteer is to leave this planet in another, less salubrious way.

The embezzlement story had that macabre quality about it that was difficult for the news outlets to leave alone: Christmas ruined, destitute clients, trust violated, missing woman last seen dressed as Philanthropy Barbie.

I scanned the front page as I finished my second cup of coffee the morning after the party. Anne and Harold landed on the front page. In the photo, they looked appropriately shocked. Their quotes were of the "we had no idea" variety.

Shelter Closed. Hundred's Affected. The homeless have nowhere to turn. Salvation Army reports spike in cases. The tragedy of it all blared in huge font and capital letters.

The professor, Marcel Von Drake, looking dapper and elegant, had posed for a photo in front of his shelter RV. He smiled happily. He had also obliged with an interview. He rattled off names of clients and offered comments about each one, their story and where they could be found. He insisted that he did not have the locations of the other mobile shelter units. He was appalled at the President and CEO's behavior and hinted that if the board had been more diligent, then perhaps this wouldn't have happened. Oh good, throw the board members under the bus. Or RV.

Three other shelter recipients were eloquent in their praise of the place. One client interviewed by Chris Conner had listed the homeless members he knew personally: Elton, John, Bono, Michael, Stevie, and Ricky. Chris Conner had written every name down with no comment, and published same. That she didn't even do it with some hint of irony was disappointing. Where were the intelligent reporters? Not here.

The story continued on page five and featured a photo of the redoubtable Martha Anderson, who looked disgusted. Maybe it was because she had been relegated to page five, surely an insult.

The non-profit offices were temporally shut down pending investigations. There was even speculation that the President and CEO himself was the serial killer and the missing Cyndi was his latest victim.

Carrie did not take the news well.

"I tried to tell someone, but no one, especially Martha Anderson, would listen." Carrie could sit up today. She was swathed in a silk yukata Katherine had given me a few years ago, but it was too small, so I gave it Carrie.

"How did the party go?" She asked me.

"You were missed," I said. "Oh, and you had a relapse and Ben and I had to leave right in the middle of the pirate gift exchange. I was forced to forfeit the brandy I brought. It was quite a blow."

"What kind of relapse did I have?"

"Health related," I grinned. My mother barely noticed my exit. I only heard about it this morning when she called to chastise me for not staying after the party and helping with clean-up.

"How did Richard do?"

"He too, left in the middle of the pirate gift exchange, but he went upstairs."

"Passed out."

"Safer than when he imagines he's the life of the party."

She shook her head, both at Richard unattended problem, and at my lack of enthusiasm for holiday festivities. "Some people think the pirate gift exchange is great fun. Our seniors do it with home made gifts. Cookies are the most coveted."

I sank into the chair that Patrick usually occupied. "I'm tired of it all, isn't there a better way to run this holiday?"

"Well, you can get into the real spirit of the holiday, it will make you feel better. I need a favor." She smoothed down the wrinkles in the kimono style garment. "Can you drop off my Christmas gifts to the Homeless Prevention League staff? And while you're there, you can pick up that chinchilla coat you loaned me."

"No, you keep it."

"It's not mine. You'll find it on the kitchen chair."

I decided not to argue about the blue, fur coat. "But the office is closed because of the investigation," I protested, instead.

"Don't complain. I'm sure Harold and Anne stop by every day, and a gift would cheer them up."

I agreed. I can't say no to Carrie. She was still bruised.

The Monday morning traffic had thinned by the time I reached Carrie's small apartment. She lives in a granny unit perched precariously over a converted garage. Many people in the college section of town build attachments and additions for rentals. I was sure there were no permits for any of the work, never is.

Carrie's place is no larger than Beverley's closet. If anyone other than Carrie lived there, it would be dark and depressing. But it's not, Carrie turned the single room apartment into a cozy retreat, bright green walls, chintz flowered day bed and curtains. I was tempted to stay.

I found the Trader Joe's holiday theme bag and picked it up. The coat was hanging neatly on the back of the other kitchen chair. The white, satin lining glowed in the dim early light. Carrie is remarkable. I wonder if Patrick even deserves her.

I left the coat where it was. She'll need something warm and soft when she comes home.

The parking lot at the Homeless Prevention League was empty. The fog hovered overhead, and made the temperature, in the low fifties, feel colder. The door handle to the office had been replaced, but the door was unlocked and gave when I pushed it. The police string yellow caution tape around a murder scenes but not, apparently, around embezzlement sites. Maybe they should.

"Hello?" I stepped into the tiny foyer. The computers were, of course on, but neither Harold nor Anne were in evidence. It was as empty as the last time I was here, and that was not comforting.

"Hello?" I stepped around the corner – under the stairs- and checked the break room in the back. I tried the back exit door, it was locked from the inside. Over the door hung the sign with the admonishment to always keep this door unlocked during business hours.

I thought of abandoning the bags on the empty desks, and bolting. But something compelled me upwards. I slowly took the stairs. The raw morning light barely penetrated to the upper hall. I approached the President's office with caution. I gently pushed on the door. Nothing inside looked disturbed. Relieved that the only anomaly was a jar filled with deadly, pointed pencils, I stepped back out of the office and pushed open the door to what I remembered to be Cyndi's office.

Her office was dark; no natural light seeped in. So I flipped on the light, choked, and flipped it back off. Crap. And only two days until Christmas.

There were no worries about how poor Cyndi was spending her holidays. She was spending them on the front page of the River's Bend Press as the lead story for the local news. She was about to be famous, but would not be able to appreciate it. The Homeless Prevention League was already news. This would make it even worse. And I was about to help.

I called the police.

At least this ended Carrie's involvement with the Homeless Prevention League. Not a moment too soon.

"Hello? Who's in here?"

It was Anne, girl of all trades. I stood with my back to the door of Cyndi's office/home. I hadn't looked at much of the scene. But there was something different about the office room, something dramatically different compared to what I remembered of Beverley's bedroom. But I couldn't look again to find out exactly what it was, sorry, I couldn't.

"It's me, Allison Little, Carrie's friend?" I called out.

I walked down stairs to face Anne.

"What do you want?" She demanded. Her hair was uncombed and fly away, as if she hadn't conditioned, or even combed it over the last week, which could be the case. She wore jeans a size too small and a sweatshirt, advertising the local community college, two sizes too big. She looked more homeless than Cyndi ever did.

"I was delivering some Christmas gifts to you, from Carrie." I emphasized Carrie's name, I certainly wouldn't be personally bringing gifts to these guys.

"Oh," Anne moved back so I could step off the stairs.

I heard sirens. I hear sirens a lot. That is not a good thing, in terms of lifestyle.

"What are you doing here?" I asked.

"I'm getting my files and stuff," she answered honestly. Anne ignored the sirens. Of course, she didn't realize they were for her. Ask not for whom the sirens wail . . . Joan, the literature professor, would be so proud of me.

"Why didn't Carrie come herself?" Anne asked.

"Still in the hospital." I said.

"Why is she in the hospital?" Anne glanced around the office, she noticed the gift bag on her desk, but didn't comment.

"She was severely beaten and left here," I automatically gestured upstairs, bad idea, it called attention to the offices, where really, Anne should not go.

"Why didn't I hear about that?" She demanded.

"It was kept out of the paper," I explained.

"Unlike the embezzlement," Anne said bitterly. She hesitated, her eyes trained on the upstairs rooms.

The police arrived barely in time, Anne was about to discover Cyndi for herself. First in, my own officer, Robert Yarnell, the nice young man who was on the scene at Beverley's. He stopped cold when he saw me. I grimaced and gestured upstairs. He nodded and hurried up to Cyndi's living quarters.

"Oh, Hell," he said clearly as he opened the door.

"What?" Demanded Anne, "that's Cyndi's,"

"Home?" I interrupted. "It's illegal to live in an area zoned for office and retail use."

"Whatever," Anne's attention was riveted on officer Robert and what he was doing. He was giving himself a minute, I did not blame him. After composing himself, we we heard him calling for back up and the ambulance.

"It's Cyndi, she's been murdered." I am nothing, if not helpful, during an emergency.

"No," Anne said automatically. "Steven took her with him."

"No, he didn't," I assured her.

"What is going on here!" Martha Anderson swooped in and

planted her redoubtable self in the middle of the office lobby. She must monitor police calls. She was on time for the next blow to the Homeless Prevention League. I was quite glad my make-up was good, my boots were dry, and my hair was smooth. I probably was a little pale, but that couldn't be helped, considering the situation.

Dame Anderson stopped a few feet short of me, "Have we been introduced?"

"Allison Little, Carrie Eliot's friend."

She looked at me blankly.

"Ben Weiss?" I added helpfully.

"Oh, yes, you were with Mr. Wiess at the dinner. Now, why are all these police officers here? Working to find Steven I assume. But we have serious matters to discuss. Where are the rest of the board members?"

"I haven't heard from them, but Harold is on his way." Anne backed into her own small office to avoid another police officer who dashed up the stairs to help Officer Robert.

My phone buzzed, I moved behind the stairs to answer.

"That is not good enough. Call them! You!" Martha Anderson bellowed.

Officer Yarnell carefully walked down the stairs towards Mrs. Anderson. From his expression he was clearly not sure which was worse, the body upstairs, or the irate woman downstairs.

"Hi, Allison? This is Bo Freeman."

"Ma'am, I'll have to ask you to leave the building," Officer Yarnell said, carefully.

"Leave the building! I just arrived! We need to call a board meeting, this is shocking and where is Harold? If he's not here in five minutes, he's fired!"

"I want to buy the house," Mr. Freeman said.

I asked him to repeat himself.

Officer Robert Yarnell didn't even wait for Martha to finish her rant. He hustled her into the morning fog. I trailed behind, arranging to meet Bo at Starbucks the next morning. Well, good news and terrible news.

The patio at the entrance of the HPL office surrounded a

fountain that no longer ran water, even though the building complex was named Fountain Lakes. The "Lake" in the center resembled primordial soup, very ecological. very green.

"Okay," Officer Yarnell took a deep breath, "who found the body?"

"Body?" Demanded Martha. "Body? What are you talking about?"

At that inauspicious moment, Harold, the other player in this small morality play, slouched towards our little group.

"Locked out of the office?" He asked pleasantly, as if he knew this would be the case. He seemed unconcerned about the police cars, the approaching ambulance, the officers swarming in and out of his office.

"No," Martha glared at him, glared at her watch, a nice designer model decorated with a few modest diamonds. "At least we are not locked out physically. Apparently we've been locked out informationally for years."

Is that a word? I kept quiet.

Harold scratched his head and shrugged. He was strikingly calm in the face of this irate, major donor. Did he already have a ticket to a nice, warm place? Did he have his own money carefully stashed away, bit-by-bit, from various and untraceable donations? I think that's how you do it.

"Do you know what this means?" Martha demanded of the remaining staff, which would be Anne.

"We'll lose our $367.68 of United Way funding?" Anne opened her very large purse, and started to hunt through it.

"Very funny, young lady, you need spend your energy finding the President, this is a terrible mess!"

I thought that the mess upstairs was considerably more terrible, but this wasn't a contest.

The procedure was the same as it was at Beverley's house. Only I had far more explaining to do to the nice officers, Robert included. But the police officer in charge took my explanation at face value, asked if I knew where Ben Stone was – I assured them I didn't keep track of Ben every second of the day – and as a response, they bade me to wait while they talked with all the other "witnesses."

Anne pulled out a copy of the River's Bend Press from her purse and handed it to Harold. She pulled out a donut from the handbag, and took a bite.

Momentarily distracted by the ambulance and the awful black body bag, the officers abandoned us to a miasma of silence as thick as the brackish water in the fountain. I really needed a Starbucks coffee. As soon as I was released, that's where I planned to go. The cheerful acknowledgement of the joys of Christmas manifested in the seasonal red and white paper cups courtesy of the green colored franchise, was exactly the kind of holiday cheer I longed for.

"I was thinking," Harold reflected. Folding the paper in half, then half again. "We never seem to mention a solution."

"There is no solution," Martha snapped. "As long as there are human settlements, there will be members who have no interest in joining in the work of the community. We will always have homeless, and we will always have the poor. And thus, you and I will always have a job, a mission to help those who cannot help themselves."

"If we want it," Harold replied.

Anne looked away.

The adage, no good deed goes unpunished, was written specifically with me in mind. My feet were cold. My hands were cold. Fortunately, I did not have long to wait. The officer's released me first. I happily left the other three to glare accusingly at one another. I swung by Starbucks for some holiday comfort in Venti size, and bought a cinnamon latte for Carrie. It was the best I could do, they don't allow wine in the hospital.

I wanted to tell her what was happening, at least before she was released.

"I get to leave tonight," she announced, as I came in with the coffee.

"Good, I'll pick you up."

"Patrick will take me, I'm spending the holidays with his family, at their house."

The Sullivan family compound was fairly notorious. Many people think it's something they can drive by and gawk at, but it has the same kind of mystery and inaccessibility as Lucas Ranch or Neverland. You can see the gates of the place, but that's it. The Sullivans helpfully erected a sign with a tasteful rendition of their mascot, the cooper chicken (it's a rooster really, but the alliteration works better with chicken) that identifies the acreage as the family homes, but that's as good as it gets for the great unwashed.

"Take pictures," I instruct her.

"Guaranteed."

I took a breath, a big breath, because of what I really suspected, and blurted it right out. Patrick could walk in any second now, and I didn't want the sight of his poor, guilty face to complicate things for Carrie.

"I found Cyndi, she was," I paused.

"Murdered. I heard it on the news, about an hour ago," Carrie confirmed.

"That's pretty quick, I just found the body two hours ago."

"Anonymous tip. Straight to CNN, photos." She shuddered, then dropped her head into her hands.

"I said some terrible things to Cyndi," Carrie voice was hoarse. "I'm a complete bitch."

"Do you think she beat you up for it? In which case, I'd call you two even."

Carrie shook her head. "No, I did say she was an opportunist and shouldn't be sleeping with board members, or the President."

"What, there's a rule about that?"

Carrie smiled, although I could tell it hurt her to do so. I'd hold back on my jokes, for her sake, although tragedy brings out the black humorist in me.

"She was sleeping with the boss. That's not terribly unusual."

"Did she mention she had children?" Carrie continued. "Did she tell you that her husband abused her both physically, and mentally and the reason she couldn't convince the courts to give her the kids was because she had no home, no attorney and no income and he did?"

"No, she didn't mention that." I tried to re-arrange my opinion about Cyndi.

"Poor thing," I said. I studied my best friend's bruises. No, I changed my mind, Cyndi was not a poor thing.

"She did that to you," I pointed out. If Carrie had accidentally fallen into the hands of our butcher, she would not be here at all. I reached out and grabbed her hand. She squeezed back.

"She probably did, but I'll live. She must have been pretty frightened, and angry, to do this. But who did that to her?"

"The ex-husband will be the first suspect."

"They usually are, for good reason," Carried agreed.

* * *

Many people, me included, should not begin a gray day with the full media blast of newspaper, television and Internet. No one. But, after everything that happened in the last few days, I felt compelled to watch, read and listen to anything, and everything that may give me a clue to how this all will end. I wanted why, I wanted who.

The press did in fact, have a field day with linking up all the murders associated with the Homeless Prevention League. The River's Bend Press splashed poor Cyndi's story across the front page. No photos, thank god, it's a family paper, but her story was featured in every possible media outlet. Fox News featured Cyndi as a story of the mother, slain. Her homelessness was highlighted and emphasized. The grief stricken children were featured in the morning news talk show. The husband was mentioned, there was a nice photograph posted of he and his dark hair, Chilean wife. He was still in Chile, thank you.

Not even the media could blame the ex-husband and anoint him as the guilty party. All they had was speculation, so the reporters speculated paragraph after paragraph. Reporters focused on the holiday slayer, the list was growing, no one was safe. If you wanted to buy a hand saw at Home Depot, you had to show ID.

I should stop watching TV all together, but that resolution was as futile as my yearly resolution to eat something other than round foods. As if those narrow, often oblong, vegetables are so damn good for you.

The other fall out from the discovery of Cyndi's body (and I gave the discovery honors to Anne, so it was her name on the police report and thus, she will be the poor sap Chris Conner will stalk for a quote) was that the doings of the Homeless Prevention League fell under closer scrutiny.

Cyndi worked there. Beverly volunteered there and, in an amazing stretch of credibility worthy of a Cirque du Soliel performer, one of the River's Bend Press reporters – not Conner - speculated that the two other bodies found in the creek bed both last summer, and recently, could have well been recipients of services of the Homeless Prevention League.

The reporter didn't point out that all the victims were women. That fact clearly slipped right by. Photos of the bodies, all but Beverley's, were featured in a large spread on the inside pages of the paper. I didn't even want to turn on my computer, there would the same news, the same awful photos, I couldn't bear it.

The holidays were brought up as a possible scapegoat, the alienation of mankind was cited at least twice in articles, and a number of times in letters to the editor.

Carrie's attack was not mentioned for two reasons; one, she was alive, and two, Chris Connor had other people to pursue. Conner was now camped at the door of the Homeless Prevention League office, never a snappy dresser in the first place, after a day on stake-out, she was in danger of resembling one of their clients.

Still grumpy, I stopped by my own office. Patricia should have been in fine mood, what with all the murder and mayhem going around, but she was as gloomy as me.

"It's always the ex-spouse or lover." She declared in sepulchral tones. Patricia's favorite holiday, Halloween, had come and gone. Christmas wasn't so festive for her. She much preferred to spend a month dressed as a vampire and tracking all the blood mobiles in the county. She uses a color map and marks the mobile spots with tiny bat stickers.

"It's always a relative, or lover," I said impatiently.

Rosemary and Katherine were arguing in Katherine's office. The door was closed, but I could hear the words *carbs* and *protein* bandied about. Someone needed a cookie.

"Are you sure?" Patricia persisted. "I mean, how long have

you been seeing Ben? I read in a blog that he was the ex-husband of that Beverley Weiss. And it's often the ex."

"A few months," I admitted.

"See? That's not long enough at all. You have no idea what this guys' really like."

"I met his grandmother," I pointed out.

"Sometimes, the grandmother helps," she declared triumphantly.

"Or is already dead, in the basement," I pointed out.

"That's the mother."

The phone rang, and Patricia snapped it up.

The carb/protein/personal trainer agenda argument escalated, and Katherine stormed out of her own office.

"I'm right, you wait and see," she said over her shoulder.

"But," Rosemary yelled from the sanctuary of the office. "I'm the one who's five pounds ahead."

I gave Katherine a sympathetic look, but she was not looking at me.

"Uh, how are you doing?" I tried to get Katherine attention.

"Escrow fell through, the lender declared bankruptcy this morning." Katherine said shortly.

"See Inez?"

"I will, she usually has names of brokers who can find funds." She drew in a breath, and patted her hair, "worst market I've ever seen. And now we can't even hang out our signs."

"Worst than the 80s?" I squeaked.

"Oh, must worst," she glanced back at her office. "Well, not the worst thing in the world." She marched down to Inez's office, located at the back of the building.

Rosemary poked her head out of her office door, "is she gone?"

"Down to see Inez." I confirmed.

Rosemary nodded. "I'm not really losing any weight, not even my personal trainer is helping. But, don't tell Katherine."

"Are you giving up?"

"Yeah, but I'll let her compete until New Year's." Rosemary nodded with, I will editorialize here, a great deal of satisfaction.

"You can see how miserable she is," I said.

"Yeah, she's pretty miserable isn't she?" Rosemary displayed the first smile I'd seen in a month. "Want a cup cake? It's on your round food list."

"Sure." I recommend my round food diet to everyone, especially if you already feel pretty good about how you look, and are now searching for inner happiness. Nothing creates inner happiness better than a frosted cup cake.

I called Ben, but I couldn't get through. Usually, he grabs the phone before his voice mail has a chance to run its course.

This time, I got the full message.

I had the pest inspection for Silverpoint, so I was busy part of the day. When I remembered, I called Ben again. Still no answer. I called the office to be sure my phone was working. I thought about calling his house, but I didn't want to disturb or alarm Emily if Ben wasn't actually home. I glanced out at the grey overcast sky. The air looked cold and unwelcoming. So uninspiring. With no Ben to distract me, I went home at five and spent the evening hunkered down. If he wanted his own time by himself, that was fine by me.

I suffered through another restless night and opted not to start the morning with televised news. What could they say? It's almost Christmas? People steal from the poor. Women are murdered, and no one can find a good reason why.

I checked my phone, no calls from Ben.

I called his phone and got the same, all too familiar, phone recording.

I poured more coffee, and headed to the shower to distract myself.

There was a message on my phone when I emerged, all steamy and pink, but with no one to appreciate it.

I hit the details button, but there was no ID. Okay fine. I scrolled through the voice mail program and listened to the message left five minutes ago.

"Allison? This is Peter Klausen O'Reilly, (he was so distracted he forgot the third, my stomach clenched, and the coffee rose in my throat). "I'm here at the police station, with Ben, can you come down?"

Chapter 17

I held the phone, stunned. O'Reilly's voice continued, as he gave directions, plus two parking alternatives, because parking is always problem at the courthouse – something I never personally experienced, not being a hardened criminal with many appointments to keep with the judge - I was stalling. I listened to the message again, then realized I had to launch into action.

In any emergency, it's normal to throw on whatever clothing is laying on top of the pile on the closet floor, and go, go, go! I knew that a second, or even a minute or two, spent getting dressed in real clothes. would garner long term benefits, if only for me. So I hurried into a grown-up outfit as fast as I could. I managed to rip through two sets of pantyhose in the process, but I persisted. I hoped that in the satitorial hierarchy of the incarcerated, pantyhose would elevate me above the regulars.

The sky grew darker instead of lighter, and seemed to press down on me as I drove up the freeway to the courthouse. Had they jailed Ben? Had they tortured him and now he was a puddle of human flesh and broken dreams? Should I stop watching selections from my James Bond DVD collection late at night?

I parked, per the instructions from O'Reilly, and hurried to the courthouse.

I was right. The combination of elegant snakeskin (fake but still substantially expensive) pumps, pantyhose, and a suit with the slenderizing lines that only money can buy, did the trick. I was ushered, with minimal security and delay, into a back room where Ben and Peter O'Reilly were seated.

"I thought you'd be in jail." I said.

"You got here pretty quickly," O'Reilly, maybe I should call him Peter after this adventure, stood and shook my hand.

"Of course I did," I glanced over at Ben, who did not move.

"He's a little shocked," Peter explained.

"Why?" I sat down next to Ben and stroked his arm. His eyes were red rimmed. He looked drawn, even haggard. It was as if he was re-living Beverley's murder.

"They brought him in for questioning, yesterday," Peter

explained. "A squad car picked him up from his home."

"Oh no, your grandmother!"

"She's in the public waiting room," Peter explained. "I asked them to bring you around the back way."

He took a breath, "Emily was understandably beside herself. She called the family lawyer," Peter winced, as well he should, it was akin to using a cannon to take out a fly. Ben had said his family was prone to over reaction.

"Is the Concron contingency here?" I asked cautiously.

"They are on their way, as are Gloria and Ben Sr., Donald too."

"Family," Ben raised his head and I realized, too late to discreetly turn away, that he was tearing up.

"But that's good, they want to support you." I tried to sound positive.

His face was twisted more in pain, than anything else. Ah, he subscribed to the family involvement equals exponential pain, school of thought.

"Should I greet them?" I asked.

Ben nodded, "I can't." He dropped his head into his hands.

I continued to rub his arm, the only physical comfort I could offer under the circumstances.

"What was the charge?" I asked O'Reilly.

"When they hauled him off? Pre-meditated murder."

"Oh lovely. And their evidence?" I asked as calmly as I could. Patricia's dour voice ringing in my ear, it's always the husband. Well, it hadn't been Cyndi's husband, Carrie doesn't have an ex, so we have good odds the murderer wasn't Beverley's ex, either. I have no idea if that's a legitimate argument or not.

I squeezed Ben's arm, careful not to dig in with my long acrylic nails, and faced O'Reilly. The lawyer looked a bit more human, he had known Beverley too; this couldn't be easy.

I opened my mouth to ask more questions, but Peter beat me to it.

"Are you sure the signature on your listing agreement, was Ben's?'

"There was a signature. And it was his name," I said carefully. "But apparently Beverley signed documents with his name all the time."

Peter let out a breath. "Thank you. Yes, she did, so much so that Ben is in danger of having the bank reject his real signature."

"What are you going to do?"

"Get him out of here, and then talk to the DA about signatures, forgery, and motive. You were with him last Saturday night?"

"The night poor Cyndi was killed? Yes, he was at my brother's party, then with me."

"Ah, I see." I didn't appreciate the way he said that, but I couldn't snap at him, I couldn't do anything mean, he was helping Ben. And even while I appreciated the irony, I was also relieved. O'Reilly scribbled something on a, yes, legal yellow note pad.

We heard a rather large commotion from the front lobby.

"Mom," Ben said from between his fingers. I patted his tense shoulder and walked out to the public waiting room. If I couldn't face them now, I would never be able to face them.

"Allison, you're the one!" Emily, dressed in black yoga pants and a colorful sweatshirt, glared at me with hatred.

I composed myself as best I could. And avoided Emily's eyes.

"I'm Ben's girlfriend, Allison." I extended my hand to the closest person, who must have been Ben Weiss Senior, from whom Ben took more than a passing resemblance. I wondered why I didn't notice that when I saw the Senior Ben at the Lost Art Museum. Ah, because here was Gloria.

"I understand you told the police Ben was at the scene of the crime." Gloria did not shake my hand, she crossed her arms and glared at me. Well, at least she was still protective of her son, I actually held that in her favor, same for Emily.

"Mother," Ben's brother, with far less hair and a bulkier body than his brother, gently moved his mother aside and did take my hand.

"I'm Ben's brother, Donald Weiss. Our lawyers will be here in a minute, is there anything you can tell us?"

The family Stone- Weiss all stared accusingly at me. God, I was doubly glad I wore pantyhose and decent shoes. Facing this group in sweat pants and Tasmanian Devil slippers would not have held at all. Those were the easy choice items on top of my pile in the closet.

"Beverley forged Ben's signature," I said. "She did it all the time. Ben's attorney, Peter Klausen O'Reilly, the Third, is talking to the police at this very minute. I am not really involved." Except to protect Ben from his loving family.

"Then why blame Ben?" Emily demanded.

"I suppose there isn't much else to go on," I admitted, "but he has alibis for the other murders."

"They think he murdered other people?!" Gloria shrieked. Wow, she does make my mother look pretty good. I debated on whether or not to tell my mother that, then decided not to, didn't want mom to get a swelled head.

"No, they have to cover all the bases," I repeated. I held myself tightly, I would have liked to scream myself. But I didn't. I braced myself for more questions. Donald was holding Emily and whispering something to her. Gloria was standing rigidly in the center of the room, her slender body almost vibrated with pent up tension. Ben, Senior stood a foot away from his wife, as if her aura prevented him from moving any closer.

At that moment, when I was about to come up with something really inane, like – everything is going to be fine - Ben, with Peter holding him by the arm, appeared.

A riot ensued. When all the kissing, exclamations, admonishments and dirty looks in my direction, were over, Ben was whisked off for breakfast and I was left standing alone in the lobby of the county court house.

"Buy you a cup of coffee?" Peter watched the group exit. Ben didn't even look back at me.

I shook my head, and absently fluffed my hair.

"Don't take it personally," Peter said. "His family is a big, bad juggernaut, when they swoop in, it's all over for the outsiders," he made quotation marks with his fingers.

"You've known him for a long time."

"We attended the same high school. He spent as much time away from home as possible, he usually ended up at my house."

"I thought you two weren't friends."

"We aren't, but that doesn't mean we didn't help each other out, now and then."

"I will never understand men."

"Don't bother," he glanced at me. "Don't worry, he won't give you up for them. He's always made his own way, that's why they're all here. He hasn't needed them since the divorce, so this is an opportunity to smother him." Peter paused. "And be right. They love being right."

"Great," I said gloomily. I was not having luck with this family at all. Carrie was doing better with the clannishly private Sullivan family.

I took a breath and tried to subtly readjust the waistband of my pantyhose.

"Yes, you can buy me coffee."

Filled with caffeine, but not any more of Ben's past, as Peter was as cautious as Ben when it came to childhood memories, I finally arrived at my office. Patricia greeted me with the news that Beverley's ex-husband had been held over night for questioning then released.

"Thank you," I said, shortly. I stood in the lobby, there was something I needed to do, what was it?

"Where is everyone?" I tentatively glanced around the corner at Rosemary's office, but it was deserted.

"Gone, working, dieting, whatever," Patricia said dismissively. "They haven't caught the murderer yet."

They may never catch the murderer, he could be sipping pina coladas on a resort beach at this very minute, safely ensconced on an obscure, and difficult to find tropical island.

"There's a blog about how the police are puzzled about that last murder." Patricia said.

"Cyndi," I looked up at the clock, it was almost eleven, what was it that I was suppose to be doing?

"Yes," Patricia agreed. "With the odd spelling, anyway there wasn't enough blood at the scene."

I had to stop and fight down the coffee I had consumed with Peter Klausen O'Reilley the Third. Coffee, was I having coffee with someone?

Patricia did not notice how distracted I was. "They think she was brought to the site after she was killed," Patricia continued.

"Why does that information help?" I asked.

"Well, where was she killed then?" Patricia said sensibly. "Maybe in the creek, like the others."

"She disappeared after she attacked Carrie," I said, the idea forming in my still addled brain. Where would Cyndi go? Crap! Bo Freeman, the offer on Ben's house!

I engaged Patricia in an actual work. We scrambled to download the contracts, and disclosures. I raced out of the office, the purchase agreement still warm from the laser printer.

Chapter 18

I bought only a tall sized, decaf latte, and sat down to sort through the paperwork for the Silverpoint offer. I tried to take a breath, and grimaced out a smile to arrange my face correctly. I glanced at my watch, five after. Thank goodness Mr. Freeman was running behind. I was too relieved to worry that he may stand me up. But more important that standing me up, was Freeman the killer? He seemed to come out of no where, and wanted the house, with very little protesting or questions. Fine with me, cash trumps concerns over a psycho killer on the loose.

Mr. Freedman strode in at ten after the hour. He had given me exactly enough time to compose myself, and use the restroom.

"Thank you for doing this. I usually don't get this kind of attention." Mr. Freeman slid into his chair and waved away my offer to buy him a high caloric, but oh so delicious, Starbuck's special peppermint, mocha drink.

"Really?" I said, trying to look disbelieving. I mean, the man looked more homeless than the professor, or even Cyndi. Poor Cyndi.

"Yeah. Well, here is my check, and my letter from my banker that says the check is real. You know the drill." He handed me the check, and leaned back in his chair.

I certainly did. What surprised me was that he knew the drill. I took the check, the note, and filled in the rest of the offer.

While I worked, he tapped his fingers on the table top, and jiggled his foot clad in those ugly, but apparently comfortable, rubber clogs. They were the kind of shoes my grandmother Prue would wear, I wore my third best boots, years old, but the spike heel was still serviceable.

Bo signed the purchase agreement, here, here, and here and we were in business. I promised to get back to him soon. Christmas eve loomed, and Ben had only technically three days to counter, or accept the offer, but exceptions would be made for Christmas. In my world they are made all the time.

"Can you get an answer by Christmas?" He asked suddenly.

"By Christmas?" I repeated. "Well, I don't,"

"It's a gift for my sister," he explained hastily. "I want to present it to her on Christmas Day."

My coffee went down the wrong way. I coughed and coughed. He waited patiently but did not offer to bang me on the back, for which I was grateful, cash or no, he was still pretty odd.

"She supported me when I was starting out. I thought I'd return the favor," he explained as if it was the most sensible of ideas.

The very thought of one of my siblings making such an outrageous gesture was, well, unthinkable.

"You are sure she won't mind the stories of the murder? People around her will remember, they will ask questions, want details," I warned him. I shouldn't warn him, I had the signed offer, but I did anyway.

"She's not that sensitive, and she's always wanted to live in the Villas. The address is important to her. And if it's important to her, than that's what she'll have."

He not only had enough cash to buy a house, he was giving it away, as a gift. Perhaps he didn't just emerge from a Unabomber shack after all.

"Why was she so supportive?" I finally asked. I didn't feel all that compelled to make a new friend, he still frightened me, but I was curious.

"I'm an artist. Here." He fished out a crumpled piece of paper and handed it to me, "here is a sketch of what I'm working on, see?"

I regarded the sketch, and then looked at him again. "Will you sign it?"

He nodded. We had a deal.

I did not even stop at the office. I hightailed to Ben's place in Dry Creek, and laid in wait until he came home. I was a little nervous about walking in unannounced and greeting the angry and upset Emily, on my own. I was sure I was persona non grata as far as she was concerned. So I parked outside the main gates, and when his truck appeared, I followed him into the driveway.

"Hi," I greeted him with a kiss.

"Hi. You could have come inside, I think Grandma is home."

"No, I was okay, I, uh , had some calls to make," I hedged.

He glanced up at the imposing façade of the house. "Yes, well, they aren't that mad at you. The police have dropped charges, thanks to O'Reilly."

"Does that mean you're even?"

"For what?'

"For what he did to that friend of yours, Cassandra." I took a stab at it and from his expression, I was right.

"Oh, that, no, we are not even, but he came pretty damn close today." Ben paused, had his family finally won? Did he want to throw his lot in with them, live with Emily all his life?

He pulled me into his arms and hugged me so hard, and for so long, I was having trouble taking a breath. I could feel his heart, banging up against my breasts double time. He had not recovered from this morning, not by a long shot.

"What did you do for the rest of the day?" My voice was muffled against his chest.

"Hammered things. Then I used a sledge hammer to break up some cement, then I bent up some aluminum siding for recycling."

"With your bare hands," I guessed.

"That's right," he released his grip a little. "Don't ever get hurt. Don't ever go away," he whispered.

That was enough for me.

"Okay, well," he recovered slightly. "Come inside."

I followed him around the house into the entrance that led directly to his own part of the house. I hadn't noticed before, but he did not have a Christmas tree, or even bowl of oranges on his small coffee table. No signs that we were smack in the middle of the most wonderful time of the year.

"You don't decorate for Christmas," I commented.

"No," he said absently. "I wrestle out the tree for Emily and she decorates enough for the both of us." He pulled off his sweatshirt splattered with sawdust and caulking smears and headed to the washer and dyer, adjacent to the bathroom.

"I have an offer," I called after him. "And you should take it."

"Already?" He ran his fingers through his hair and shook

himself like a dog scattering bits of detritus from his body. He always threw himself into his work. It was an appealing thing about him.

"I told you I was good."

"Yes, you are. What's the offer?"

"Full cash, he's buying it for his sister – as a Christmas gift! Here's a pen." I said wearily. "This is a God send."

"Or a gift from Santa." He said, glancing at the contract. "Where do I accept?"

"Why can't all my clients be like you?"

"Because, I am the only client you're sleeping with."

"Well, yes," I conceded.

I called Bo Freeman right away. Instead of being a murderer, he was actually an artist.

Bo answered the phone on the first ring.

"Merry Christmas," I said.

I turned my phone to vibrate. All the important business had either been taken care of or was in front of me. We ordered pizza as a late lunch/ early dinner. Ben did not suggest we convene in the main rooms of the house, we kept to his cozy apartment.

"I met Beverley at a holiday party, I think it was a service oriented one." He considered it for a moment. "Boys and Girls Club? I think that may have been it. The place was filled with elderly men who insisted on calling it the Boy's Club and Beverley spent the evening correcting them – it's the boys and GIRLS club - she'd point out. All night."

He smiled. Ah, here it was – there had been attraction, there had been something, a spark, some chemistry. It was actually better, than thinking the poor man had been simply duped.

"So, it was love at first sight?" I asked, and took a third piece of pizza.

"No, that was with you," he was matter-of-fact. "This was more love after three or four or five dates, but she was flattering, and I was complimented. You remember what O'Reilly said, she made you feel needed, important. She needed your big, manly, protection. You know how it is."

I blushed, I could feel my face turning as red as my jacket. I had encountered a lovely man a few months ago. He paid attention to me, took me to dinner, lavished me with compliments, and in the end, betrayed me. And that was only the most recent example.

A long, long, time ago, I had actually made it all the way to the altar before my last serious relationship blew up, very publicly, in my face. We both lost our hearts. Maybe we could help each other find them again.

I snuck out of Ben's house first thing in the morning, I still didn't want to run into Emily, and I did not wish to encounter her first thing, in the morning. I wanted to spare her that.

I checked my phone. No messages. I switched it back from vibrate to ring.

If Beverley was escaping the county to meet someone, and I assumed it was a man, why hadn't he contacted her? Wasn't he concerned that she hadn't shown up to the rendezvous? They must have agreed on a rendezvous point, yes?

Or, had Beverly's phone buzzed and buzzed, but no one heard it? Many people who attend endless meetings keep their phones on perpetual vibrate. Where had I left her purse?

Katherine called me as I snaked my way south, through the worst of the morning traffic.

"I'm quitting, I can't diet at this pace. And those grass drinks really upset my stomach!"

"You drank wheat grass?" I asked.

"Rosemary suggested it."

"She also recommended the personal trainer, and you almost killed him."

"It would have been in self defense," Katherine protested. "But at least I wouldn't have cut him up into little bits."

"Don't," I protested.

"Sorry, don't tell Rosemary, I'm going to let her compete until St. Patrick's Day."

"That's noble of you."

I felt the universe was back in balance.

The stop and start south bound traffic gave me time to think. Beverley had a phone. Everyone has a phone. And it followed that Beverley had the latest phone, the thinnest phone, the cutest phone, the kind of phone you can't find in your purse until the last buzz buzzes, and the caller goes to voice mail and complains that you are never there to answer your phone. That kind of phone.

I detoured to the Silverpoint property.

I keep lock boxes on my listings until escrow closes, so it was easy to get back into the house. I shivered, the grey days had cooled the house too much. I flipped on the heat to take off the chill.

The phone was indeed well hidden. It was tucked into a padded phone pocket on the outside of the Chanel bag. It was very easy to miss. I had missed it the first time, but I wasn't looking for a phone the first time I went through her purse. Even now, I couldn't even feel it when I squished the bag.

I flipped it open and scrolled through the numbers looking for traces of missed calls. Yes, here was the list, seventeen missed calls. Same number.

I pressed the most recent missed call, but did not get a helpful ID, yet the call dialed through anyway.

"Hello, hello!" said a male voice. "Beverley," ah, he had caller ID on his side.

"You are late!" he continued without bothering to confirm that the caller was, in fact, Beverley. Was that arrogance or idiocy?

"What happened?" He continued. "Where are you? Your stuff arrived by the way, where am I suppose to put all this?"

I still didn't recognize the voice, but I had my suspicions. "Yes, she is late, Mr. Bixby."

Silence.

Got him.

"Who is this?" he finally said, well, at least he didn't hang up.

"Her Realtor, yours too." I had represented the buyers for Mr. Bixby's house, and the sale went through despite some last minute problems - like finding Mrs. Bixby floating face down in the hot tub.

He dismissed my last comment. "Where is Beverley? She was supposed to sell the house, and join me, uh, here, by

Christmas eve."

"How romantic. And you haven't heard from her since Thanksgiving, weren't you worried, say, three weeks ago?"

"We agreed not to communicate until end of December," he explained innocently. His easy admissions were astonishing. I could be an under cover agent, I could be FBI, I could be . . . someone who could actually do something about all this.

But I was not. I did, however, have a question.

"Did you kill your wife?" I had actually met his wife, Debbie Bixby – another Debbie, go figure – this one didn't fare well. I count myself lucky that Debbie's was one of the few bodies I hadn't personally discovered.

"I didn't kill her per se," he said honestly. "She passed out in the hot tub. And I may have accidentally closed the lid, not realizing she was still in there." He was even unconvincing over the phone.

"That can happen to anyone." I said sarcastically.

"Where is Beverley?" He repeated.

"I take you are somewhere warm with no extradition treaty with the US?"

"Something in that category," he agreed.

"Beverley is dead," I announced, brutally.

He had the courtesy to pause, and I head sounds of coughing and choking.

"What? How? How can she be dead?"

"I don't think it was easy. Check the Internet. You do have the Internet where you are?"

"It's difficult, all dial up," he said absently.

"Have a good life," I clicked off.

He was not anywhere he could be reached. I knew that, he knew that. Got rid of his first wife, lost his future second wife. Perhaps that means he lost? Was the President of the Homeless Prevention League with him? Had Steven escaped to the same warm island? Maybe they worked out something together.

I regarded the slender phone in my hand. Now, my fingerprints were all over Beverley's phone. That didn't look good. I scrolled through the names – men, women, I couldn't tell who was important, and who was not. She had all of Ben's numbers, and a home number with the San Francisco area code, probably Ben's parents.

It was a pretty phone – the latest model. I suppose the numbers can be traced and another call would garner Bixby's location. But would that drag Ben back into the fray? Bixby did not kill Beverley, he merely ran away with some - not all, apparently- of the Homeless Prevention League monies. And ran away from a murder.

I hefted the phone, a shame really. But it would guarantee Ben and his family would be haunted by this for years to come. I walked to the largest Cuisinart, dropped in the phone and punched the chop button.

Don't try this at home.

Carrie's admission into the private shadows of the Sullivan compound was a good news, bad new scenario.

"I feel I'm that Japanese princess who enters the royal palace, and never comes out," she said over the phone.

"Is it that bad?" I asked.

"No," she rushed in. "But Patrick is feeling very paranoid and responsible, and won't let me out of his sight, and since it's almost Christmas and I'm on medical leave anyway, I figure, I may as well enjoy my rest."

"So, it could be worse," I said.

"The Senior Center is fine. I asked Linda from accounting to take over the front desk, but with no staff at the shelter, I'm worried about the clients. I was suppose to drop off some blankets to the RVs. Martha is in charge of bringing the Christmas turkeys to each mobile unit, and I'm in charge of the blankets, I would hate to have her get there before me."

I did not say anything. I knew what was coming, then again, Carrie would be meeting Martha at every event she attended, if she looked irresponsible now, she would never hear the end of it.

"We personally deliver to a shelter of our choice, it's to keep the board members involved in a hands on way," she said, unconvincingly.

"But you're not staying on the board, remember?" I pointed out.

If someone can sound severe and judgmental over the phone, my friend can. "That's beside the point, people are cold. They need their food and blankets. I would help them even if I was fired from the board."

The whole world needs about a million more editions of Carrie Eliot. "So you want me to bring the blankets to the shelter." There was no way I was avoiding this. "Okay, where are they?"

She knew I meant the blankets. "Probably at Target."

"I have to buy them as well?" I shrieked. Target on Christmas Eve? A massive florescent lit monolith packed with men desperately searching for that special, last minute, obligatory gift item for their loved ones? Cars honking, people yelling. The whole holiday snafu?

I was the Grinch. I really belonged on top of a mountain, not down in the chaos of the Who-ville. I'm the one who would to steal the blankets from the homeless, that would be more in keeping with my holiday spirit.

"How many blankets need to be delivered?" I said in complete defeat.

Have you visited Target on Christmas eve – well, afternoon? Don't. Don't go anywhere, don't do anything. Run, save yourself. Go to a nice island and hang out with felons. But, don't shop the day before Christmas. It occurred to me that this was probably a big reason why my grandmother opted to live in Claim Jump. Maybe, that's why Emily did too. Maybe, I have more in common with these elderly ladies than I thought.

The revelation did not cheer me.

I found the blankets, and marched into line behind a tall man dressed in kahki slacks and white tennis shoes. Something tugged at my memory, had he come to a recent open house? Not at Silverpoint, I knew that.

He looked back at me, and smiled.

I automatically smiled back. His cart was stuffed with toys and a blanket similar to the ones I clutched to my chest.

"Last minute shopping?" I asked, casually.

He regarded the pile in the cart, "I am behind, work was a bitch this week, didn't have time for anything else."

"Who is the blanket for?"

"Oh, my wife."

I glanced at my soon-to-be-purchases; they were the cheapest I could find. It was one thing for a homeless recipient, quite another for a loving, well considered, holiday gift for your wife.

I glanced at my watch. I didn't have that much time, but for heaven's sake! "No," I told him, "you are not giving that blanket to your wife, come with me."

No good deed goes unpunished, but I couldn't let him give such a thing to his wife. I felt if I didn't help, I would be violating the secret pact of the sisterhood: prevent crummy gifts at all cost.

I said as much as we cautiously made our way back through the choked store. I avoided the baby strollers packed with product, the baby nowhere in evidence.

"But she wouldn't know how much it cost," he protested.

"Yes, she will. We always know how much the gift costs." I guided him back to the blanket aisle.

"Here," I pulled down one of those deep, lush, throws in dark eggplant. "If you must present your wife a blanket, at least give her something that feels luxurious."

"Why are you being so nice to me?" He dropped the cheap blanket on the shelf and picked up the boxed throw and set it carefully on the cart.

"Maybe a friend of mind is rubbing off on me," I admitted.

"That would be Carrie Eliot?"

I dropped the blankets and backed into the hard, metal shelves. They rattled, but held.

"How do you know that?"

"Detective William Morris, Bill. I'm working on the Weiss murder, as well as the assault on Ms. Eliot."

"And you've been following me."

He was not a potential client at all, a stalker of sorts, but at least not the murderer.

"Not really in a serious way, I wanted to keep an eye on things. You were a suspect of course, but not a very convincing one. I decided to switch from catching you, to keeping you safe. You take a lot of chances, don't you?"

"Hazard of my profession."

He rearranged his cart. "It would seem so."

"Then who is the main suspect?"

He placed his hands on the throw. "Wow, that is nicer, thanks!"

"You're not going to answer my question."

"It's not your boyfriend."

I gathered my own blankets.

"Do you think she'd want one of those watches with jewels?" He asked.

"I'm sure she would."

"Look, we haven't arrested anyone, yet. So be careful."

"I'm always careful."

"No, you're not. Happy holidays," he pushed the cart around the corner and disappeared.

"Am too," I called after him.

I was due up at Ben and Emily's for Christmas Eve dinner. I was even invited to spend the night, by both of them, which was a compliment I took to heart. Maybe I could get on Emily's good side after all? I hoped so.

Distracted by that thought, and worried Emily wouldn't like the four red wine goblets I found for her gift, I pulled around the back of Target to the only RV I knew about, where the professor lived.

My phone buzzed as I was exiting the car. I pulled back in and answered.

"I think I want to buy that last condo." It was Owen.

"The last condo?" I said, trying to buy some time, which condo? We saw so many, which one?

"You remember," he said, a bit belligerently. "The one with the deck out back. I want that one, what do I do?"

"Meet with me on the 26th, and we will write up an offer." I said. It was almost too good to be true and so, I wasn't going to get all worked up about it, not yet. Owen and I have been down this path before, and the path always seems to be marred by an unacceptable crack in the pavement.

"First thing?" He said.

"Ten o'clock at my office, Owen." I promised.

"I don't want to lose any time," he said.

I wrote a note in my day planner to stop by the office on my way to Richard's house, and print out the purchase agreement.

That would a good treat, two houses sold during the traditionally worst time of the year to buy or sell a house.

Go Team Little.

I drummed my fingers on the steering wheel and stared at the RV. In the light, it looked copper, then a little green. Very pretty, it was probably that Flex paint. Ben told me that the golf club loved their Flex paint jobs because the cart changed colors depending on where you stand. The cart can look green, or blue, or copper colored.

Washing the same RV over and over.

I suspected I only needed to deliver blankets to this one RV, and I would have the whole program covered.

I took a deep breath, called forth my latent philanthropic traits, gathered up the blankets and walked up to the RV. The air was damp and heavy, more rain was on the way. I hurried up a two-step metal stair pushed up against the side of the vehicle. It served as the gracious entrance and porch. I wobbled on my heels and knocked on the door.

"Who is it?" he called out. Did he have roommates? I thought he might, but I wasn't sure.

"My name is Allison, I'm here from the Homeless Prevention League. I have your Christmas gift." There, a little mystery is always helpful. Open the door, take the blankets, and I'll be on my way, my good deed carefully executed.

The professor, Marcel I think, jerked open the flimsy door and looked me up and down as if I were the derelict, and he was the righteous volunteer. I wore a beautiful velvet skirt and my favorite boots - finally discovered at the back of my closet - I was certainly not a derelict.

In honor of the holidays, the professor was clad in a dirty tee shirt that stretched over his ample stomach, and a shiny, worn, suit jacket. He was barefoot.

It started to rain. I twitched as it settled on my hair, but held onto my blankets and made a mental note to be careful and not slip on the metal steps when I was finally allowed to move.

"Blankets," he did not bother to hide his disgust.

"It was the best they could do," I was defensive on the HPL's behalf. Honestly, the way people complain about free stuff boggles my mind.

He sighed with exaggeration. "Come in, set them over there."

I complied. The interior was pleasant enough, the lights fixed under the tiny kitchen cabinets lent a soft glow to the whole room - kitchen/dining/living/study/formal dining and entertainment center, all within arm's reach.

I dropped the blankets on the built in banquet, and straightened up. I filled the small room and as a result, I was not comfortable. Cozy, in this case, translated to cramped.

But something stopped me. What was that smell? It was faint, but still horrible, and distinctive. Oh God, Oh God. I swallowed and composed my face.

I turned slowly to face the professor and to re-orient myself to the door, there was only one exit from the space. It was to my left, one big lunge away.

"It was a great story," he said conversationally, looking me in the eye. "The homeless mother from a wealthy family, it can happen to you, kind of angle." He said with some satisfaction. "I finally got something on the front page."

"Good, then you got what you wanted, yes?" I stepped towards the door with confidence that I did not feel at all. Get out, I thought. Don't turn your back, don't hesitate. Just get out. I didn't need to do any more than that, no one will expect any more than that.

It sang in my head like an unpopular tune that won't go away. Get out, get out.

"The television news picked it up right away. I'm sure it was the children, and the photos, we are such a visual culture, photos are absolutely essential. I should have thought of that sooner. Of course, I had to take them myself, another miscalculation."

I swallowed. The portly, professorial, gentleman morphed into someone far more menacing that I had ever thought possible. He smiled happily at me. He had all his teeth, but they were yellow with age, and his smile did not help mitigate the over all impression of a mind gone awry.

"Yes, they did." I acknowledged more calmly than I felt.

I took a small step to the left, I could almost reach the door. "That should make you happy right? Mission accomplished?"

He took a step towards me, and I had no choice but to take a step back, away from the door, so tantalizingly close. I tried to remember where my car was parked. Had I locked it? Where were my keys? In my pocket.

I said the first thing that came to mind. "I don't have children."

"That's okay," he acknowledged pleasantly. "Still, you are tremendously newsworthy, I recognize you from the tribute to poor Beverley. You are an excellent victim, especially if you're killed during an amateur investigation, doing your part to expose Beverley's killer. The current girlfriend helping the dead ex-wife. Very interesting angle, in addition, you have notoriety, I read about you in the paper all the time." He casually picked up a knife, a large triangle shaped knife (no, I did not recognize the brand, it was large and looked very sharp) and waved it in my direction. I arched back, but did not move, the space was too small for much dodging or ducking.

"Those are paid advertisements," I pointed out. "Different than editorial, everyone knows that." Get out.

He shook his head and looked, well kindly, except for the knife. Now, I've been bludgeoned, beaten, smacked and nearly immolated, but facing a big knife, wielded by a killer with intent, overwhelmed me, but not with adrenaline, rather by a sense of terrible loneliness. To die alone, no one near, how truly awful. I felt for poor Beverley and Cyndi. Great, another learning experience. I suppose this will build character,

I took another step, the incessant music in my brain: get out, get out. I had faced unhinged mad men before, but not one so completely sensible. The rain roared onto the trailer, water cascaded down the small windows as if we were in a car wash.

"Come on," he waved the knife and slowly approached me. "It won't hurt a bit, you'll feel a little tug, then blessed darkness, and the rest," he shrugged, "the rest is up to me and you won't care at all."

He eyed me, "but you are much larger than the other three." He glanced at the knife, and I held my breath. I did not have an exit strategy (except for get out), and the thought of him chasing me through a slick, and empty parking lot in the pouring rain, was not a good one. I would become a horror film heroine, I would not get into my car fast enough, he'd follow me into the front seat, and we'd end up wrestling for the knife in an even more confined space than the RV.

He frowned at the size of the knife, versus the size of my, well, me.

But, apparently it was not a problem. "I was disappointed there were never photos of Beverley."

"And you worked so hard," I realized now why the police never released details about the murder scene. I was one of the only people who knew how poor Beverley had ended up. Me and the murderer.

"It was so difficult to get her head off. And there we no photos." He spoke as if relating how hard it is to open wine bottles stuffed with synthetic corks.

"You made quite an effort." I swallowed. I knew ten seconds before, but his comment confirmed it. The real deal. I had found the murderer, all by myself. And there in lies the problem. I was all alone.

"I did," he gestured with knife. "All that staging, wasted. I may drive away, this is not working out as well as I hoped."

"Sometimes murder is can be that way," I agreed.

I backed away a whole inch, it was a far as I could go. The rain beat down. Sheets of water obscured the windows. I couldn't see anything outside, and of course, no one could see in.

He advanced, completely confident of the outcome. A murderer with tenure.

My phone rang. I had to ignore it, as much as I wanted to brandish it, claiming it could be a buyer and would he understand if I took this?

I backed up and hit the built in banquet.

So who saves Allison? Who comes in at the last minute? Does someone come at the last minute?

Yes, someone does. The imperious Martha Anderson. She didn't even bother knocking on the RV's flimsy door, but pulled it open as if she owned the place. A steaming hot turkey proceeded her into the doorway.

"Good," she said loudly. "You're ready to carve."

The professor looked down at the knife in his hand.

"Martha!" I greeted her loudly enough to be heard over the rain. I pulled her into the RV because I couldn't very well push her out backwards. Once she took a step inside, I grabbed the turkey, barely balanced in the flimsy aluminum tray in the first place, and threw it as hard as I could straight at the professor.

He dropped the knife to defend himself against the steaming white meat and hot grease, and in that second, I pushed Martha back out of the RV (forward, it gave her a more fighting chance), and followed her stumbling bulk, pushing the door closed behind me.

"What are you doing!" Martha yelled at me from the safety of the parking lot.

I kept my hand on the door handle, and my body weight pushed against the door to hold it closed. It would only be a second before, here he was.

The professor banged on the door, but I didn't budge. The rain plastered my hair down and quickly trickled down the back of my jacket. Call me the human doorstop.

I looked around for something to secure the door, but the parking lot was empty of random pieces of wood.

The rain made the handle and the little metal steps leading to the door, too slippery for a good purchase, especially long term.

"Your car!" I yelled at Martha.

"What?" She stood solidly in the lot, looking at me as if I were mad. Which could be, but I had a killer inside. Did he have the keys to the RV? He must, he drove Cyndi's body to the Homeless Prevention League and back again. I could slash the tires after I secured the door.

"Get in your car. Drive it here!" I called to Martha.

"What? That was a perfectly good turkey, donated by Cooper Milk," she announced.

"Believe me, they will understand. Your car, I need to block the door."

"But then the professor can't get out!"

"Exactly." The door heaved against me from the professor's efforts. I pushed back and held onto the handle, as I worked to keep my feet wedged on the stair step.   Martha hesitated, still not processing what happened. She eyed the bulging door and the sounds of the man knocking against it. In a fair fight, I can take him, and for me, this moment was completely fair. The door smacked against me. I wedged my heels under the steps and braced myself with all the energy and pounds at my disposal.

I gestured frantically to the door, and pointed to her car. She finally moved, in slow motion it looked to me, but I was pumped through with more desperate energy that she, my perception of time was quite different.

The door handle was slippery. A nail broke as I tried to maintain my grip, my shoulder slipped but I steadied myself and pushed harder. At least the song had disappeared, I was out, not finished with him, but at least outside, and away from the knife.

After about a thousand years, Martha (I think I can call her Martha, after all we've been through), started the motor and pulled the car closer. Closer.

The door gave and I slipped. He must be looking for another exit. I pulled out my phone and scrolled to the second number on my screen, the police.

I waved her closer. She had no idea what I wanted to do, but I did. Closer.

I had my hand on the handle, he came back with new force and pushed and yelled.

She looked at me through her windshield, still completely puzzled.

"Please!" My hair was a mess, I had turkey drippings all down my skirt. It would be ruined if I didn't get to a dry cleaners quickly. She probably thought I was a lunatic.

"Push the car up against the door."

I kept my hand on the door, as soon as her bumper was close enough, I jumped to one side and kicked away the stairs. I threw my arms towards the door as if I was pointing out the view, imagine this city scene at night. Here, I gestured. I hope she got it by now, that she needed to pull her car up against the door.

She paused, the rain whipping against the windshield. "Go!" I yelled. "Block the door, now!"

She did, the grill of her Cadillac banged into the side of the RV and effectively covered the bottom half of the door. It bent under the impact, but held. The professor howled from inside.

I stepped away. Two finger nails had completely popped off and I was due at Emily's in an hour. I hate when that happens.

The professor had quite a vocabulary of swear words.

It's really sad that the River's Bend police is number two on my most called list.

* * *

"Umm. Hi." Ben let me into the side door. I couldn't risk encountering Emily in my current state.

I staggered into the library, and sat down on the first inviting piece of furniture.

"You look like you've been busy," he ventured. He was a very good man. And despite some of his inabilities to handle aggressive fundraisers, he knew how to handle me.

"I broke two nails," I announced.

"Ah," he shoved his hands into his jeans pockets, and rocked on his heels. "And what were you doing that justified sacrificing your lovely and expensive fingernails?"

The calming cocoon of shock that insulated me enough to speak to the police, nod to Mr. Morris, who waved me on, sign a hastily written report, leave my business card and assure everyone I was not leaving town. The calm that helped me drive north, putting up with holiday songs on the radio that all seemed to mention turkeys. The calm got me here to this chair, suddenly split open and fell away.

"I found Beverley's killer," I wailed. Tears overwhelmed me now I was safe.

I don't think I've ever cried in front of Ben. But I didn't have enough fortitude left to stem the tide, and pretend to be strong. I was not strong. I kept walking in on horribly mutilated bodies and tonight, I almost joined their ranks.

That thought made me cry harder.

"I'm going to delay dinner," I hiccupped.

"Oh baby, it's crab, it will keep." He sank down next to me, wrapped his arms around me and held me tightly against his chest. He felt good. I clung to him as only a ravaged, upset heroine can, and sobbed out the last four hours.

At least Martha Anderson was impressed.

She didn't stay in the car, once she blocked the RV door. She struggled out, shoes first, the bulk of her last. Her raincoat caught on the door, she jerked the coat free and slammed the door in fit of pique.

"What are you doing!" she waved at the RV, now rocking suggestively due to the professor's exertions. "He's still in there."

"Yes he is."

Sirens flared up from around the corner. Excellent. The professor was still beating against the door.

The only coherent words I heard were "this is an outrage." Yes, it was.

"He is the murderer," I announced.

She put her hands on her hips and glared at me. The rain had let up some, but water was still pouring out of the sky, and I swear, Martha Anderson's hair was completely unaffected.

"Now, how did you come to such an unsupported and spurious conclusion? Just because he's homeless, is that it?" She demanded, still indignant, I assumed, about the sacrificed roasted turkey.

Two police cars, red and blue lights flashing, illuminated the wet, black asphalt and skidded so close to me, the tires sprayed water on my boots.

Guns drawn, they politely asked Martha to move her car again. In a huff, she did.

I thought for a second that the professor could have escaped from a window. But the windows are small and he is round, it would not be an option. I happily stepped to one side as the police extracted the professor, appropriately with guns drawn and handcuffs ready.

"He told me," I said to Martha.

"He told me," I repeated to Ben.

"No good deed goes unpunished." Ben declared. Which was my holiday theme.

He led me to the shower and left me in peace to wash away the afternoon, but he was ready with his thick terry cloth robe when I emerged. Barefoot, my hair in a ponytail because that was all there was to do, I found two blue SpongeBob band-aids in my purse, and wrapped my damaged, nail-less fingers. Sure, applying first aid made the loss of the two nails more obvious, but much more cheerful. I buried my hand into the pocket of his robe and was ready to endure a festive Christmas Eve.

We walked down an inner stairs, and into the family room that blended seamlessly into the inviting kitchen. A large fake pine tree barely cleared the high ceiling. It was festooned with frosted grapes and miniature wine glasses, along with gold dipped grape leaves. Purple and red lights made it glow. It was startlingly elegant.

"Oh my goodness you poor thing!" Emily greeted me warmly, more warmly than I deserved. "Come here, sit down. What possessed you to walk into the den of a murderer?"

"It was an RV," I hitched up the robe and regarded her a bit warily. Since we last spoke, she had warmed, did I trust it?

"Ben told me you found out who killed Beverley." She guided me to the kitchen table, two large ceramic bowls were filled with crab legs and bodies. Two empty bowls were ready for the carnage to follow. It's kind of odd to massacre a crab in honor of Christmas, but December is Crab Season and we Californians love our crab.

I had a choice of melted butter or mayonnaise. Ah, a woman after my own heart. I relaxed a little more.

Ben poured me a glass of white wine. I didn't bother to scrutinize the label.

"It was an accident. I didn't guess he was the murderer, until he told me."

You may not believe that I really do find these murderers and killers completely by accident. Perhaps, I should have my chi re-calibrated, or whatever Rosemary does periodically. Or I could spend the day at the spa at Sonoma Mission Inn; that would work well in the re-calibration department.

"Why?" Ben asked. He passed me the crab parts, I took a white piece of body and two large legs. I broke them open, and started fishing out the moist meat.

I knew what Ben was asking. "I think he wanted the attention. And murder, something gruesome, had the best chance of getting covered by the media. He didn't count on the media, at least in River's Bend, to be sensitive to both the victims, and the survivors. His work was not reported on as thoroughly as he hoped."

"That was it? Why didn't he publish a book or something?"

"Do you have any idea how hard it to get a book contract?" I countered. I swirled my delectable crabmeat into the clarified butter, and popped it into my mouth, if there is a heaven; they are serving Dungeness crab.

"The professor knew that Beverley was popular and famous, at least locally. It made sense to think her death would be a big deal in the community."

"Okay, how did they get in?" Ben demanded, calmly. I did not take offense, he needed answers and I was not myself, I knew I wasn't delivering information as quickly as he needed.

"She simply let him in. She knew him, why not? There were rumors about board members fraternizing with the clients, nothing concrete. I don't think it was only about Beverley and the president."

"Beverley and the president of the Homeless Prevention League?" Ben drank down half his wine.

"Sorry, I thought you knew."

Ben shook his head and gestured with a crab claw for me to continue. Emily expertly pulled apart a crab body and listened.

"Remember, we overheard that Beverley hired the homeless? She needed to paint over Thanksgiving weekend, who else would help her? The Professor probably showed up for some spending money, and apparently decided to stay and get himself fifteen minutes of fame."

"That, he got."

"You have been working on this for the last month," Emily concluded. She poured more wine for all of us.

"With Ben." I pointed out.

Emily shook her head. "I don't think anyone's ever done something like that for Ben, ever."

I acknowledged her compliment silently. Considering what I've done TO Ben I wasn't sure that doing something FOR Ben put me back in the black as far as doing good deeds was concerned, but I was happy to take her praise. I was very happy to accept her praise.

Emily toasted me with a crab leg. "Welcome to the family."

Chapter 19

Even though it was gruesome, what with Richard and Allen racing around the house, fighting over the toys, stealing each other's candy, tearing open gifts, including mine, in a orgy of greed, I do miss those childhood Christmas mornings.

On the other hand, it was delicious to wake up with someone, Christmas morning.

Ben served me coffee and the paper in bed.

The headlines in the River's Bend Press under *Happy Holidays*, read: "The Professor is the Madman." Someone who reads real books, actually works at the Press.

Murderer found! Stalwart Donor Halts Escape. A blurry picture of Martha's car, the high centered Escalade, occupied the rest of the page. Towards the bottom, the headline "Not a Merry Christmas for the Homeless Prevention League" took up the rest of the front page.

"Didn't even get his photo in the paper," I commented.

"So much for the fifteen minutes of fame." Ben poured me more coffee.

"I can see why you give to the arts."

"A more boring choice, certainly. Until the museum you support purchases stolen art."

"That would be a problem," I agreed.

Beverley was named again, clearly one of the victims of the madman. Her house, however, was not mentioned, nor was I. I escaped the scene of the capture before Chris Connor appeared. Ah, Merry Christmas to me.

Chris Conner had only the police and upright (and stalwart), Martha Anderson to interview. That suited me fine. I was infamous enough.

The professor was being held for psychiatric evaluation.

"Come on," Ben tossed the papers on the floor, and took my cup for me. "The best part of the day is the morning, we need to go down."

I had been too busy and too distracted to leave stuff at his house – only that one bag from Thanksgiving and those clothes had been overused. So I sucked it up and went downstairs dressed in only his robe.

Emily greeted me with a hug. She wore a cashmere robe, but no slippers. Her feet were twisted and deformed from years of wearing pointed high heel shoes. I hoped I wasn't looking into the future of my own feet and toes.

Emily served some rolls that pop out of a can, and which I love, and more coffee. She also served up Christmas stockings for Ben and Allison.

"Grandma, where did you find these?" Ben stroked his stocking as if remembering it by touch.

"I found them yesterday," Emily said with great satisfaction. "I think they've been here for years, obviously your mother never missed them." Emily gestured with her coffee mug to my stocking, "that one is for you, hope you don't mind, it was Donald's."

I shook my head, the old fashion knit stockings were delightful because they were such a homely contrast to the rest of the sleek Craftsman, modern, and completely tasteful home. Ben's stocking featured a lively elf, mine, a snowman. It was perfect. Emily had stuffed the stockings with Godiva chocolates, oranges and small toys. We each found a miniature car that ran on the floor by dragging it backward and releasing it. Ben unwrapped a yo-yo.

I almost cried again.

By eight o'clock, the sun came out, and illuminated the brown stakes of the grape vines. The mustard between the lines of vineyards had turned green, from all the rain. I sat in the living room, curled up with my coffee and gazing out the windows.

"We usually start out this way, the two of us." Emily sat down next to Ben on the couch. "Ben indulges me by acting the little boy, and appreciating my silly toys."

Picturing Emily as silly was difficult, but I kept a straight face.

"A single moment of happiness." Emily stroked his hair.

Ben and Emily were scheduled to drive down to the City for their family Christmas and early dinner. as was I.

"Merry Christmas," Emily gave me a warm hug as we all left

- them in their finery, me in yesterday's clothes. My skirt still reeked of turkey grease. It had been the best twelve hours of the season.

"I think she trusts you," Ben nuzzled my hair, "that"s exceptional."

I drove to my house under the hazy shade of winter. Low mist dragged through the valley, but the sky was clear, the roads were dry. What a lovely beginning. Emily was kind to include me.

I took my time changing my outfit at my own house. I ate more Godiva chocolates and put together the paper work for Owen to sign. All I'd need to do was print at the office.

Rosemary's Mercedes was parked in the otherwise deserted parking lot.

I stepped into the office and Rosemary flipped from her solitaire game to the opening screen for our local MLS.

"Oh hi," she greeted me.

"Hi." I remembered Rosemary commenting that her family was away for the holidays. "away" being the whole of her geographic explanation. For a woman who traveled the world, she was fairly vague as to the location of her own offspring.

"So you have an escrow," she said as a way of greeting.

"Yes, I put in the papers a couple days ago. All cash, it should go pretty quickly."

I headed to my own office to access the paper work for Owen Spencer's Purchase Agreement.

"Good for you," Rosemary called.

I was tempted to call back, don't forget the black seven on the red eight. We are all very good at solitaire, there is little else to do while waiting for the phone, or waiting for the client who is running late, or waiting for someone to call the office. Some agents play so many games of solitaire they play to beat their own time. I once suggested an office-wide solitaire tournament, but no one will admit how good they were at the game.

Owen has made no fewer than seventeen offers on seventeen different condos. So I wasn't holding out for a miracle on this, the eighteenth offer, but I was willing to take another chance that this time, Owen was sincere. That's the hallmark of our business

– we are always ready to re-shuffle the same deck and start a new game.

I pressed print, and wandered back to the lobby to chat, while I waited for my papers to print.

"So have you thought of being friends with Katherine?" I suggested.

"She's a snob," Rosemary said dismissively. She started a new game and began clicking on cards as she talked. "And she teases me about my hobbies."

"Come on, the time you erased your computer hard drive with your healing magnet bracelets was pretty funny."

"Those bracelets are a wonderful way to balance your energy field." Rosemary pulled up to her full height – she's five foot seven - and gave me a haughty stare.

"Sorry." I retrieved the papers and folded them into a New Century Realty binder. This would be a most excellent gift – the exiting of Owen Spenser from my immediate concern.

"Well, Happy Holidays."

Rosemary nodded, concentrating on her new game. "Merry Christmas, Allison."

One could ask, during this holiday season, Allison, do you have any clients you actually enjoy? I enjoy Ben.

"You're late," Debbie greeted me and she wrenched open the front door. Jingle Bells raged around us because Debbie stood smack in the center of her holiday floor mat. Debbie's sweater read Merry, Merry, Merry.

"This is suppose to be a family gathering, and you are part of the family, you could at least come on time." She accused.

"Had to work," I said succinctly. Had to cuddle with Ben. Had to drink some more coffee and admire the old vines that swooped up and down the rolling hills right outside Emily's living room windows. Had to cuddle some more.

I stepped over the mat to avoid another raucous chorus of Jingle Bells, but mid-step, I felt inner muscles pulling, protesting and refusing to cooperate. I recovered as best I could, and limped towards the kitchen.

Debbie's nostalgia Christmas tree loomed in the corner of the formal living room, big glass ornaments in pale colors winked in the afternoon sun. The pile of gifts spilled out from under the thick branches like a glacier overtaking the floor. My six nieces and nephews snacked on cookies as they hovered at the edges of the glacier.

"Oh Allison, look at your nails." Mom, dressed in a festive light green cashmere twin set and charcoal gray slacks, bustled up to me and eyed my bruised face, and of course, the missing nails.

"I had an accident," I explained.

"Really Allison, you should be more careful," she chided me. "Now hand me those rolls, there's barely enough room in the oven to heat them up. You're late, we're about to open the gifts and eat."

I glanced at my watch. Oh, my, it was almost one o'clock. That's the latest I've managed to be for a family event. It felt pretty good.

"I had to work." I called after her, but mom was already bustling about. She gave Mary some instructions, called for all the granddaughters to come and help and otherwise took over the kitchen. Mom can't cook, but she loves to bark out random orders.

"How is that nice Ben doing?" Dad approached me, a glass of eggnog in his hand. I gave him a hug and wished him Merry Christmas.

I grabbed a nephew and kissed him on the head, because he hates when I do that, so I always do.

"He's fine," I said. "We're meeting up at four o'clock to exchange gifts."

Debbie hustled over to me and relieved me of my gifts, all bagged and tagged, I don't bother much with wrapping paper.

"I'll put these under the tree. The boys will act as Santa, it will give them something to do. Merry Christmas Allison." She delivered a dry kiss to my bruised cheek and didn't comment on my appearance, because Debbie never does. I am an affront to all she holds dear: family, organized children, clean house, soccer team duty, dieting. I think of her life in terms of those home focused magazines that feature a recipe for a seven layer coconut cake smack up against the diet article promising that you can lose fifteen pounds in twenty seven minutes. Debbie always tries the diets, never the cake.

"There are a few hors d'ouvres left." Debbie instructed. "Go to the kitchen, we're all in there, and in about seven minutes," she check her watch. "We will open the gifts."

"Fran," Debbie called out, "we'll open gifts in about six and a half minutes. Richard! Where are you!"

I managed to get to the kitchen, grab one chip with onion dip before Debbie hustled us back into the formal living room. My nephew, Tom pulled a Santa hat low on his head and quickly distributed the grown up gifts with the practiced acumen of a Vegas dealer. Richard appeared, looked a little worse for wear, and carefully joined Debbie on the couch. With exaggerated patience he set down his martini glass, then grinned at me as if to show that everything was simply fabulous.

Well, at least, he didn't tip over, and nothing had caught fire.

Gifts were duly opened and thank yous delivered.

Debbie eyed the small gift bag from me, out of place next to the elaborately wrapped gifts from Mary and my mother. Mary followed Debbie's gaze at the small bag with the words "Debbie" written on it, and looked up at me, and winked.

I grinned back.

Debbie saved my gift for last. For the most part we all give each other gift cards worth fifty dollars. Everyone was pleased with their gift cards.

Debbie delayed as long as she could, then finally accepted defeat, and picked up the small bag, the last gift. She pulled open the bag and pulled out the tissue paper.

"This better be good Allison."

"It could be a gift card. I'm really happy with mine," I responded.

Debbie pulled out the first bracelet and gasped, then the second, then the third.

"Where did you? Oh my God, these almost look real!"

"Almost," I said quickly. "A little something I picked up. I thought of you." If they were real, well, when she lost one, it would be that much more tragic. Made me happy thinking about it.

She was silent for a full minute as she gazed at the bracelets. Then she slipped them over her hand and jangled them on her wrist. I had a hit. I hoped to never chose her name again.

Dinner was fine. Richard was quiet. Allen did not go near the fireplace. I ate olives and the bread because Debbie overcooked the turkey and there was no way I was touching the creamed onions. No one did. Debbie had to take a spoonful to be polite.

I was happy to have to leave by three thirty for my "Four o'clock time with Ben." The magic word, Ben, galvanized my mother, and she propelled me out of Debbie's house. She was so happy I had a man this holiday season, she didn't even admonish me to stay to clean up. What can I say? It was an extra gift for her.

Ben came to my house, halfway between the city and Emily's. Emily was spending the night down in San Francisco, her token of holiday conciliation for her daughter. I had Ben to myself.

I greeted him at the door, formally as of we hadn't woken up together, "Merry Christmas." I kissed his cheek.

"Merry Christmas." He pulled me into another breathtaking bear hug. I snuggled into his chest and was prepared to spend the rest of the afternoon in his arms - corny, but completely true.

"Come on, let's get a glass of wine and exchange gifts."

My gift to Ben was large and - un-wrapable, so I had hid it behind my chair and sort of draped it with one of my throws.

I poured him wine, set out an assortment of cheeses and crackers and then, when he was settled, I pulled out his gift and whipped off the shawl.

"Ta da!" I said with a flourish.

He squinted at the picture. He didn't move, he stayed in his seat and simply stared.

"Is it okay?" He was too quiet.

He set down his glass.

"Allison," he reached out and gently touched the frame, he pulled it closer so he could study the swirling blue and purple brush strokes.

"Where did you find this?"

"It's a Bo Freeman."

"Isn't that's the guy who bought the house?" He didn't say his house, which I found comforting.

"Yes, and he's the artist of that painting you bought years ago, I recognized a sketch he made."

"But he's," Ben trailed off. I could tell he liked it and was surprised by it. I loved being able to surprise him.

"He's very popular now," I agreed. "Which is why he can buy a house for his sister with cash, but I didn't think that would change how much you appreciated his work."

"That you'd remember," he trailed off. He stood to set the painting safely on a far wall, but where he could still see it. "Should I ask how you managed it?"

"No. Your job is to accept it."

"Okay, I have something for you." He handed me two flat envelopes. Did I want a small box with a ring nestled inside? Isn't that the Christmas fantasy? It is, but not on my list. Maybe on my mom's list – for me.

I opened the first envelope. It was a colorful brochure featuring a charming Victorian Inn and five sets of theater tickets.

"Ashland, next September." Ben explained.

"And this?" I held up the second envelope.

"Open it."

It was a gift certificate for $1,000 to Bloomsbury Books in Ashland.

"I've never been to Ashland." I touched the brochure, the picture of the Victorian style county Inn was almost impossibly perfect. And a $1,000 for books! I blinked back sudden tears.

"I guessed that. We need to get you out more," he agreed. "And, it would be nice to watch drama on the stage, not in our lives."

"I agree," I sighed. I would love to have normal, but I don't know what that looks like anymore. And Ben probably rues the day he showed up at my listing in Marin, ready to fix a guest bath room and instead, discovering me.

"It certainly hasn't been boring." He read my thoughts.

"No," I agreed. "Not boring, dangerous, but not boring."

He picked up his wine and sipped. "I miss you when you're

not with me."

"You're with me, now."

"Nice," he responded sarcastically. "Really, I don't think I want to be apart from you."

"Remember, we agreed to postpone any feelings conversations until Valentine's Day?" I reminded him.

I didn't want to ruin a lovely moment with too much talk.

"It doesn't get any better than this," I insisted, hoping to forestall anything he may suggest that would change my suddenly precious status quo.

But, if we don't throw in something new once in a while, there would be no story.

"You haven't been here," he gestured to my living room, taking in the whole house in his comment, "much."

"Your house is pretty comfortable," I said innocently.

"You could stay there," he said.

"I have been," I pointed out. Was I purposefully obtuse? Why, yes I was.

"No, stay there, with me," he struggled, "all the time."

"Move in with you?" I repeated dumbly.

He nodded, relieved that I guessed. "Yes."

* * *

My favorite day of the holiday season is the day after Christmas. Everything is over save for the shouting. The stores are still clogged with amateurs, but they are all corralled into Customer Service lines, loaded with returns. That frees up the rest of the store for the real shoppers.

I was pleased Carrie managed to spring herself from the Forbidden Palace, and meet me for lunch.

Owen Spencer had signed the purchase agreement papers, first thing in the morning. He even presented me with the updated paper work from his mortgage broker who, I'm sure, will be as happy as me to see the last of Owen Spencer.

After lunch I planned to spend my certificates from the New Century Party and the family Christmas, at the bookstore. I'm only telling this so you don't think, after everything that's happened, that I'm completely pathetic and have no happy moments.

There is a particularly good Japanese restaurant in town, Nagasaki, where Carrie and I met for sushi and decidedly un-holiday food.

I walked into the restaurant and took one look at my friend, with her flushed cheeks and stereotypically shinning eyes, and I knew that my announcement about the house, Ben's delight over his gift, my very brief contact with his family, was all going to be dropped like the egg in our soup.

"Patrick proposed," Carrie announced as soon as the waiter had retreated with our order. She dug into her purse, pulled out a velvet ring box, opened it, and pulled out the ring.

It was (this is my best guess) a five carat, canary yellow diamond, flanked by more than enough single carat clear, diamond baguettes. The light caught the center stone and splintered shards of light around the restaurant; an erratic disco ball. Three women across the room looked up. All eyes immediately went to the ring. It was like lighthouse in a fog-shrouded coast. The other women lurched forward, drawn irresistibly towards the light. Carrie was too pleased with her bauble to shoo them away.

She gestured to the other patrons, "come, look."

"Oh my God," exclaimed one woman. "That's the size of,"

"A creamer" I suggested.

"A hubcap," said the other one.

"That's not very romantic," I defended my friend. "It's more like the size of," I floundered for a word, "satellite dish."

Carrie slipped on the ring. "It's pretty, isn't it?"

"Oh my." I said, wishing for my Dragon Roll right now because I could use something in my mouth to keep it from unattractively hanging open.

She held her hand out, her fingers splayed to better see the ring. "He has great taste."

I looked at my friend, how happy she was, pleased with her gaudy bauble which meant far more to her than the giver would probably ever understand. I noticed that of all Beverley's acquired jewelry, there wasn't one diamond. Not a single ring.

"He does have excellent taste."

She looked up from the ring, startled. "Thank you. You're not disappointed are you?"

"About the ring?"

"No, about me getting married before you, because you're older."

"That has nothing to do with anything." I snapped back, then stopped. I did feel older, mayhem, bad people, and my relatives during the holidays, will do that.

"I meant. . . " Carrie was saved by the waiter bearing a pink bottle of sake.

"I'm sorry," I apologized. This is about her. It should be all about her.

Carrie gestured to the wine glasses and the waiter poured. The rice wine was sweet and cold.

I toasted her with my glass.

She clicked her glass against mine. "I ordered it before you came in, I thought it would be more festive. You do feel festive don't you?"

"It's a beautiful ring," I said. "You deserve the ring, the man and the life, better than anyone I've ever known. And yes, I feel festive." Once I recovered from the shock.

"You found the murderer didn't you?" She took a sip of her wine.

I nodded.

"Was it Professor Von Drake?"

I stared at her, my sake half way to my mouth. How did she do that? Every once in a while she popped off with the answer. She is far more intelligent than she even gives herself credit for.

"You do realize, you sent me right to him, burdened with blankets that I have half a mind to give you the receipt for."

"But you won't," she toasted me with her sake. Her ring caught the light and glared painfully into my eye. I blinked.

"And I didn't ever think it could be him, I mean, the professor was so charming, really lovely to me, he said I reminded him of Beverley."

"And you took that as a compliment?" Our first course arrived, and we slurped salty soup between sips of sake.

"No, but I did use the professor's comment yesterday when Patrick and I were discussing the honeymoon."

"Damn you're good," I said admiringly.

"Allison," she set down her soup bowl and leaned forward. "I would never have sent you to the RVs if I thought anything was wrong. I didn't really figure it out until later. When all the excitement over the ring and the engagement died down a bit, Patrick and were talking about the murders and what was involved, and that's when we came to the conclusion that it was the professor. Patrick had a lot of insight about erratic behavior."

"It was also in the paper that morning," I pointed out.

"Yes, but Patrick said he was always uncomfortable with the way the professor was so easy to anger, and how he got worked up about the lack of recognition, things of that nature. Plus, we thought that maybe since Beverley hired some of the Homeless Prevention League clients to do odd jobs, she probably hired the Professor to come during Thanksgiving to paint. And when we thought about it a bit more, we realized that the professor probably had help."

"Probably." I hadn't thought about that, he had made his work sound like a solo act. Of course he would, he was working on being the star, any of the little people who had helped him, and I didn't really want to think of it any further than that, would remain unnamed.

And they would be still free, but leaderless.

"Now, you can start the new year clean," Carrie encouraged.

I thought about Ben's proposal, no less weighty for lack of jewelry. Did I want to move in? Rent my house? Change my life? Did he want to move into my house? Should we get a place together? That's what I would suggest to any other couple, but I rarely take my own good advice.

At least, and I'm going to give myself full credit for this, I did not react badly to Ben's proposal, in that I didn't dismiss him, didn't say, give me time, let me think about it. I was pretty straight forward. I said, "great, I would love to have you to myself 24/7. Your place or mine?"

It was the perfect response. It bought me some time, because the question, your place or mine, is fraught with complications.

It's going to take a bit for us to figure this out.

For Carrie, there are no questions. The princess will be drawn into the family compound and I hope that won't be the last I see of her.

"Will this change our friendship?" I asked.

She made a face. "Never. Besides, Patrick likes Ben, we'll be together, a lot, I think."

I couldn't help it, Carrie's diamond drew me in, as if it was one of Rosemary's magnets. "It's amazing." I said, absolutely sincerely. Carrie is going to have to return to the gym, she'll need to work out so she can pick up her hand.

"We're holding an engagement party on New Year's Eve. You and Ben are invited of course."

"Of course," I said. Damn that thing was the size of well, one of my fake rings, or all of them, put together.

"It's at the French Laundry." Carrie said. "Patrick reserved the whole restaurant."

The French Laundry is so exclusive and expensive that even I hadn't been there. The three star restaurant is located in Yountville in the Napa Valley; where the rich live, and the wines are pretty good, but this is from a Sonoma county resident, we only grudgingly appreciate of any wine not from our own vineyards.

Anyway, a person, any person, can't walk into the French Laundry off the street and order dinner. A person must make reservations two months to the day in advance, and if that person is planning on eating more than bread, he or she should check the equity line of credit on the house, to make sure dessert is covered.

"New Year's Eve? Are you kidding me?" I blurted out, because all that last information went through my brain faster than it took to explain it to you.

She glanced at her hand. The ring, really, was rock star huge. Ginormous.

"Allison. What have I done?"

Epilogue

Christmas Day is quiet in the Wal-Mart parking lot. The bargains had been purchased, the specials fought over, the dollar bins cleaned out and stuffed randomly into stockings hung by the fire with increasing obligation and decreasing wonder.

She considered herself, ironically, a member of the disenfranchised, if it could be said that the disenfranchised have a membership. She was at loose ends, and decided to walk in the watery, chilly sun. Even if she hadn't intended to head in that direction this morning, Anne watched enough television to realize it was only a matter of time before she was inextricably drawn to the scene of the crime. Many crimes, she had to admit. Who knew that the story of Homeless Prevention League owning only one shelter instead of thirty or thirty-two or thirty-five (she couldn't recall exactly how many she had promised over the years) would break, and people would care? Yesterday, their story had made the front page, she could actually read the opening paragraph through the window of the paper kiosk. They were above the fold. She was inordinately pleased with that. Even if it was bad news.

"All we ask, is spell our names right," she murmured.

It wasn't raining, that was nice. She settled her purse on her shoulder and walked down to the last place she had left the RV.

She was surprised to see it. After years of claiming a fleet of mobile shelter systems, seeing the phantom shelter units so clearly in her mind, so she could convince any donor that the network was enormous, it was almost startling to see the real thing. But that was silly, she knew their one RV intimately. Now that she was more removed from the immediacy of her job, she marveled at the hubris that led her to her park it, one last time, in the center of the Wal-Mart parking lot.

She stood on the rough worn asphalt clutching her bag, wondering. A breeze tossed an empty holiday sticker shell, the outlines of red bells and green holly momentarily caught her attention, before it tossed away to the edge of the lot.

"So," Harold walked up and stood next to her, "it's still here."

"It should be admitted for evidence, scene of the last murder, but the police couldn't guard everything on Christmas Eve." She glanced sideways at him, how did he find her? On this day? At this hour? No one hangs around a parking lot. Not even the professor would stoop to that. All the homeless would be at some dinner or another. Fed for this one day.

She however, had no place to go.

"Last place anyone would look." She surveyed the oil stained parking lot. "It fits right in, don't you think?"

He said nothing. He silently stood next to her in the noon light. He thought of her as being like the swallows. She had to return to the RV, at least for one last look, before she moved on to something else. And he'd never see her again.

"You're taking it pretty well," she ventured.

He narrowed his eyes against the sun. The professor was gone, in a safer place, a harsher regime to be sure, but still, three meals a day, still the guest of the tax payers.

That's how it is.

"Adversity looks good on you." .

"Well, thanks, but I don't think I'll be able to write a book about it."

"Nor I."

They both stood and looked at the RV. The door to the living section was smashed, but it still closed. One back room was probably a horrible mess and would need through cleaning.

"Color TV," she said.

"Really? Still there?" Harold was surprised.

She nodded. "I locked it right after the police removed the professor."

"And how did you come to lock up after the arrest?"

"I was his phone call."

He nodded, and squinted at the RV again. "He once suggested driving away in it."

"Of course he'd be arrested before he left town. Besides, we don't keep much gas in it. But now the gas is all gone, almost all gone," she amended.

She had enough gas to get it to the Wal-Mart, in the pouring rain. No one noticed her at all. She seemed to be the only one who noticed the dark stains in the back of the bus, the police were probably now learning about that themselves.

"I think he killed Cyndi, too. Then drove her back to the offices," she said.

"To point the finger at us."

"He had nothing to lose."

Harold ran his hand over the clean side of the van and walked around to the front where the door stood locked against all do-gooders and criminals alike. From this new angle the RV glowed copper color.

For twenty-four hours it had rested here, ignored, while reporters and Chris Conner, wasted their energy and their Christmas morning scouring the county for the other RVs. No one thought to ask he or Anne

"Here," Anne fished out something from her enormous handbag and pulled out a key ring. She handed him the keys.

He looked down at the shiny objects in his hand, surprised, as if she were a magic genie handing him all the wishes in the world, the magic lamp, the magic compass, the magic ring. Keys unlocked mysterious doors with old runic writing, they unlocked the front gates of castles, they unlocked secret boxes that often were best kept closed.

"We would be stopped."

"Cyndi was pretty haphazard with her filing system." Anne dug around again in her voluminous purse. He sighed automatically. What would she come up with? An egg? Photos of someone else's children? Sausage and cheese ball? Shrimp?

She pulled out the pink slip to the RV.

His mouth fell open as if she had levitated, finishing up the magic trick during which leopards and woodland creatures disappeared before your eyes, then appeared again at the back of the theater.

"Cyndi was always a little casual in her filing system. I found this last year and kept it, just in case."

"In case the board members asked to see all the ownership slips for the thirty one vehicles?"

"Thirty two, I would have told them the pink slips were in the safe." Anne said with confidence.

"We don't have a safe."

"We don't have fleet of RVs, either."

He hefted the keys in his hand. "You want to come?"

She shrugged her bag onto her shoulder more securely. "Sure."

the end

Made in the USA
Charleston, SC
23 September 2011